CERRADO

LEIF J. ERICKSON

Table of Contents

UNITED STATES OF AMERICA

ISBN: 978-0-9962804-2-6

The night was crystal clear as an incalculable amount of stars twinkled in the cloudless sky. A father and son walked along a small dirt trail that followed the contour of a lazy brook. The boy, dusty and snaggletooth with wild brown hair, had his eyes glued to the night sky as the tall, proud father held his little hand as they walked through the night. With only the full and bright silver moon as their guide, the pair walked in silence. The boy didn't bother to notice the brook to their left or the red stone wall holding the forest back on their right.

The smells of harvest lingered in the crisp fall air. It was not cold enough yet to see your breath, but cold enough to warrant an extra layer of clothes and a pair of gloves. The leaves beneath the pairs' feet crunched loudly as they walked along, making no attempt to quiet their movement. The father looked at his young boy with pride. The boy hadn't taken his eyes off the sky since they'd left their house. The young boy stopped, forcing his father to stop with him.

"What's the matter, Son?" the man asked.

"Father," the young boy began, with a quizzical look on his face. "If there are so many stars in the sky, are there other worlds up there that contain people?"

The father smiled at his son. He was used to questions like these—questions that all six-year-old boys ask, boys who are curious about everything around them. The father looked to his son with a smile in his eyes. "Son, you don't need to look to the sky to find another world."

The young boy nodded confusedly as he continued to walk along with his father, his eyes still scanning the heavens. The boy had dreams of going to a different world—of being on a star, looking down on earth and looking back on his home and his friends. He dreamed he would be vast distances away—distances no other adventurer in history had traveled. As the boy looked, a shooting star shot across the sky, leaving a rainbow of color in its tail. The star burned out in the night while the boy's eyes enlarged as he quickly formulated his wish.

"Shooting star, shooting star," the boy said, as he stopped and bowed his head in prayer. "How I wonder what you are. I wish I may, I wish I might, have this wish I wish tonight. I wish to find another world, and have an adventure greater than any adventure anyone has ever had."

The boy looked back up to the heavens to see that the shooting star was no longer in the sky but its tail was still hanging like a mist in the atmospheres. The boy smiled as he looked up to his father.

"Kale Risdell," the father said, sternly, to his son.

"Are you going to tell me not to have my head in the clouds?" Kale asked his father. "Like Mommy tells me?"

"No, I'm not, Kale," the father said, getting down on one knee to look his son in the eye. "I'm going to tell you that when you find that world, when you have your grandest adventure of all the world, there's one thing you need to do."

"What's that, Father?" the boy asked.

"You need to return to this spot on a clear night like this with billions of stars twinkling in the sky," the father said, "And you need to thank the shooting star you just wished on."

"I will, Father," Kale said. "I will thank that star when I have my adventure."

Kale Risdell never forgot that night, nor did he ever forget his dream of finding another world. In fact, he was so enthralled with the concept of seeing a new world and having an adventure that he spent his teen years studying everything he could about the stars. Kale received a scholarship to attend the foremost university of astronomy in London. It was there he used the biggest telescopes in the world to view the skies.

Although his heart was true and he worked harder than anyone else in the university, Kale was never able to discover a new world. He spent every waking moment trying to find something—something that wasn't there. His peers began to see his endurance in his theories of new worlds and they began to mock Kale over his beliefs. 'Everyone knows there's only one world—this world!' his schoolmates would say, mocking him for their own entertainment. Kale wouldn't give up, he knew his wish upon a star would come true. Not because of the particular star he wished on, but because his father believed in him.

As his passion for a new world consumed him, even the professors of the university worried about Kale. He never socialized with his classmates, and while his friends were spending time with their girlfriends, Kale was searching the skies. Kale was awkward and had a timid face with nervous eyes, but there were still girls longing for him to escort them to a dance—he never noticed. It got to the point where the leaders of the university decided Kale needed to have a break. They told him to return home for one month's time and stated if he wanted to continue with his education he would have to put his ideas of other worlds out of his head and focus on his studies.

Kale returned home to his family's sheep farm. His parents were happy to have him home, hoping that he would stay and be a shepherd like his father, his father's father, and all the men in the Risdell family. Kale knew his parents wanted him to be like them—content herding sheep, living the simple life of a shepherd.

Kale simply couldn't accept that his wish upon a star wouldn't come true. He knew if he worked hard enough, he would find his other world and the adventure that came along with it. Kale took a walk to clear his head and try to figure things out. He didn't notice he was walking along the same lazy brook on the same road he and his father had walked together so many years ago. When Kale looked up to the sky on that crystal clear night—stars everywhere—his father's words came back to him: You don't need to look to the sky to find another world.

Kale never before pondered what his father meant by those words. If I don't need to look to the sky to find other worlds, where in the world would I look? Kale looked around where he was at. To his left was the lazy brook and to his right was a red stone wall holding back the Moon Forest. Kale had heard about people who went into the forest and had an adventure. He heard there were things in the forest that weren't human— nor were they animals.

Kale noticed a gate in the red stone wall, and in that moment he decided he would walk the forest and see where his path would take him.

Kale stepped through the gate, looking over the dark forest. There were very few places the trees allowed the shafts of light from the bright silver moon to come through. Kale didn't know how he would find his way but something told him that he would. Timidly, Kale entered the forest.

After trekking only a few minutes into the woods, Kale wasn't sure where he was at or which way he had come from. He knew in that instant he had to make a choice that would change his life forever—should he continue on through the forest or should he turn back and go home. It seemed like it should be such a simple, small choice but something told Kale that the weight of that decision and its consequences would be with him the rest of his life.

As Kale was about to take another step forward into the Moon Forest, something happened that he didn't expect. About twenty feet in front of him, Kale noticed two trees had seemingly fallen together, forming an arch over a patch of dirt. The trees themselves nor the arch weren't the strange thing. The strange thing was the fact that the arch seemed to be glowing a cool green color. It was like nothing Kale had ever seen. Kale fidgeted as he looked at the arch. He didn't know what to do— but then something came over him, prompting him to run into the arch.

From the cloudless night came a crack of thunder and a bolt of lightning which lit up the entire forest while the thunder shook the ground with its force. The next instant, the Moon Forest was quiet again. Only soft sounds of the animals—an owl, a fox, and crickets making noise. Notably, Kale was no longer in the Moon Forest.

Where he went or how long he was there, only Kale can say. No one from this world was there with him to understand the adventure that he had. His parents began to worry and many people searched the Moon Forest and surrounding areas but there was no trace of Kale, no one knew what happened to him. Every night, his mother and father would stand on their porch, looking out at the sky, hoping their only child would return to them.

After what seemed like a lifetime to his family, but was only six months, there was a bolt of lightning that lit up the entire Moon Forest. It was followed by a crack of thunder that shook the ground. Everything grew silent just before another bolt of lightning and crack of thunder. Standing by where the trees had formed into an arch was Kale, smiling a true and happy smile for the first time in a very long time.

Standing next to Kale was a figure in a black hooded cloak. The figure was almost as tall as Kale and had a shapely and curvy figure. Long, shiny, thick black hair protruded from the hood of the cloak. A tiny bump was starting to form at the figure's midsection—barely there but enough to be noticeable. As the figure turned, what part of the face wasn't hidden by the hooded cloak, was bathed in the silver moonlight—revealing clear complexion skin glowing with youth and vigor, full pouty lips slightly pursed below a tiny button nose, and a smile that lit up the forest.

Kale took the hand of the figure and led her through the forest, past the red stone wall, and toward his parent's farm. As they started walking home, Kale stopped and looked up to the amazing starlit night. Kale smiled as a shooting star streaked across the sky as he took a deep breath, "Thank you star, thank you."

As the pair started walking again, Kale saw his father rushing down the road. When his father reached them he almost knocked Kale down when he embraced his son. His father noticed that Kale looked different somehow—braver and stronger. Kale's father looked at the figure with Kale, looking over her face before looking down toward her stomach.

"Kale," his father began. "It appears you had quite an adventure."

"Like you wouldn't believe, Father," Kale said. "I don't think my room is going to be big enough for me anymore, for us I mean, as this is my wife and she is expecting."

"I gathered that, yes. Adventures can change a person, Son. Are you sure being a shepherd will be enough for you?"

"Father," Kale said. "I've seen things I didn't know were possible. I've experienced things I never thought I'd experience. And I've lived a life I didn't know I could. I know now that our little village is not the worst place in the world. I'm sure one day I'll want to have another adventure, but for now we will be content to raise our child here on our little farm."

"Your mother will be happy to hear that," Kale's father said. "When we heard that thunder and saw the lightning, the same thunder and lightning that marked the day you left, your mother had me rush here to see if you had returned."

"I am back, Father," Kale said. "Tomorrow we will find a proper house for my wife and me, but tonight let's celebrate my return."

Kale, his wife, and his father all smiled as they started to return to their home. Kale and his wife made a very successful run on the farm and Kale never returned to the university. His child was born and his parents passed away, the arrow of time points in one direction only, and Kale never spoke to anyone about his journeys beyond the arch—only telling people that he met his wife a few towns over.

The pair had a handsome son, Krispin, who they raised to follow in the family footsteps of being a shepherd, but they also instilled in him knowledge and values that most shepherds don't need. Krispin grew into a strapping but scrawny young lad. A lad who, like his father, longed for adventure...

Chapter 2

On a bright and sunny day, where only whips of white fluffy clouds hung lazily in the sky, Krispin Risdell, a tall and lanky, scrawny lad with bright eyes, unknowing of the world as his thick brown hair cascaded past his shoulders, slept with his back to a tall old apple tree. He was in the family's south paddock, a swell of grasslands that was surrounded by a three foot high gray stone fence that contained most of the family sheep. As he slept, Krispin dreamt of adventures in the world, pirates on the high seas, treasures and gold in the Klondike, and mysterious buildings in the desert.

The sheep grazed peacefully on their own, feeling protected by the wall which would not allow them to see the wolves gathering outside trying to find a way to sneak in while the powerful and handsome Kale Risdell walked along the wall. Kale was on his way home from the market after selling the winter wool crop, his wallet was fat with the bounty of a good year. The trees and grass had that spring green look, that special hue of green that looks so good after months of being covered by the white snow.

Kale arrived at the old apple tree where his son took his nap. Kale smiled while shaking his head, looking at his boy, knowing that Krispin was destined to greater things than tending a flock of sheep. Kale decided to play a small joke on his son.

"The sheep are out!" Kale yelled, not more than a few feet from his son. "The sheep are out and there's wolves out there!"

Krispin instantly woke up, grabbed his staff, stood quickly, and tried to take off but tripped over his own feet. In confusion, Krispin looked up to see his father offering a hand to help him up while at the same time chuckling at his joke.

"That wasn't funny, Father," Krispin said.

"Never allow the chance for a joke to pass," Kale said, as Krispin got to his feet. "You may not have another chance to have that joke again. Tell me Krispin, how are the sheep today?"

"Months away from being a meal and a sweater, but they still fatten themselves up thinking they are living the good life in our paddocks," Krispin said. "Ah, Father, the sheep are fine. They were fine yesterday and they will be fine tomorrow. We have the best walls in the country, Grandfather built them himself. The sheep will not escape nor will the wolves enter."

"I sense you're upset."

"Whatever gave that away?"

"Son…"

"Don't give me the lecture again, Father," Krispin said, as he looked over the flock of two hundred sheep. "I know, everyone in my family has been a shepherd. We are a family of shepherds who take pride in have the best sheep in the countryside. I just feel like there's so much more out there, that something is calling me to be something more than a simple shepherd."

"Are you saying that a shepherd doesn't have a noble occupation?"

"I didn't say that at all, Father," Krispin said. "It's just that I'm not a shepherd. I'm something more."

"What?"

"I don't know yet," Krispin said. "I haven't had the ability to find out yet because I'm always watching the sheep. I want to go out and explore the world, Father. There has to be more here than just our little farm with our little village."

"And if you were to go, where would you go?"

"Paris or London," Krispin said, looking dreamily into the sky. "Maybe I'd go to the Klondike and pan for gold, or I could go to the Caribbean and protect ships from pirates. I could go to the desert and investigate the strange buildings and tombs being found. I could go climb a mountain or cross a sea. There's an adventure out there for me, Father. I know it. But I can't find it if I'm trapped here on this farm."

"Don't let your mother hear you say it like that."

"But I've heard the stories," Krispin protested. "You went to university and studied the skies. They said you were gone for four years and when you returned you'd already married Mother and she was expecting me."

"You're right," Kale said. "I did go to university and met your mother. Krispin, your mother and I only want you to be happy but we need you on the farm. There are more important things than having an adventure. I'm sure you'll find your bride here. I'm sorry, Son. I can't let you go off on an adventure. Not yet anyway."

"Father," Krispin said, turning to look his father in the eyes. "I have to move on soon. I can't keep watching the flock. I need something more than this."

"What would you do with more?"

"I don't know," Krispin said. "I'll know when I see more, experience more. It's my time, Father."

"You don't choose when your calling is, Son," Kale said. "Krispin, one day you will get your adventure, but not today. Why don't you walk the wall again and make sure there are no gaps where a wolf could get in."

"Okay, Father," Krispin sighed heavily as he climbed onto the wall.

Krispin walked on the top of the wall as he checked over the wall's integrity. Like always, the wall would stand through anything, built strong and true. Krispin couldn't believe his dad was so unwavering in his desire to keep Krispin on the farm. As Krispin was walking, something caught his attention. On the road, walking toward him, was Holly Porter. Holly was a tall, thin girl, with a shapely body, long eyelashes, bright big blue eyes that were sometimes hidden by her long golden curly locks. She was walking down the road, deep in thought.

Krispin instantly noticed that Holly wasn't walking with the usual skip in her step, that energetic step that would drive all the boys wild as she passed by in her fancy dresses and matching hats. Her bright eyes were focused on the ground, like she was trying to figure something out, her face held in a confused, questing expression that Krispin had never seen before. As Krispin was watching Holly, he wasn't watching where he was walking and walked right off the wall, hitting the ground with a thud, right in front of Holly.

"Holly," Krispin said, quickly standing and brushing the dust off. "I wasn't planning on dropping in on you today but I saw you walking and I thought, why not?"

"Krispin," Holly said, in her light, angelic voice. "How dreadfully charming. Please, today is not the day for your jokes."

"What's wrong?"

"Everything."

"Come now, Holly," Krispin said, hopefully. "A beautiful woman like you cannot have that big of problems. Tell me what's going on and I'm sure I can figure it out for you."

"I don't know, Krispin," Holly said. "I don't think you'd want to know."

"I'm going to find out sometime anyway," Krispin said. "You'll go home and tell your little friend Hannah, simply because you tell her everything, and Hannah will tell everyone in the village."

"You're right," Holly said. "Okay Krispin, but remember you pushed me to tell you. I received a marriage proposal today."

"What?" Krispin almost yelled. "How…what…from who…what?"

"Chester Van Brunt," Holly said.

"Chester?" Krispin asked in disbelief. "That Neanderthal? These sheep would make a better husband than Chester. Why do you even spend your time with that brute?"

"He may be brutish," Holly said. "But he has his charms. Oh Krispin, my knees get weak every time Chester flashes those fire-intense eyes at me. I get butterflies in my stomach when Chester takes my hand. I get…"

"I get it," Krispin said. "He's a swell fella. Holly, there's a lot of men that would like to marry you."

"Believe me Krispin," Holly said. "I know that. I'm the most beautiful girl in all the village, plus my father is the largest grain farmer and I have no other siblings. A man that marries me gets not only an amazing woman, but more money than they could imagine."

"I want to marry you, Holly," Krispin said, optimistically.

"I know," Holly said. "But I owe it to my family to marry a man who will not only take care of me but also run the family farm in a way Father would approve of. I need to be with a strong man who can protect me. I need a man who knows how to treat a woman."

"I know how to treat a woman," Krispin said. "Better than Chester ever would."

"Can I make a confession to you?"

"Of course, Holly."

"I don't want to marry Chester," Holly said. "I really don't want to. The reason isn't why you think. Chester's content to be here, to run a farm and drink ale at parties but I want more than that. I want to see the world. I want a man who will take me to the new world. I want a man who will take me to London and show me the museums. I want to go to Paris and see a real play. I want to sail the seas."

"Holly," Krispin said. "That's exactly what I want to do. I'm going to have an adventure one day. I'm going to have an adventure that will go down in history as the greatest adventure of all time. Remember when we used to walk home from school together? I would tell you about the adventures I would have. I'm going to have one of those adventures, Holly. I will."

"Oh, thank you, Krispin," Holly said, laughing heartily. "I needed to hear a good joke. You are not the type of boy who has adventures. You are a shepherd just like your father and his father. You will stay in the village and tend the flocks your entire life. You're grade-school fantasies will never come true."

"I won't be a shepherd, Holly," Krispin said, dropping to one knee. "Holly, marry me."

Holly was shocked by Krispin's proposal. She did know he cared deeply for her and she'd even used that care to get Krispin to cater to her before. Holly was in a tough place, she just had two proposals from men she really didn't want to marry but she knew her parents wanted her married before her twenty-first birthday, which was only three months away.

"I have to marry someone I know will be a good match for me, Krispin," Holly said.

"I will be the best match for you," Krispin said, still on his knee. "When we get married I will sell part of my flock and take you on a one-year tour of the world. We will have grand adventures that will be the talk of our village for years to come. We will see all the major sights of the world."

"I still just don't know, Krispin," Holly said. "I don't know if I even want to return to our village…it's so small and plain."

"Holly," Krispin stood and took her hand. "My father always says people have no limits on what they could achieve if they work for it. He had an adventure and met Mother while he was away. I could have an adventure grander than anything he ever did. You never know what turn of events could happen to a person. In a few years I could even be king."

"Oh please," Holly said, taking her hand away and laughing harder than before. "You, king? I doubt that any one would ever bow to you Krispin. You talk big but I don't hear any conviction in your voice. You don't believe the words that you say. I'm going to marry Chester. He may be couth but I will be taken care of and rich. I can talk him into trips and adventures. It would be best for everyone."

"Not for me, it wouldn't," Krispin said. "Give me a chance, Holly. I will show you and everyone in the village that I'm capable of having a grand adventure."

"Okay," Holly said. "Why not? I will get married on my twenty-first birthday which is three months from now. If you have an adventure, and I mean a grand, amazing adventure, I will marry you instead of marrying Chester. I will alone decide if your adventure is grand enough for me to marry you. Do you accept those terms?"

"I do, Holly," Krispin said. "I will leave for an adventure that will amaze everyone."

"You do that, Krispin," Holly said, as she began to walk away.

Krispin rushed back to the wall and jumped on top of it, throwing a quick glance over his sheep before leaning against his staff to watch Holly skip away. Whatever he'd said, it gave her that spring—that skip, back to her step. His mind raced with all the things he would need to do before going on his adventure. As he watched Holly, he regretted only one thing, one thing he didn't say. He watched Holly disappear around the bend as he whispered, "I love you."

Chapter 3

As Krispin day-dreamed about his adventures and his upcoming life with Holly, trouble was brewing in the magical Kingdom of Cerrado—a place Krispin couldn't get to from where he was at. Within the walls of the Cerrado Castle, a massive sweeping castle that sat in the middle of the village Bauer Rock, the largest village in Cerrado, Duke Asmout sat in his wealth-encrusted throne room upon the Honor Throne. The Honor Throne was carved from a single block of granite and covered with an opaque greenish pink Jade façade.

Attending to the duke was his most trusted advisor, Mystic Seven the Red. The two men were polar opposites when it came to appearances. Duke Asmout was a large man—bold and powerful, with a balding head, big bright eyes, and a loud personality, whereas Mystic Seven was a stick of a man—ugly, looking almost as a scarecrow who'd jump down off the post and fled the field. His eyes shifted quickly and often while his stringy gray hair almost seemed to shift shades according to his moods. Seven was still a young man, only forty. Duke Asmout had seen many more winters at almost sixty, and the men had been through almost twenty years of ruling the Kingdom together. Asmout as the duke holding the Honor Throne until the Former King returned, and Mystic Seven providing guidance.

Duke Asmout sat in the throne, staring at a map of the kingdom. He was vexed by the sights Mystic Seven had seen. Mystic Seven had seen sights before, had predicted trouble before, but this time it wasn't the kingdom that was in trouble, it was Duke Asmout himself—and his family. Duke Asmout had faced troubles before but nothing like this.

"Tell me, my mystic," Duke Asmout boomed loudly, like he always did. "Tell me again what you've seen."

"I see your children gathered around your grave," Mystic Seven replied in a raspy voice. "Three months from now when snow is falling, the first snow of the winter. Your children are upset and crying, and they all swear revenge on the man that killed you."

"Will they get it?"

"They will die trying," Mystic Seven said. "All four of them. They will die cold in the wastelands of the kingdom. A new family will hold the throne—a new master will sit on the Honor Throne, my liege."

"I cannot allow that to happen, Seven," Duke Asmout said.

The Duke stroked his salt and peppered beard as he stared at the map of the kingdom. He was deep in thought, debating all his options. Duke Asmout had once before sent his children to the edges of the kingdom to prevent them from falling into a trap set for him. The duke was still convinced that if he hadn't done that they would all be dead.

"I know what you're thinking," Mystic Seven said. "Send the kids out into the empire, it will make no difference. You will die. And once you do, their fates will have been written."

"We must hold Cerrado until the Former King returns," Duke Asmout said. "He charged me with protecting the realm and defending its people until his glorious return. Is there any indication of who is coming for me?"

"I see a hand holding a dagger made of pure gold," Mystic Seven said. "The hand I confess I have never seen before. The point of the golden dagger finds your heart. You are surprised by the person holding the dagger. You never envisioned this coming."

"The kingdom has been at peace for ten years," Duke Asmout said. "I have ruled a peaceful and prosperous kingdom. There have been no threats or grievances. Who would want to do this, Seven? Who?"

"Princess Ashlynn has raised questions about the shared rule of her territory," Mystic Seven said. "Along with Ornthal, the supreme ruler of the Bandits."

"Princess Ashlynn and the Bandits don't concern me," Duke Asmout said. "They each have their place in this kingdom. We have battled the bandits many times but they don't have the ambitions to take the kingdom. Princess Ashlynn has a very weak claim to her throne to begin with and she knows better than to press her luck in an assassination attempt."

"Greed is a powerful motivator my lord," Seven said, straightening his red robe. "And under your rule, Cerrado has become a very wealthy kingdom."

Duke Asmout looked over his advisor. Mystic Seven's red robe was made of a heavy fabric and the mystic would often grab the edges and wrap them around his body when he walked the castle halls, covering the black bodysuit he wore underneath. Asmout repositioned his mellow fox jacket, a jacket made from the bluish tinted fur of the mellow fox, who made its home on the southern grasslands of Cerrado. The jacket barely covered the duke's girth which was being held in place with blue trousers and matching regal top.

"I would trade all the wealth the kingdom has for peace and security for my family," Duke Asmout said. "Before their mother died I promised her that she would greet me on the other side before any of them. Do we know of anyone with a golden dagger?"

"There are legends."

"There's always legends," Duke Asmout said. "I want to know if any of them have any real merit. Do we know of anyone who possesses a golden dagger that could harbor ill-will toward us?"

"We do not."

"Advise me, Seven," Duke Asmout said, as he straightened in his throne. "What course of action do you recommend we take?"

"I would recommend that four objects need to be found," Mystic Seven said. "To protect you, your children, and the kingdom, we need protection. I would recommend obtaining first, a unicorn's horn. Second, water from the Immortal River. Third, the sword of the Former King. And fourth and finally, Necromancer Oliver's Knowledge of Cerrado."

Duke Asmout was stunned silent. He didn't know how to respond to his advisor.He knew not if his advisor was being serious or putting him on. Asmout remained silent as Seven tried to read the response to his advice. When the mystic couldn't take the silence anymore, he spoke.

"Your silence tells me that you do not approve," Mystic Seven said.

"Very hard quests," Duke Asmout said. "The easiest would be to obtain the unicorn horn. Unicorns reveal themselves in the Blue Cerrado Forest on quiet nights with full moons. I believe that one could appear to my youngest daughter as she is still pure. Waters from the Immortal River would be the next easiest task to complete, if the river is real and not just a legend. Next is the legend of the sword of the Former King; after defeating the evil Queen Mala, the Former King told me he needed to leave, that there was something he needed to do, and that he would return one day to rule the kingdom. I will know him by the sword he carries—a sword he hid somewhere in Cerrado, in a location only he knows. Finally, the last and most difficult quest, the Necromancer Oliver's Knowledge of Cerrado. The kingdom's most powerful necromancer, Oliver, takes all the knowledge of evil things in Cerrado and puts it in a book. It is a cursed book that only powerful necromancers can read. Four impossible tasks and three months to complete them in,"

"It is the only way, my liege," Mystic Seven said. "With these objects, no one in the kingdom will be able to challenge you."

"How would we use these objects? How would we use these powers?"

"A unicorn horn can extend life," Mystic Seven answered as he began to pace. "It is said that a person can become an immortal with a large enough horn. The waters of the Immortal River can also grant immortality along with rumors of massive healing powers, the power to heal any wound or illness. The Knowledge of Cerrado contains many spells and incantations that grant protection or destroy enemies. We could use it to place protective charms on you and your family."

"And the sword of the Former King?"

"It is said that the sword has magical powers. It could be very useful in defense of the kingdom and your family. Also, if you possess it, it could bring the Former King back or it could scare any attackers if they think the Former King is truly back."

"Interesting theory," Duke Asmout said. "If this worked it would guarantee the safety and continuation of the kingdom. Who would we send on these quests?"

"Your four children," Mystic Seven said. "Prince Alos, Princess Ambriss, Prince Atin, and Princess Arctic."

"Hmm."

"They will not refuse any quest you send them on," Mystic Seven said. "When they know what they are fighting for they will not fail. They are all old enough to face the challenges of the kingdom on their own, and you can send them out with your military generals. They will be protected on their quests."

"It is a big decision," Duke Asmout said. "Send for my children."

"You will send them on the quest then?"

"No. I will consult with them and discover if they have better actions we can take."

"Time is of the essence, my liege."

"A man in a hurry doesn't see the cliff until it's too late," Duke Asmout said. "Send for my children and we shall discuss our options."

Not twenty minutes after the call had gone out, Duke Asmout's four children were in the throne room with their father. Prince Alos, the fox prince, stood at the front of the room. In his mid-thirties, Prince Alos was tall and handsome, with a Greek-God body seemingly chiseled from solid muscle. His blonde locks cascaded around his broad shoulders, framing a strong face with sharp angles, piercing blue eyes, and a world-weary smile. Prince Alos had spent much time in the kingdom and was wise with the ways of the world.

The eldest prince wore only white animal-hide trousers with a blue robe draped over his shoulders, allowing his bronzed chest to be revealed to all. The robe was secured with a golden, ruby-encrusted brooch that was shaped into a fox. The back of the robe was adorned with a fox, sewn in with golden thread and silver accents. At his waist the prince carried a golden-handled sword—a sword he won at a knights' tournament when he was only sixteen. He was the youngest person in the kingdom to ever win a knights' tournament. Next to his sword was a silver-handled dagger that had a fox carved into the blade. The dagger had been forged by the fox prince himself.

Standing a pace behind Prince Alos was Princess Ambriss. The hawk princess was almost as tall as her older brother, but she was twig skinny, with golden curly locks breaking almost to her waist and partially covering her narrow face. The hawk princess allowed her hair to flow over her high, regal forehead, wide set blue eyes, tiny nose, thin lips, and pointed chin.

Princess Ambriss wore a blue strapless dress made from the finest satins in the kingdom, with a robe that formed the shape of a hawk's wings and tail. The hawk princess adorned her body with golden and ruby jewelry that was formed into the shape of hawks. The princess had often been called the most beautiful woman in the history of the kingdom and there were very few people who would ever argue that assessment.

Near the rear of the of the throne room, standing away from the others, was Prince Atin, the wolf prince. Atin, who was still in his late twenties, was shorter than the others but still a big man. His body was large—not as muscled as his brother but not as fat as his father. Atin had a shaved head, big eyes, a wide mouth, and a tempered disposition.

The wolf prince wore a regal suit of blue and black with no robe. He carried two daggers and no sword. When the wolf prince was in his younger years he'd lost his sword in a fight, and since then he'd never carried a sword, but he became the kingdom's foremost expert with daggers. Never one to reveal his true intentions early, the wolf prince was known as a formidable man who was destined for great things.

The last of the children, at only eighteen, was Princess Arctic, the snow princess. She was born during the worst snow storm Cerrado had ever seen. Petite all over, Arctic was much smaller than all the other members of her family. The snow princess had golden hair, thick and wild, that fell to her shoulders and surrounded her button nose and thin red lips.

The snow princess's most well-known feature were her eyes—her bird bright, ocean-blue eyes. Her eyes were soft and young, but had a fire-like intensity that could make a man melt—if her father allowed any men near her. Every man in the kingdom had made offers to the duke for his youngest daughter's hand but he'd refused them all. Just looking into her eyes, it was obvious she was going to conquer the world one day, if she was only allowed to leave the castle.

The snow princess wore satin white clothing with snowflakes subtly sewn into the fabrics—tights with a haltered top under an open robe cut to resemble a snowflake. And secured around her neck was a snowflake shaped, platinum brooch. Princess Arctic tried to project confidence, but her lack of experience was overtaking her desire to show a strong front for her family.

The children had listened to their father and his mystic while they explained the vision. The children were frightened for what this meant for their future.

"A misstep here could be catastrophic," Prince Alos said, his hand on his sword hilt. "We cannot risk the kingdom on speculation. We must hold Cerrado until the Former King returns."

"You are correct Prince Alos," Princess Ambriss said. "But we cannot risk father's life either. We must move with certainty on both fronts. The Former King never gave us any indication as to when his return would come, no indication as to where he needed to go. We've defended his kingdom for almost twenty years but there's been no word from him."

"We've fought enemies before," the fox prince said. "We'll fight enemies in the future. We've had peace for the past ten years—no wars, no violence. It was inevitable that something would happen. We have an army that can defeat anyone in the kingdom. Cerrado will not fall in a day."

"We have to ask a question, Brother," the hawk princess said. "Would our efforts be better spent questing for the objects or should we protect Father and try to learn where this threat develops before the threat strikes?"

"Mystic Seven the Red has never misled us before," Prince Alos said. "How many wars have we avoided or won because of his sight? How many enemies have we defeated before they were able to harm us? How much has he saved us?"

"This is true," Princess Ambriss said. "Mystic Seven, use your sight, if we stayed to protect Father, what would happen?"

Mystic Seven the Red moved to the center of the throne room and sat in a meditative position. He closed his eyes and went into a trance, his body gently rocking back and forth as his eyelids shuttered. After a moment the mystic opened his eyes and stood up.

"Remaining would be a costly mistake," Mystic Seven said. "The duke, Prince Alos, and Prince Atin would be killed, I see their bodies hanging in the courtyard, snow falling on them."

"And what of my little sister and myself?"

"I see you both birthing children for the new overlord of Cerrado," Mystic Seven said. "You will be taken and impregnated before being banished to the dungeon to die broken and alone."

There was silence in the room. No one wanted to be the first to speak. The gravity of the situation was beginning to set in on everyone. Prince Alos looked over his siblings. Princess Ambriss had a formal façade that was hiding fear, Prince Atin's face was unreadable as always, tossing a dagger between his hands like he was ready for a fight in the throne room, and Princess Arctic was flushed with fear, her little body trembling as she listened.

"Princess Arctic," Prince Alos said. "You haven't made a peep. What are your thoughts?"

"The wolf prince hasn't spoken either," Princess Arctic said. "Why do you ask me first and not him?"

"Because they know what I'm thinking, little one," Prince Atin said in a deep, controlled voice. "Kill."

"Ever since Prince Atin lost his sword in the knights' tournament," Prince Alos said, "his actions have been very consistent. I'm asking you, my littlest sister, what are your thoughts?"

"I've never had to deal with something like this," Princess Arctic said. "Even Princess Ambriss was outside of the castle during her teenage years, learning different aspects of Cerrado, working with the horse masters and the farmers, taking her lessons while sailing on the rivers and seas. My brothers have fought in tournaments, trained with the armies, and had quests. I've never left the castle walls."

"You still didn't tell us your thoughts," Prince Alos said.

"I'm scared!" Princess Arctic shouted.

"We all are, little sister," Princess Ambriss said. "But there were times before when we were scared and we got through them, as we will get through this."

"I think we can win this," Prince Alos said. "Cerrado will not fall in a day. The Former King will return and when he does he will reward us for holding the kingdom for him. We shall quest for the objects. Princess Arctic, you are the only one of us who a unicorn would appear to, correct?"

"Correct," Princess Arctic said, with pride.

"Then you shall quest for the unicorn's horn," Prince Alos said. "The most dangerous quest is the Knowledge of Cerrado. I've face necromancers before and know their powers. I will seek the cursed book out and return it."

"That leaves the sword of the Former King and water from the Immortal River," Princess Ambriss said, looking to the wolf prince.

"Pick your poison," Prince Atin said.

"I will quest for the Immortal River," the hawk princess said. "I will bring a flask of the magical water back."

"Couldn't this be much simpler?" Princess Arctic asked. "In my recent lessons I've learned of genies. If we found a lamp a genie could set all this right."

The room roiled with laughter.

"What?" Princess Arctic asked.

"Genies are notoriously dangerous," Princess Ambriss said. "They are not to be trusted and are very dangerous—more dangerous than the tasks at hand, little sister. We will go on the quests as Father has requested."

"Then it is settled," Duke Asmout said, standing. "Sleep well, my children. Tomorrow morning at first light you will leave for you quests. Remember what's at stake here... the survival of Cerrado."

Chapter 4

Krispin paced in the sitting room of his family's small cottage. The cottage was basic—simple, with a few pieces of homemade furniture and a wool rug on the floor. Everything in the décor was wooden, earthen, and without fancy accessories. There was a stone fireplace in the corner waiting for the winter chill to return so it could warm the cottage.

Krispin nervously fidgeted with his hands, alternating between rubbing them together and tugging at different parts of his clothing. He seemed to be trying to rehearse a speech but the words weren't coming to him. Krispin was frustrated as he paced—his pace quickening in the small room.

"This is just something I have to do, Father," Krispin said, to no one. "No, he would never buy that." Krispin pondered some more. "This is my calling. This is my call, Father. I have to go...no, no, no, he won't listen to that either."

"What's the matter, my handsome son?" a soft, feminine voice rang out behind Krispin.

Krispin turned around to see his mother Mary standing in the doorway between the family room and the kitchen. Krispin looked his mother over. Mary was tall and fit, with a powerful presence that commanded attention in any situation. She was an exotic beauty with tanned skin and shiny black hair surrounding her dark features and seductive eyes. Many people in the village thought she was Mediterranean, and that Kale had been to the islands and seas to the south. Some thought maybe she was Spanish, and spent her days on the ocean beach, but Mary would never confirm where she was originally from. Krispin realized his mother was waiting for him to speak.

"Nothing's the matter, Mother," Krispin said. "Why does something have to be the matter?"

"Please, Krispin," Mary said, in her silky, elegant accent. "I know when my boy is melancholy. Tell me, what troubles you? Why are you blue this fine evening?"

"It's Holly, Mother."

"It's always Holly."

"She's going to marry Chester."

"They'll make a good couple."

"MOTHER!"

"It's true," Mary said, moving to her knitting chair. "They will make a fine couple and Chester will make a good farmer."

"But I want to marry Holly."

"She's not the girl for you dear."

"Mother?" Krispin said, exasperated. "How can you say that? Holly and I would be a grand couple—an amazing couple. It would be true love between us."

"Oh please," Mary said laughing. "I'm so sorry to laugh Krispin but Holly is not the girl for you. There will be a better girl, a much grander woman. A mother knows these things."

"I'm almost twenty-one, Mother," Krispin said. "And I still live at home. I still am a shepherd on the family farm."

"So is your father," Mary said. "If it's a good enough occupation for him, why isn't it for you?"

"Mother," Krispin said. "I want an adventure. Holly says if I have a grand adventure then she'll marry me instead of Chester. I know I can have an adventure. I know I can win her heart."

"Having an adventure alone is not the way to win a woman's heart," Mary said. "Trust me, I know."

"How did you and dad meet?" Krispin asked. "I've never asked before but I always hear the rumors in the village. Dad went to the sea and was on a ship that was protecting the harbors against pirates. They said that a pirate ship had captured you from your home when you were only fourteen and you were forced to clean the ship for the pirates. Dad saw you on the ship and instantly fell in love with you but the pirate ship got away. He spent two years chasing the ship down and saved you. You and Father were married by the captain of his ship the moment he brought you back to his ship...is all that true?"

"Not a word of it," Mary said, with a knowing smile. "Oh Krispin, your father did save me, we did have an adventure together, but it didn't involve pirates—well, the pirates didn't play that big of a role in the adventure, and they really weren't pirates per se, but seamen none the less. It's difficult to explain..."

"But there was an adventure."

"Why are you so intent on having an adventure?"

"Why not?" Krispin said. "I don't want to live my life and look back regretting the fact that there were so many opportunities in front of me that I didn't take. I want to have a story to tell my children when they are getting ready to leave the home. I want to know what else is out in the world."

"Do you really think Holly would make a good wife for you?" Mary asked. "If she doesn't want to marry you as you are now, only if you have an adventure? Does that sound like a good way to start a marriage?"

"I have to go on an adventure," Krispin said, pleading. "I have to do something. I cannot stay here any longer. I love you, Mother, but I need to grow. I should have before but I didn't. This is my time and I have to go. Oh Mother, the only difficult thing will be convincing Father."

"That will be the challenge," Kale's voice filled the room.

Krispin quickly turned around to see that his father had been standing in the doorway. Kale had a dejected look on his face but there was something in his eyes, something Krispin didn't notice, but let Mary know he knew this time was coming.

"I can see that your time here in our village and farm is limited," Kale said.

"I don't want to leave," Krispin said. "I want to marry Holly and go on an amazing honeymoon then return here to run the family farm, similar to what you did."

"I do believe it is time that you spread your wings," Kale said. "There's only so much that you can achieve here. There comes a point when you have to go out into the world and seek your destiny."

"Really?" Krispin said. "You'll let me go?"

"I don't know if we can contain you much longer," Kale said.

"Please tell me about the adventure that you had, Father," Krispin said. "Please tell me how you met and fell in love with Mother."

"That's a long story, Son," Kale said, with a knowing smile. "But there were some exciting times when we were dodging evil and trying to save each other."

"Where should I go?" Krispin asked. "Which direction should I head?"

"In the morning I will give you a heading," Kale said. "I will give you a path to start on and an idea of what you should look for."

"Thank you so much, Father," Krispin said, hugging his father. "You too, Mother." Krispin gave his mother a hug as well. "I need to tell Holly. I'll be back shortly."

Krispin rushed out of the cottage. Mary gave Kale a disapproving glance as Kale watched his boy rush toward the village. Kale just gave her a smug smile.

"You don't approve Dear?" Kale said. "I can see it in your eyes."

"He's young," Mary said, standing. "He isn't ready for the world…not yet."

"He's old enough," Kale said. "By his time on this Earth he's considered a man, but by his actions and accomplishments he's still a boy. This will be good for him."

"Can he handle it?"

"He's our son," Kale said. "We raised him well. He will have his grand adventure."

Krispin rushed along the dirt streets of the little village. Many of the houses were dark but there were still a few that had candles burning in the windows. In the house at the end of the main street was a house that had a candle burning in an upstairs window. Krispin skidded to a stop outside the lit window and looked around the ground for a small stone to throw. Krispin found a small, round, smooth piece of granite and tossed it at the window.

Krispin waited with baited breath for the window to open. When it did, Holly stuck her head out the window and looked around the street to see Krispin there. Her excited anticipation was replaced with indifference when she saw Krispin standing on the street.

"Krispin," Holly said, sounding bored. "I thought it was Chester coming to call."

"My father's giving me a heading tomorrow morning," Krispin blurted out loudly. "I will have my adventure. An adventure that will be the talk of the village for years to come."

"Oh Krispin," Holly said, with a chuckle. "You're so cute at times. You're a great friend. Remember, to win my heart it has to be a grand adventure—something better than anyone else in the village has ever experienced. Where do you think you'll go?"

"I don't know," Krispin said. "I think I'll make my way to the Mediterranean, like Father was rumored to have done. I can find a caravan headed that direction, then sail the seas fighting pirates."

"Just don't come home with a wife and child like your father did," Holly said, with a smile. "Then your adventure wouldn't mean anything to me."

"Don't worry, Holly," Krispin said. "My heart belongs to you. I will prove that to you with this adventure."

"Thank you," Holly said, as she started to close her window. "I look forward to hearing about your adventure. Goodnight."

Holly closed her window as Krispin headed home, adventures swimming around his head. Krispin slowly made his way out of the village and down the dirt road between the lazy brook and the Moon Forest. Krispin looked to the heavens at the billions of stars that were twinkling in the clear sky above. Krispin imagined that very soon he'd be looking up at this sky but not here—not outside his little village and farm. He'd be looking at this sky from the seas or mountains.

As Krispin's eyes were glued to the sky, a shooting star streaked across the night sky, its tail leaving a multicolored streak against the black of the sky. Krispin smiled as he formulated the perfect wish.

"Shooting star, shooting star, how I wonder what you are," Krispin said, excitedly. "I wish I may, I wish I might, have this wish I wish tonight. I wish to have a grand adventure that brings me a loving wife who falls madly in love with me and we live happily ever after. That's what I wish for, shooting star. Thank you."

Almost as if in response to his wish, another shooting star flared across the sky in almost the exact same path the first had taken. Krispin smiled as he continued walking home, knowing that now that he'd wished upon a star, he was going to have an amazing adventure that would bring him happiness with Holly.

Chapter 5

The morning air was warm with the smell of a nearby rainstorm, although there were no clouds in the sky. The first rays of the sun bathed the shimmering stone of the Cerrado Castle in brilliant golden light as Duke Asmout's four children prepared themselves for the task at hand. The children were wasting no time getting their supplies ready for the trip they were about to take.

Prince Alos, in his blue and white royal suit, with an elegant flowing robe behind him, had a team of soldiers—loyal footmen he'd commanded in the past. The troops were ready for a long trek through forests and over grasslands to reach the Windswept Castle where Prince Alos believed he could find a copy of Necromancer Oliver's Knowledge of Cerrado.

Princess Ambriss, in her blue leather riding outfit, mounted atop her large brown steed with a white patch over its eye, was flanked by her riding women—a team that could perform amazing exhibition riding performances and cover vast distances in short times. The women had plans to ride like the wind to the north, where dark forests concealed many strange things—possibly an immortal river.

Prince Atin, wearing non-royal blue animal hides, had three very shifty looking men and a woman with him—all dressed in blacks with no symbols of royalty or allegiances on their garments. The group could move like thieves in the night, striking before anyone knew they were there. The other children didn't know the names of the wolf prince's companions and some of them thought it was a good thing they didn't know them.

Princess Arctic, in her snow white tights and haltered top, sans robe, was with Hibit—a flustered little man who was advisor to the king and educator to the children. And Snowflake, a snow white puma with blue patches over her eyes and feet—one of Princess Arctic's best and only friends. Hibit had strict instructions to lead the snow princess to the Blue Cerrado Forest, lead her to the Hidden Meadow within the forest, and wait until a unicorn appears to her. Snowflake was there because she was always with Princess Arctic.

Duke Asmout with Mystic Seven the Red beside him looked over his children as they prepared for their quests. He could see the fear and

33

concern in their eyes—none more afraid that the young Princess Arctic. The duke worried that the snow princess had been sheltered more than the other children, being the apple of his eye, and that she wouldn't be ready for a quest of this nature.

The duke looked over his advisor Hibit, who was only slightly taller than Arctic and didn't weigh much more than his little daughter, although Hibit was in his late forties. Hibit wore a blue suit with gold metals that indicated his rank of advisor with a brooch of a snowflake to indicate he was associated with the snow princess. Hibit had an ornate knife that he kept in a sheath in his left boot, but the duke hoped the knife wouldn't need to feel the open air on this mission.

Princess Arctic was busy putting some supplies into a bag she'd attached to Snowflake's back. The puma was a big animal, heavier than Arctic herself standing three feet tall and six feet long, not including the tail. The puma had a smile on her face, as she always did when Arctic was playing with her. Snowflake had been trained to protect Arctic and had been with her since the day she was born.

"My children," Duke Asmout called out. "Gather 'round."

The four royal children complied and gathered around their father while their travel companions stayed back, away from the royalty.

"You must not fail," Duke Asmout said. "The quests I send you on today, I don't send you on lightly. I will pray every day for your safe returns. Although there's been peace within the kingdom for over ten years, there are still many dangers out there. Remember that I've cultivated many friends within the kingdom but there are still enemies out there. We do not know where the dagger will come from…whose hand holds it. Proceed with caution—be alert. And please, my children, come home safely."

"We will not let Cerrado fall, Father," Prince Alos shouted. "We are strong and will have victory."

Prince Alos shouted a command and his foot soldiers fell into line behind him as they started marching out of the courtyard. Princess Ambriss's riders took off like the wind in a sweeping formation. Prince Atin and his small band simply vanished outside the castle walls, disappearing like shadows in the night. Only Princess Arctic, Hibit, and

Snowflake remained in the courtyard. Arctic was on the verge of tears as her father approached her.

"What is wrong, my little one?" Duke Asmout asked, hugging his daughter.

"I'm scared, Father," Princess Arctic said, wiping a tear from her eye. "I've never left these walls before. I've never been away from my home before. There's always been at least one of my siblings near me."

"I know, my little daughter," the duke said. "Every person needs an experience like this. Everyone needs a chance to grow. This will allow you to see something you've never seen, and meet people you've never met. Look here Princess Arctic, this will be a good experience for you."

"I don't know what I'll find out there," Princess Arctic said.

"That's part of the fun," Duke Asmout said. "Part of the experience. You've got Hibit to guide you and Snowflake to protect you. You will go to the Blue Cerrado Forest, see a unicorn, and your quest will be done. You might even see one tonight and then you'd be able to return home without spending a night away. It will be an easy quest, my daughter."

"Okay," Princess Arctic said, as she wiped her eyes again. "I will be brave for you. Thank you, Father. I love you."

"I love you, too, my youngest," Duke Asmout said.

"Come, Snowflake," Princess Arctic said, to her happy-go-lucky cat. "It is time to experience what's outside the castle walls."

Snowflake gave Princess Arctic a quizzical look before falling into step behind her—her tail wagging like an over-excited puppy. Hibit looked to the duke as he started to follow them but the duke stopped him.

"Hibit," Duke Asmout said. "She is my youngest."

"The Blue Cerrado Forest is a safe place," Hibit said. "And the hidden meadow is a magical place that's protected. Only a person like Princess Arctic could enter. She will be safe, my Duke."

"I trust you know what will happen if she isn't safe," Duke Asmout said. "But do make sure she experiences something new."

"I will, Duke Asmout," Hibit said. "Fear not, a unicorn will appear to her before nightfall and we will be back in the castle without a night away from our beds."

Duke Asmout nodded toward Hibit as he scrambled to catch up to Princess Arctic and Snowflake. Mystic Seven approached the duke as he watched his youngest walking away.

"There is no reason to fear for her, Duke Asmout," Mystic Seven said. "She is in good hands. I should think Snowflake alone could have been her defender."

"That may be true, but it's not her I have the greatest concerns about," Duke Asmout said.

"Prince Alos?"

"Prince Alos," Duke Asmout said. "He is the strongest warrior and knight in the land. He is wise beyond his years and could make a formidable king. There is no limit on how successful my oldest son could become."

"Then why are you concerned?" Mystic Seven asked.

"Because he walks into the den of a very powerful necromancer," Duke Asmout said. "A powerful she-witch that has powers and abilities far beyond anything he's faced before. It's one thing to take a knight to the ground in the games, it's another thing to be faced with magic and dark powers that have no concern for morals or ethics."

"He is powerful and wise," Mystic Seven said. "He will proceed with caution and use his best judgment on how to obtain the book."

"I hope so, my mystic," Duke Asmout said. "Come, there is much work we need to do before my children return. We must get defenses in place in case this attack comes before we think it will."

Duke Asmout turned and began walking toward the castle as Mystic Seven watched Princess Arctic and her team disappear through the city. Seven smiled to himself—almost chuckling, as he turned and rushed toward the duke.

Krispin excitedly finished putting the final items in his brown sack, cinched the cords, and swung the pack over his shoulder. Krispin took one final look around his small bedroom, taking a deep breath before walking toward the door to leave the room. His mind was so full of the adventures that he'd be having, he couldn't think of anything else. The thought that this could be the last time he'd ever see his little room again didn't even register, nor did the fact that if he returned here, he'd be a fundamentally changed man.

Krispin made his way to the front porch of the cottage where his parents were waiting for him. Mary put a small bag of food in his bag before kissing him on the head and embracing him in a tight-squeeze hug. Krispin hugged her back, unaware there were tears in his mother's eyes. Krispin shook his father's hand.

"Son," Kale said, looking out over the bright, sunny morning. "There is much advice that I should give you before you head out on your quest. I could tell you that not everyone has had a life as good as yours with as much abundance as you've had—but on the other hand, many have had much more than you could ever imagine—so try to see things from their perspective before you criticize or envy them. Or I could tell you that not every person you meet is going to be a friend, but friends are easy to find, if you know how to look for them. Or I could tell you that the world is a huge place, no matter how many people try to say that the world is getting smaller and there's no way you could know everything there is to know. Those are things that I could tell you about but here is only one piece of advice that I want to give you, Son. Something I wish someone would have told me before I left on my quests. You see, when I went to university, all I was focused on was finding a new world. I wanted so badly to discover something that hadn't been discovered, to go somewhere that no one had ever gone to before. My father told me that I didn't need to look to the sky to find other worlds. I never understood what he meant, but what I think he meant is that we live in our own sheltered little world right here on the farm, Krispin. People in the city have so many different experiences than we do, and people who don't live in merry old England have vastly different experiences than we do. There's a whole new world right outside our doorstep, Krispin. So don't focus so much on where you're going to end up."

"What are you trying to say, Father?"

"Don't focus on the destination, Krispin," Kale said. "Don't worry so much about where you are going to end up. Instead, focus on the journey that takes you there."

"I understand, Father," Krispin said.

"Actually, you don't, Krispin," Kale said, with a smile. "You can't understand that yet. Not until you've experienced a little of what I'm talking about. Then it will make perfect sense. Be brave, my son. Remember everything that we've taught you over the years."

"And do make sure to have a good time," Mary chimed in.

"I will, Mother," Krispin said. "And I will return before the wedding. I will have an adventure that will be the grandest of them all."

"I'm sure you will," Kale said. "Now, I promised you a heading...in three days' time there will be a full silver moon inside the Moon Forest. I've heard rumors that many strange things can happen on a full silver moon in the Moon Forest. Go there and see what you can find."

"The Moon Forest?" Krispin asked, skeptical. "I was hoping to see the ocean, the seas, and maybe pirates. The Moon Forest is a place that I played as a youngster."

"You must take small steps to start your adventure, Son," Kale said. "I promise you that your adventure starts in the Moon Forest on the night of a full moon."

"Then I will go there," Krispin said. "And I will return. I promise you that."

Krispin hugged his parents again. Mary didn't want to let him go, squeezing him tight and planting kisses on his head. Kale had to help Krispin escape his mother's grip. Krispin began to walk down the familiar trail that led between his house and the village on his way to the path for the Moon Forest. His parents watched, hoping for the best for their son.

"Will he find what he's looking for?" Mary asked.

"I'm sure of it," Kale said. "There's magic in that forest. It's no coincidence that he receives a calling three days before the full silver moon. You know what's about to happen."

"I do and I'm afraid for him. We should be with him, Kale. He's not ready for something like this on his own."

"Everyone must grow into their own shoes one day, Mary. This is his day."

"What about Holly and the wedding?"

"My hope is that when he gets back he no longer has those feelings for Holly."

"And if he does?"

"Then I'm sure she will love him back."

Mary gave Kale a disapproving glance before he kissed her on the lips. They looked back out to see their son go around a bend and out of their sight. Mary breathed a heavy sigh before turning and heading back into the little cottage. Kale watched for a moment longer before he followed his wife inside and closed the door.

As Krispin walked happily down the trail, his mind working quickly trying to process everything his father said while at the same time being disappointed that his adventure started in the simple Moon Forest, he didn't realize someone was following him. Krispin's mind was swimming with information when someone rushed up from behind and threw Krispin to the ground.

Krispin scrambled to roll over onto his back and get into a defensive position. He looked up and saw Chester Van Brunt—a tall, muscular, brutish man, standing over him. Chester looked ready to bite the head off a nail as he stood breathing heavy over Krispin. Chester wore an unbuttoned white shirt, exposing his smooth, powerful chest. The shirt was tucked into his dirty brown trousers. Chester didn't wear shoes, preferring to show how tough he was by always walking around barefoot.

"If you ever talk to my wife again, Risdell," Chester boomed as he shook his fist at Krispin. "I'll throttle you so hard they'll have to have the sheep tend to you."

"Clever," Krispin said, trying to stand, but Chester pushed him back to the ground. "Holly is her own woman and she can choose who she marries."

"She's marrying me!" Chester yelled. "She's the most beautiful woman in the entire village and I'm the most handsome man. There isn't another man in the village that's deserving of her. I'm not going to tell you again, Risdell...you stay away from my wife."

"Chester, just let me go," Krispin said, meekly. "I have an adventure to go on."

"Then go on your adventure," Chester said. "I'll give you one piece of advice, be like your father and find a girl to knock up so she's stuck being your woman."

"My parents love each other!" Krispin yelled. "They've always loved each other."

"Yeah, right," Chester laughed. "You just make sure to select someone else to be your woman, Risdell, you stay away from my Holly."

Chester kicked some dirt into Krispin's face before he walked away. Krispin slowly stood as he wiped a tear out of his eye. Krispin brushed the dirt off his pants and shirt before he began walking toward the Moon Forest.

As he continued his walk, Krispin began to pay attention to his surroundings. He'd walked this trail hundreds of times during his life. Krispin knew every twist, every turn, and where ever pothole was, yet this was the first time he truly paid attention to the surroundings of the road. There was the twisted tree that Krispin and his friends would swing off of when they were little, but looking it over now, Krispin realized the top of the tree was spread out with lots of leaves, but the tree didn't look as strong as it once did.

Krispin noticed the old man Hanson's barn was in desperate need of a painting and the fence surrounding it needed patchwork done. Krispin saw the Van Brunt's wheat fields were growing nicely, as they always did, and the wheat was grass green, swaying in the light breeze. All these things had always been there but Krispin never noticed.

Krispin began to wonder if this is what his father had meant—not focusing so much on the destination but on the journey that was going to bring him there. He still wondered what his father meant about finding other worlds. All those thoughts quickly got pushed out of his head when he realized he'd just arrived at the gate in the red stone wall. Krispin looked over the Moon Forest that was being held back by the old wall. Krispin knew that when he stepped through that gate, his adventure would begin. It was a big step for Krispin, but after a minute of hesitating, Krispin entered the forest.

Chapter 6

After three days of wandering through the depths of the Moon Forest, Krispin was beginning to wonder if he'd made the right decision. So far his adventure had been very plain, simple, and mundane. He'd yet to encounter any strange beings, yet to discover a new animal, and he hadn't seen anything that he'd never seen before. Krispin was walking along a narrow dirt path, one that barely cut its way through the giant trees of the forest, when he happened to see the first person in the forest.

The person was a beautiful girl wearing a strapless tight green dress with an incredibly short hem. The girl was very pale, tall, and thick, with curly blonde locks that extended just past her waist and were decorated with various leaves and flowers. She had the deepest blue eyes Krispin had ever seen. She almost seemed to dance around as she moved. As Krispin got closer and could see more of her face, he realized the woman was in her early thirties. She seemed to be looking for something.

Krispin watched the woman as she moved between trees, looking near the ground, almost as if she was tracking something she'd lost. The woman was oblivious about Krispin watching her. She was intently looking around the trees, remaining absolutely silent as she moved around.

"Are you looking for something?" Krispin asked, immediately realizing how obvious her actions were and how dumb his question was. The woman jumped, startled by Krispin.

"You scared me, good sir," the woman said, smiling, and taking a couple steps closer to Krispin.

The woman stepped into the shafts of light that were coming through the canopy of trees. The golden light bathed the woman. She seemed to be glowing—sparkling with an energy that Krispin couldn't figure out. The only thing he knew was that this woman was the most beautiful woman he'd ever seen.

"I'm sorry for that," Krispin said, sheepishly. "I saw you there and couldn't help but notice you. There's something about you that's amazing."

"I'm sure there is," the woman said, smiling.

"My name's Krispin Risdell," Krispin said. "Can I help you find what you're looking for?"

"You might be able to, Krispin Risdell," the woman said. "I'm not from here."

"You must be from the islands," Krispin said. "I would have guessed Sweden since they say Swedish women are blonde, pale, and stunningly beautiful...but you don't dress like they do. Your dress looks to be from a much warmer area. They say the islands are hot, and the most beautiful women in the world come from there."

"You're a strange one," the woman said, smiling. "No, I'm not from the islands or Sweden. You don't know where I'm from."

"Where is it?" Krispin asked. "How could we get there from here?"

"You can't get there from here," the woman said. "Tell me, Krispin, have you noticed anything strange in the forest in the past couple days?"

"As a matter of fact I have," Krispin said. "Last night, well, just before dawn really, the entire forest lit up like daytime from a single bolt of lightning. It was accompanied by a crack of thunder that shook the entire forest, but there wasn't a single drop of rain. What's even stranger is I climbed a tree and looked into the sky, and there wasn't a single cloud up there...only a billion twinkling stars and a full silver moon. Is that the strange thing you are looking for?"

"In a sense, yes," the woman said. "You see, that was an indication of something that happened—something magical. That is the magic I am searching for."

"You're a magician?"

"In a sense, yes."

"In a sense?"

"In a sense, yes."

Krispin stared at the woman who'd resumed her search for whatever she was looking for. The more Krispin stared at the woman, the more he realized how amazingly beautiful she was. He couldn't take his eyes off her, her green dress that seemed to fit her perfectly, her blonde hair that hypnotically swayed in the breeze, her stunning legs…

"You might help me look," the woman said, with a smile so powerful it could melt the coldest of hearts.

"I wouldn't know where to begin," Krispin said. "Or what I'd be looking for."

"You'd be looking for something magical," the woman said. "Something that shouldn't be here."

"I've never been here before, so how would I know that it shouldn't be here?" Krispin asked.

"I'd suspect that once you set your eyes upon it," the woman began. "You'll know in that instant it isn't supposed to be here. Magical things have a way of almost glowing…sparkling, in a way that indicates they shouldn't be where they are."

"Kind of like how you are glowing and sparkling in the shafts of sunlight right now?" Krispin asked.

"Yes, exactly," the woman said, looking herself over. "Exactly like this. Let me ask you something…is your father Kale Risdell?"

"Yes he is," Krispin responded, stunned.

"Then your mother is Mary, correct?"

"Yes. How do you know that?"

"Lucky guess," the woman said, with a smile. "Krispin, I do need your help. Continue on this trail, looking for something that shouldn't be where it's at. Don't stop until you find the out of place item. Once you find it, I want you to do something with it."

"Anything," Krispin said. "What do you want me to do with it?"

"I'm not sure," the woman said.

"You're not sure?" Krispin asked, skeptically. "How can you not be sure?"

"Because I'm not sure what it is," the woman said. "You will know what to do with it once you find it."

"I don't understand," Krispin said. "I'm supposed to walk this path until I find something that's not supposed to be there, which I don't know because I don't know what's supposed to be there anyway, and when I find that out of place thing, I'm supposed to do something with it, but we don't know what that is either?"

"Sounds like you understand perfectly," the woman said. "What's the problem?"

"Okay…"

"Trust me, Krispin," the woman said. "When the moment is right, you'll know. There'll be something in the back of your mind that tells you that it's right. When you feel that, just go for it. I promise you that if you do well, you will be well rewarded."

"Rewarded?" Krispin asked. "How are you going to reward me?"

"I will give you something," the woman said, walking right up to Krispin, putting her hands at his waist. "I will give you something that you've always desired but have never been able to find." The woman softly kissed Krispin on the lips. Krispin's eyes shuttered with delight from the magical kiss. "I will give you an adventure that you'll never forget."

With that, the woman took a couple steps backwards into the shadows of a tree and seemed to disappear. Krispin looked around quickly for her but there was no trace of the woman. Krispin looked into the dirt, hoping to track her footprints like he'd done with sheep in the past. But to Krispin's surprise, the only prints in the dirt were his. There were no female footprints. Krispin was stunned but he decided to quickly get on the trail and compete the task she'd given him.

Krispin rushed down the narrow dirt trail, dodging in and out of trees and up and down the contours of the land. He was watching intently for anything that was out of place but everything seemed to fit perfectly into the forest. The woodland animals all looked content in their homes and Krispin didn't see any other signs of humans in the forest.

After an hour of searching, Krispin thought he heard the faintest of sounds. He looked around and realized that somehow, in all his travels, he

45

was back by the red stone wall. He could just barely make the wall out through the few hundred feet of trees. Dejection began to overwhelm Krispin. After all this time searching and looking, he'd somehow looped around.

Krispin could still hear something. At first, he thought it was the water of the lazy brook, but the more he listened to it, the more he realized that it sounded like a person softly crying. He couldn't figure it out, there didn't appear to be anyone near him. Krispin breathed a heavy sigh. All he'd wanted was an adventure but here he was, after three days, back where he started. Krispin felt foolish, sheepish, and in that moment, he thought about going home. If this was all the further he was going to get, if all his efforts were going to be for nothing, then what was the point of continuing?

As Krispin started to walk toward the red stone wall he could hear the sounds of someone weeping getting louder. Krispin had already made up his mind to leave the forest and return home when he looked to his right.He thought that he saw someone sitting on a log. Krispin debated walking over and seeing what was wrong, but instead, walked toward the wall again. As he looked back, he noticed that the light seemed to hit the person sitting there. The person was glowing—sparkling in the light. Krispin remembered what the strange lady had said, so he started walking over to the weeping person.

When Krispin entered the clearing he saw the most curious looking girl. She was very petite, with shoulder length blonde curly hair, wearing formfitting white tights with a haltered white top, both with snowflakes subtly sewn into the material. The girl looked to be no older than eighteen years old and she had her face buried into her hands as she softly wept. Krispin noticed that as more light from the sun breaking through the canopy immersed the girl, there was an energy about her. It was something Krispin had never seen before.

"Why are you crying?" Krispin asked softly.

The girl looked up at him, her eyes puffy from crying. She had such a sad look on her face that Krispin's heart melted. He didn't know what to say or do, all he knew was that he had to help her.

"What's wrong?" Krispin asked again.

"Everything is wrong," the girl said, standing.

Krispin looked her over. She only stood about five feet tall but was amazingly beautiful. With her skin-tone and hair. She was also pale and blonde. Krispin thought this girl might be the daughter of the woman he'd seen earlier. The only thing that didn't fit was that this girl was so petite, and the woman was tall and thick.

"Did you get separated from your mother?" Krispin asked. "I believe I saw her not too far back in the forest."

"My mother passed away when I was very young," the girl said. "And I am not so little that I would be weeping over getting separated from my mother. I'm eighteen years old."

"Then please," Krispin said, taking a step closer. "Let me help you. My name is Krispin Risdell. Who are you?"

"My name is Arctic," she answered. "I am lost."

"Where were you trying to get to?"

"I am trying to find a unicorn."

"Unicorn?" Krispin asked stunned. "Aren't you a little old to be searching for unicorns?"

"I guess I am," Arctic said. "Unicorns will only appear to a girl who is pure, and not spoiled by a man. Most girls are married by eighteen but my father wanted to wait with my wedding so I was kept until a suitable match was found."

"Okay," Krispin said. "Not the answer I was expecting."

"Why would you be expecting an answer?" Arctic asked. "You don't know me or anything about me."

"Good point," Krispin said. "A unicorn though? That still doesn't tell me why you were crying."

"I was with my protector Hibit and my cat Snowflake," Arctic said. "We were walking in the Blue Cerrado Forest and all of a sudden I was here, without them. I did what Hibit had told me to do when we first left on our quest...if I got separated, I was to stay in one spot and they would

47

find me. Snowflake is a good tracker, even though she's a cat. Her nose is better than most dogs'. I can never beat her in hide and go seek."

"How long have you been here?"

"A few hours. I got here right at dawn."

"Do you remember anything else?"

"No."

"I've never heard of the Blue Cerrado Forest before," Krispin said. "This is the Moon Forest."

"I've never heard of the Moon Forest," Arctic said. "I'm from Cerrado."

"Cerrado?" Krispin asked. "Never heard of that before either."

"Well, it's where I'm from," Arctic snapped. "Please, good sir…can you help me find my way back to my friends?"

"I would love to help you," Krispin said. "I'm on an adventure. Helping someone who's lost could be a good addition to my adventure, Arctic."

"You're having an adventure?"

"You see, the most beautiful girl in all my village is getting married in about three months' time and if I have a grand adventure, she will marry me instead of the jerk that she is planning on marrying. I have to have a story that will captivate her mind and lead her to my heart."

"Is that how love works where you are from?" Arctic asked. "That's very strange. In Cerrado, people marry because they are in love with each other."

"That's how it works here too," Krispin said. "But Holly just doesn't realize that I'm the man she loves. When I have my adventure it will all work out."

"I hope it does for you," Arctic said. "Although I don't understand why you would need to have an adventure to win a woman's heart. Onto my problem, though…how do I find my way home?"

"How did you get here?"

"I was walking in the Blue Cerrado Forest," Arctic said. "I had asked Hibit and Snowflake to stand guard while I walked in an open area of the forest. Father had charged me with finding a unicorn horn and I needed to see the unicorn on my own, he wouldn't appear if Hibit or Snowflake were by my side. I walked along an open area and...I don't remember what happened after that. I was in this forest and this isn't the Blue Cerrado Forest."

"It's the Moon Forest."

"You said that before," Arctic said. "Now I don't know where my friends are. I called out for them but they didn't come. There was thunder and lightning, but no rain. I don't know what to do, Krispin. Please help me."

"I'll help you," Krispin said. "But I'm unsure of what we should do."

"What does your heart tell you we should do?"

"It says we should walk," Krispin said. "Take my hand, I'll lead you."

Arctic held out her hand and Krispin took it. When their hands met, both Krispin and Arctic felt a jolt of electricity, something that neither of them could explain. They instantly locked eyes with each other. Krispin felt as if there was a cord of light going between them—something he'd never felt before and was pretty sure that Arctic hadn't felt either.

Krispin smiled. After a moment, he started to walk away from the red stone wall. With Arctic in hand, the pair walked on a small dirt trail. Every time they came to a fork in the road, or when there was a trail that led off in a different direction, there seemed to be a sparkling glowshowing the pair which way to go. Krispin felt as if the woman he'd met earlier was somehow guiding them.

As the pair walked, they felt something between them. Neither of them commented on it, but they both felt it. As they made their way into a clearing, they saw two trees that were leaning against each other, forming an arch between the trees. The strange thing was that the area between the trees was glowing with a cool green color. The green was sparkling and looked very strange. Arctic looked at the glowing arch with a confused look on her face, before something in her mind clicked.

"That's what happened to me," Arctic exclaimed. "I walked through an arch like that. The arch is what brought me from Cerrado to here."

"That's impossible," Krispin said. "Why didn't you know that until now?"

"I don't know," Arctic said. "But I know that's what happened."

"Then Arctic," Krispin said, looking her in the eyes. "Then walk through the arch and return home."

"I'm scared," Arctic said. "Come with me."

"But what if I can't return to here?" Krispin asked. "What happens if I'm trapped in Cerrado, if that is a real place?"

"You said you would help me get home," Arctic said, in a whiny tone. "Walk through the arch with me and help me on my quest to find the unicorn. I'll make sure that you can get back here and then we can tell your Holly about the grand adventure that you had."

"It would make for an interesting adventure," Krispin said. "But I need to stay here. I'm sorry Arctic, I can't go with you."

"Yes, you can," Arctic said, as she started running toward the arch.

Arctic held Krispin's hand tight, bringing him through the arch with her. There were two bolts of lightning, and two cracks of thunder, before the trees separated and the glowing green between them disappeared just as Krispin and Arctic disappeared through the arch.

Chapter 7

In the moments after Krispin and Arctic entered the arch, the Moon Forest returned to its normal self. There were birds chirping, animals humming, and the smells of the most wonderful flowering trees filling the air with a spectrum of fragrances. The clearing where the arch had appeared showed no signs of what had happened.

It was then that a figure made its way in the clearing—the woman in the green dress that Krispin had received information from. She smiled a very pleasant smile as she looked over the clearing. She was no longer looking for something, instead she was looking directly at the location where the arch had been.

The woman smiled again before twirling her fingers. It was a sight not seen in a very long time. The air around the woman began to swirl as leaves and dust kicked up from the clearing. A whirlwind swirled around the woman and as quickly as it had started, it stopped. The woman was gone, and the clearing was empty.

The woman landed in an area not dissimilar from where she had left. It was a forest, but not a forest that anyone from earth had ever been to. The trees were...different. The plants were...different. The animals were...different. The woman looked over the area and called out. It took a moment but a whirlwind began to form near her. In the air was the unmistakable sound of a clock, tick-tock, tick-tock.

When the whirlwind subsided, a man was standing where the wind had been. He looked like a wizard—he was tall, had a long white beard and hair, he wore a gray hooded-cloak that went to the ground, and held the most curious of objects in his left hand, opposite a walking stick— an hour glass.

The woman in the green dress walked up to the man with loving eyes and kissed him. The man wrapped his arms around the woman and embraced her. The pair pulled back and looked into each other's eyes before kissing again. The pair parted and the man leaned against his staff while the woman paced.

"We've been married for I don't know how many millenniums," the man said. "Yet, you still manage to warm my heart every time I see you."

"And you make my knees weak, my love," the woman said. "We were designed for each other."

"And on that note," the man said. "I know when you are troubled. What's the matter?"

"Events have been placed in motion," the woman said. "And I don't like the possibilities. There's so much that could go wrong. A misstep here could be disastrous. We could lose many worlds now."

"There's only so much damage that they could do," the man said. "Time will take care of the damage done. You've already gotten involved too much, my love. You sent the boy into Cerrado with the girl. They will have their quest and either live or die. It's not for us to say."

"But the magic there will overwhelm them," the woman said. "I've been in contact with the pirate of the high seas, the man who sails the rivers."

"Is it true that he's romantically linked to our daughter?" the man asked.

"That's the question you ask now?"

"It's a valid question."

"They are," the woman said. "He's been waiting in Cerrado for the return of the Former King. He had a hand in it, too."

"I only hope that he can help our daughter make something of herself," the man said. "I've been so worried about our children. Where did we go wrong with them?"

"It's our lifestyle," the woman sighed. "We didn't have the time for them when they needed us."

"They don't live their lives in an honorable way."

"One does," the woman said. "The one with the captain."

"The other three don't," the man said. "If we are going to get involved then our children should do it. Having something to do would be good for them."

"They've never worked before. They wouldn't know what to do."

"Then it would be good for them," the man said. "Summon the children now and let's have a talk with them."

"Okay, my love."

The woman kissed the man before twirling her fingers. As she did, four whirlwinds began to form. It took a moment but the whirlwinds got stronger and stronger. The man watched as figures started to form within the whirlwinds.

The first whirlwind to stop revealed a stunningly beautiful girl, around sixteen years old with a dress of the finest satins that was a deep cherry color, strapless and very short. The girl had matching elegant boots with large black buckles and four inch heels. The woman was short with long hair that was the same cherry color as her dress and boots. Holding the hand of the girl was another girl, around the same age, in an elegant black dress, black formal shoes, and shiny black hair.

The woman in green gave the two girls a disapproving glance as she continued to create the other three whirlwinds. The next gave way and standing was a handsome young man, sixteen years old, in a cinnamon-colored three-piece suit. The suit was very formal, and an identical match to his long cinnamon-colored hair. In his hand was a golden chalice that was filled to the brim with the finest wine. The man sipped his wine as he looked at the woman who brought him there.

The next whirlwind formed into an identical looking man who was wearing a cobalt-colored suit. He was identical to the other man in every way, except his hair was cobalt colored, whereas the first man's hair was the color of cinnamon. This man seemed to be lost in thought, almost as if he wasn't even there and didn't realize he'd been taken to a different location. This man was surrounded by three women. The women were all the same age, all exotic beauties, and all dressed in the finest garments to escort royalty. The group was taking turns inhaling from a golden, long-stemmed pipe.

The final whirlwind produced a girl identical in looks to the first girl,but her long hair was jade colored. The girl wore jade-colored, flowing, billowy pants that danced around her legs in the gentle breeze. She wore a matching sequenced bandeau top that revealed all of her tone midriff. Over the scant top was an open, jade-colored, jade-sequenced leather jacket. The girl looked to be fitter than the other kids, and more intelligent than the others. She wore a pair of daggers in sheathes at her waist. There was a look of concern on her face as she saw her siblings, the other quintets, standing with their parents.

"Cherry, Cinnamon, Cobalt, and Jade," the woman said, looking over her children. "This is a family meeting. Your friends will have to go."

The woman twirled her fingers and the girl with Cherry and the group with Cobalt disappeared into Whirlwinds. Both Cherry and Cobalt were upset over the departing of their friends.

"Why did you do that, Mother?" Cherry asked. "She was my best friend, my strength and inspiration as I make my beautiful music."

"I know what she is," the woman said, in a scolding tone. "Your father and I have witnessed events that have been set in motion. When you were of age we gave you each a job to do. Cherry, you were to tend the grasslands. Cinnamon, you were in charge of the desert. Cobalt the forests, and Jade the rivers. As far as we can tell, the only one who's done their job with any degree of competence is Jade."

"That's only because she spends her time with the pirate," Cobalt sneered. "She is always on his ship."

"We sail the rivers looking for lost souls," Jade said, in her soft, angelic voice. "We tend to the wounded and guide those who've died on my rivers. We also make sure that no one harms my rivers. That's more that anyone can say about your forests, Cobalt. Evil things have overrun your lands."

"Why do we need to do this?" Cinnamon asked, sipping from his wine glass. "You and Father are more than capable to handle these sorts of things. We have our own lives to take care of."

"I have many things to do," Cobalt said. "I don't wish to be troubled by this."

"I agree," Cherry said. "I want to spend time with my friend."

"I have heard enough," the father roared. "It's time that you children learn the ways of other worlds. At least, both worlds involved in this particular quest. So far you've only spent time in Cerrado. A boy from another world has entered Cerrado and is now on a quest. This will permanently affect both worlds. No matter how hard you try, this is a fact that you cannot escape."

"I am willing to fight," Jade said. "I know that we can defeat whatever is placed before us. I am strong and brave and will lead any charge."

"How do we know what is good and what is evil?" Cobalt asked.

"You have only experienced evil, Brother," Jade said. "I have lived in the good but taken walks with evil. I know right from wrong. I know how to experience what's wrong in the world. I've walked the path my sister has, caring only for pleasures of the flesh. I've experimented with both your vices and Cinnamon's. Mind altering liquors and drugs. I know what evil is and I choose to spend my time in the light. I spend my time helping good triumph over evil."

"That's a cute speech, dear sister," Cherry said, mockingly. "But I love my situation as it is. I love how I live my life and what I do isn't your business."

"You're right," Jade said, "what you do isn't my business but what you do with your time is about to change forever. If evil takes control of Cerrado then there will be no hiding from it. The evil will find an arch and go to other worlds as well. They will be defenseless to stop what's coming."

"And what is coming, dear sister?" Cherry asked. "How do you know what's coming?"

"It's not hard to tell," Jade said. "We've seen what this evil has done in the past and there's no reason to think that they'll be any different this time. Remember how the people suffered?"

"We didn't suffer," Cinnamon said, as he sipped from his wine. "We've never suffered. That evil can't harm us."

"He's right, Sister," Cobalt said, through his haze. "We are immortal. There's nothing they could do to harm us."

"You don't know that," Jade said. "I, for one, cannot sit back and watch as someone destroys a land...destroys people...while I enjoy pleasures and a lavish lifestyle. I will fight the evil just as our parents have since the beginning of their time. Our parents have given us this gift. They could have sat back and let evil destroy everything, but they fought and gave us the lives we have now. I will fight as they did so that one day, when I have children, they can have a pleasant life."

"Mother and Father have fought evil before," Cinnamon said. "Let them do it again."

"We are old," the father said. "And don't have many years left."

"Don't have many years left?" Cherry asked, skeptically. "You are Father Time and Mother Nature, you cannot die. You will live forever, just as we will."

"You will not live forever," Mother Nature said. "You will die just as we will if this evil is allowed to return. This evil is older than you could imagine. It is older than your father and myself. That is why we couldn't defeat it the first time. That is why we had to have children. You have our powers. You can use them to help those questing to defeat this evil. That is the only way."

"And if we choose not to help?" Cobalt asked. "We won't get to continue our lives? We will die?"

"It's fight or die, Son," Father Time said. "There is no other choice. You hold the key to your future. You four have a choice that only you can make. You are destined for greatness, so that your names will be written down in history as the ones who help save Cerrado. Or you are destined for infamy in that you were the ones who let Cerrado fall to its doom."

"We could join the evil," Cherry said. "I'm sure if we helped them they would reward us greatly. We could live even better than we are now. We could have everything we want."

"While being slaves to their twisted ways," Jade said. "Brothers, Sister, we have no other choice. We must take action to save the land. I promise you that we can do this. Our tasks won't be that hard. I have a plan already in place."

"Is it your plan or the pirate's?" Cherry asked.

"We worked it out together," Jade said. "It's a good plan. We all will have our parts to play and there is risk involved. We don't know how powerful the evil has become. There are other unknowns to us but we can win. And he's a captain, not a pirate, Cherry."

"Isn't there another way?" Cobalt asked. "Is there anything else we can do?"

"There isn't, Brother," Jade said.

The four children looked at each other. It had been such a long time since they'd been together and they'd each changed so much. Jade could hardly recognize her brothers. They were both still tall and royal looking, but some of the leanness of their bodies was giving way to fat. Cherry was the same. They had all discovered the rare and fine delicacies of the world and were no longer willing to live as their parents had taught them.

Jade was different though. Jade was the fighter of the group. With her pirate captain boyfriend, she'd sailed the rivers, protecting them from harm. Jade carried herself with a confidence that came only from experience. She was masterfully trained with swords and knives, and she always had her daggers at her waist, ready to defend in the blink of an eye. The captain taught her to defend herself and others.

Although Jade was the strongest of the children, she prided her knowledge over her strength. Jade had studied the history of Cerrado, knew about all the kings and rulers, and had studied mathematics, science, and astronomy. Jade understood politics and how the kings and queens ruled their kingdoms. Jade knew that beyond a shadow of a doubt, she could help the questers defeat the evil. She wanted to involve her siblings to get them off their current lifestyle and to make sure that the evil didn't seduce them.

Jade noticed that all of her siblings and her parents were looking at her. Jade smiled before slowly taking her leather jacket off and hanging it on an extending tree branch. Jade made her way to the middle of all of her family and motioned for them to back up. Jade stood statue still, so still they couldn't even notice her breathing. In the blink of an eye, she had her daggers out, and was putting on an exhibition for her family. Jade rushed around the circle that had formed around her, demonstrating dagger and fighting techniques with a shadow partner. Jade showed off her speed and expertise with the daggers.

When she had finished, Jade was in the middle of the circle, not a hair out of place, with no sweat on her perfect skin. She slid the daggers back into their sheaths. Jade smiled, knowing her siblings and parents were impressed with the show she had put on. Jade reasoned that a small show of skill would make her siblings realize that they could participate and win this challenge.

"That was nice," Cherry said, as she lightly clapped. "If we ever get into battle with the air we'll be sure to send you in."

"Pick up a sword and face me then," Jade said. "Or if you wish, have a proxy fight for you, if you're unwilling to fight for yourself."

Cherry was stunned. She had expected Jade to react, but not like that. Cherry wanted to get under her skin, not get drawn into a fight with her. Cherry knew she wouldn't stand a chance against her sister and she didn't know any fighters that would fare much better. She had to act quickly to get out of this.

"Merely a jest, my dear sister," Cherry said, in a lighthearted tone. "No offense was meant. Obviously you are physically superior to me...and to our brothers."

Cherry looked, hoping her plan had worked. She thought if she said Jade was the strongest the brothers would contest and the fight would be moved from her to the others, but surprisingly, both brothers agreed with Cherry's statement. In looking over her brothers, Cherry realized that Cinnamon had drunk too much wine to stand in a fight, and Cobalt's mind was in a haze from the potions he liked to smoke.

Cherry looked back to Jade who'd already put her jacket back on, knowing there wasn't going to be any fight. Cherry sighed, accepting the fact she had no other choice but to listen to her sister. Cherry didn't want to get involved but she knew they weren't going to let her sit out.

"Very well," Cherry said. "I will help."

"Good," Jade said. "Brothers? Cobalt, Cinnamon, what will you do?"

"I shall help as well," Cinnamon said.

"And I too," Cobalt said. "But perhaps we should wait a couple days. Let our heads and bodies clean out so we are prepared for action."

"We will wait," Jade said. "Our timing has to be perfect. Come with me."

Jade twirled her fingers and four whirlwinds appeared above the four kids. It only took a moment for them to disappear and for the whirlwinds to vanish as quickly as they started. Only the mother and father were left in the clearing. The pair kissed.

"They will succeed," Mother Nature said.

"I had no idea they'd slipped so far," Father Time said. "And I had no idea that Jade was so powerful."

"She has learned to use all of our powers, my love," Mother Nature said. "She is more powerful than you, than I, or than both of us combined. If the others try to help the evil, Jade will stop them."

"Then we shall soon have peace."

"In time, we shall."

The pair kissed again as Mother Nature twirled her fingers and a whirlwind descended on them. When the whirlwind was gone, the forest clearing was empty, save for the breeze, whispering between the trees.

Chapter 8

Princess Ambriss and her team of women riders rode like the wind, in a tight formation, pushing their horses over the land as fast as the horses would go. The women were all dressed the same—sky blue leather riding pants, a sleeveless sky blue button-down tunic, covered partially by a matching sleeveless leather duster. The hawk princess had a hawk embossed on the back of her duster and a tiara on her head, while the other women had wide-brimmed hats that matched their outfits.

The women riding with Princess Ambriss were of different ages, sizes, and races. But the one who rode closest to the princess, in the second position behind Ambriss's lead, was January Hiem, Princess Ambriss's second in command, training partner, and best friend. January was dark skinned with long shiny black hair extending to her mid back. She was a thick woman, yet very tone and tall. She wore a blue and white mask that covered her eyes, extending from the bottom of her forehead to the tip of her stubby nose. January always had a smile on her face, no matter the situation. With her eyes hidden behind the mask, she was impossible to read.

The hawk princess and her team were riding north, toward some of the darker forests in Cerrado, where things that didn't want to be found could hide without fear of someone being foolish enough to look for them. In the dark of the northern forests were all the rumored evil things that liked to come out at night. Ambriss didn't fear them though, not with January and her team beside her. The woman had fought battles before and could survive.

As the women cleared a field and entered a winding trail through a pleasant, green forest, Ambriss held her hand up for the group to slow down. They began a trotting pace, single file as they moved into the forest. A younger girl, Rose Follow, red-headed and skinny, took the lead position. She scanned her eyes in every direction looking for trouble as Ambriss, January, and the rest of the team followed behind her. The riders appeared around a corner as Rose held her hand up to stop. Ambriss and January pulled up beside her to get a look at what she saw.

"What is it, Rose?" Princess Ambriss asked. "What do you see?"

"There is someone behind the trees up there," Rose said, pointing. "I cannot tell who or how many."

"SHOW YOURSELF!" the hawk princess shouted. "WE MEAN YOU NO HARM!"

The women braced themselves as they noticed more movement from the trees. Ambriss had her hand on her dagger hilt as a shadow danced out from behind the trees. The shadow was draped in black, moving quickly, decisively, as it worked its way toward the women. Ambriss blinked and in that instant, she lost sight of the shadow. The princess took her dagger out and held it close to her chest as she scanned the tree line rapidly, looking for any sight of the movement that had just been in front of her.

From behind a large, old, gnarled willow tree emerged a shadow of a woman. Princess Ambriss immediately recognized the woman as the one who was with the wolf prince, Atin, when they had left the castle. The woman had choppy black hair that swept in front of her face, hiding some of the heavy black makeup she had surrounding her eyes. The woman wore a black leather top that revealed much, a black leather skirt that was studded with stones, and tall black boots. She had a long, thin, curved-blade sword strapped to her back and black leather gloves that went up to her biceps.

The woman stood near the tree, staring at the riding women. Ambriss, January, and Rose all had their daggers at the ready. Although they knew this woman was with Prince Atin, they didn't put their weapons down. Princess Ambriss had never learned this woman's name, even though she knew the woman had been in her brother's circle for many, many years. The other kids even thought that Atin and this woman were romantically linked.

"Put your daggers away, Sister," Prince Atin said, from behind them.

Ambriss and her team turned their heads to look behind them and saw the wolf prince standing on a swell of land between two tall oak trees. Ambriss couldn't read his face. Atin wasn't sweating, didn't look worn out. She had no idea how he and his team had gotten to this point before them, without horses. What was even stranger, was the woman they'd been looking at was standing at her brother's side. Ambriss looked back to the old willow tree on the other side of the road but there was nothing there.

"Prince Atin," Princess Ambriss said, jumping down from her horse and walking to her brother. "You seem to have been moving fast. Where is the rest of the team you left with?"

"They had other…things that needed tending to," Atin said. "A side venture, if you will."

"And these ventures are more important than the safety and security of Cerrado?"

"The quests they are on will guarantee our victory," Atin said, in his deep growl voice. "Trust me, Sister…we will have victory."

"How did you arrive at this point before we did?" January called out as she got off her horse and walked to Ambriss's side. "You do not have horses. What method of travel did you use?"

"That's my little secret," Atin smiled.

"Maybe your friend here should have helped the snow princess…Princess Arctic, on her quest," January said. "I'm sure a unicorn would appear to her."

"Don't make light," Atin said, as the women stood statue still. "She lost the ability to see a unicorn many, many years ago. We wanted to stop you to speak about an alliance in our quests."

"An alliance?" Ambriss asked. "We're siblings. We are aligned with each other through thick and thin, dear brother."

"Don't be so naïve, my sister," Atin said. "There are many things that come in the way of us. Here is what I propose to you…we travel together to Hammerbrite Castle in the far northern forests."

"Hammerbrite?" January asked. "Why would we want to travel there?"

"It's a good plan," Ambriss said. "In Hammerbrite, it is rumored that there are maps of everything in Cerrado. They have thousands of maps protected in their vaults. If the Immortal River existed there would be a map of it in Hammerbrite."

"Then what do you seek in Hammerbrite, Wolf Prince?" January asked.

"I need maps to Yorehill Manor," Atin said, through a wolfish smile.

"From the legend of the Former King?" Ambriss said.

"The very same," Atin said. "If the manor exists there will be maps of it at the Hammerbrite Castle."

"But we would need to give the princess of Hammerbrite a massive tribute to be allowed to look at their maps," Ambriss protested. "And she would ask us why we were looking for what we are looking for. I'm sure we could come up with excuses and lies about our motives, but that wouldn't seem right to me. I don't know, Brother. I think there are too many variables that would make Hammerbrite out of our reach."

"You have to be joking," Atin said, flatly. "The princess of Hammerbrite owes me many favors. I have done work for her in the past."

"Work?" January asked. "What work?"

"That is not for you to know," Atin snarled. "She cannot resist my requests. Even if she did I know secret ways into the vaults. We could look through them without anyone knowing that we were ever there."

"I don't like his deceptive ways," Rose said. "He could lead us into trouble."

"I don't care for them either, Rose," Ambriss said. "But his idea is the best we've got. Instead of riding through the forests looking for a river that may or may not exist, we can look over every map ever made of Cerrado and see instantly if anyone has seen or mapped out the river."

"We must be cautious," January said. "We cannot get caught."

"And if you follow what I tell you," Atin said. "We won't get caught. Trust me."

Princess Ambriss looked over her brother and his female companion. She could tell by the way the woman was standing and looking at him that the pair were lovers. They may not admit to each other the feelings that they had, but they had definitely been together for some time. Ambriss could tell the woman was very powerful and had been in fights before—a vining scar above her left eyebrow seemed to indicate that she'd gotten to close to a sword point. The hawk princess was nervous about how the woman hadn't taken her eyes off January since they'd seen each other. Ambriss knew that January was powerful as well, and the woman was sizing her up.

"I agree," Princess Ambriss said. "We shall travel together."

Atin nodded as he let out a loud whistle. From the trees came two large black thoroughbred horses, each with a stunning blue saddle. Atin and his female companion quickly mounted the horses and took the lead positions as the riding women fell in line behind them. Prince Atin pushed the horses fast, not at a gallop, but faster than a trot. As the team made their way to a wider trail in the forest, Ambriss rode alongside her brother.

"What is her name?" Ambriss asked, nodding to Atin's female companion.

"You don't need to know that," Atin said shortly.

"She's your lover, isn't she?"

"Jealous?" Atin asked.

"And what would be there for me to be jealous of?"

"What indeed?"

"I'm happy for you, Brother," Ambriss said. "We don't need to be standoffish like this. I'm glad that you've found someone to share your life with. Yes, I am jealous. I wish for a handsome, strong prince to come and sweep me off my feet the way you did to her."

"You've experienced much, but also have much to learn, Sister," Atin said. "We should ride in silence to avoid giving away our position."

"The horses aren't quiet," Ambriss said. "We are not traveling in stealth. We hardly ever see each other anymore, Atin. I wish to know about your life."

"There are questions that I'm sure you don't want answered, dear sister," Atin said.

"Oh, come now," Ambriss said. "I want to know my family. The only one I've ever been able to spend any real time with is the snow princess, Arctic. She's so fragile but has a good heart. I'm sure she'll have the adventure of a lifetime finding a unicorn horn."

"Knowing her," Atin smirked. "She'll bring the unicorn home as a pet. That is, if Father would let her keep it."

"I could see her pleading until he did," Ambriss said. "Although she never has to beg to get what she wants. Father allowed much leeway in raising her."

"She has Hibit to guide her," Atin said. "And with her cat, Snowflake, Arctic will be protected. She may have already completed her quest."

"She should be the first one done," Ambriss said. "Tell me, Brother, you are in tune with the information networks of Cerrado. You know many people and have contacts throughout the lands. Who do you think is coming for Father?"

"If pushed for a quick answer," Atin said. "I would suggest that Ornthal and the Bandits are getting bolder. They have been pushing further into the open lands, stealing bigger treasures than ever before."

"If you thought deeper about it," Ambriss said. "If you thought about it, who do you think is behind this?"

"There's been a dark shadow descending upon us for some time now," Atin said. "I can feel the evil surrounding us like wolves in the night. Very soon, dear sister, we will know who brings this darkness upon us. I have no doubt that we can defeat it. I feel that it is something very old, older than we've fought before. There's no telling where the knife will fall from—but the knife will fall."

"We will all be protected, correct?" Ambriss asked.

"We have the ability to protect ourselves," Atin said. "I would fear for Father's safety before ours."

"Why do you say that?"

"He's the duke," Atin said. "He's the one that the Former King charged with protecting Cerrado until his return. Duke Asmout is the prime target."

"You left your other companions to protect Father," Ambriss said. "Without his knowledge, of course. Didn't you?"

"They are on a very important mission," Atin said, with a smile while nodding. "One that I am not going to discuss in the open."

"I will rest well knowing that," Ambriss said. "Thank you, dear brother."

"The duke will not fall by someone's hand," Atin said. "He will die peacefully in his bed when his time comes. And Prince Alos will take the throne, if the Former King hasn't returned."

"You have no desire to hold the throne?" Ambriss asked.

"I have other ambitions," Atin said. "I find it's unwise to put yourself in the lightning-rod position. I work best in the background. Trust me, Sister, we will have victory."

"I wish I could find the confidence that you have in this matter," Ambriss said. "There's so many unknowns that it frightens me. Come my friends, let us sing to pass the time as we ride."

Both the wolf prince and his female companion rolled their eyes as the women followed Ambriss's lead as she began to sing a pleasant song.

Chapter 9

The Cerrado Castle towered over everything in the village surrounding it. The gray granite blocks once gleamed in the morning sun but now the sky had become overcast. A near-black morning sky threatened the area. Lightning hung in the air, creating bright flashes that were accompanied by ground-shaking thunder. The people of Cerrado were walking quickly, hoping to not get caught in the rain.

In the upper level of the castle was a large chamber. The chamber had maps of Cerrado hung like tapestries on the walls, and a six-foot globe on a golden stand in the middle. Duke Asmout paced the room as he looked over the maps. The duke was stressed and his face projected just how worried he was. Mystic Seven the Red watched his master before speaking.

"What troubles you, my Duke?" Mystic Seven the Red asked.

"I should have heard from my children," Duke Asmout said. "Arctic should have been back by now. The others should have given me reports of their progress. I don't understand why we haven't heard from them."

"They are safe, my Duke."

"Are you sure, Seven? Have you seen them?"

"If they weren't safe we would have heard," Mystic Seven said. "No news is the best news for us. They would only let us know if they fail, to avoid giving away their positions and intentions."

"I pray that you are right," Duke Asmout said. "There is so much that we must do before they return. How is the military coming along?"

"I have sent word to all the villages that the footmen are to gather at the castle," Seven said. "They will arrive and we will begin the training."

Duke Asmout was about to speak when a bolt of lightning and a crash of thunder struck inside the room. Asmout was blinded by the light that momentarily filled the room. The force of the thunder had knocked him off his feet. As he tried to stand and focus his eyes, he couldn't figure out what he was seeing. The duke drew his sword as he began to gain a dim awareness of who was standing in the room.

In the center of the room was a woman. She was hauntingly beautiful, well over six feet tall and very fit. She wore a stunning black dress with red accents, wild jet-black hair extending to her waistline, an abundance of black makeup, and a sinister smile on her face. The woman's face was long and pointed. She had a clear complexion, fire passion eyes, a long-hooked nose, and thin lips. The woman's eyes were completely surrounded with black makeup. The woman had no sword, no daggers or knives—nothing to protect herself with. She began laughing.

"Mystic Seven," Duke Asmout shouted as he looked over the woman. "Place a spell on her. Freeze her in position before this demon can harm us."

"Now why would he do that?" the woman said. "Mystic Seven the Red works for me. Mystic Seven the Red did see someone killing you, Duke Asmout...him actually. And he will do it when the time is right...when I command him to."

Duke Asmout staggered backwards. He couldn't believe what he'd just heard. Seven had been his trusted advisor for many years. Mystic Seven the Red had protected the duke and his family, saved them from destruction, and made sure that Asmout protected Cerrado for the former king.

"Who are you?" Duke Asmout stuttered. "You cannot be Queen Mala, although you look exactly like her. Queen Mala was killed by the Former King."

"I am Queen Mala," Queen Mala almost shouted. "This is my kingdom, my crown, my throne. The Honor Throne is mine."

"As you requested, my Queen," Mystic Seven said, bowing. "All the children are gone. None of them can bother us now."

"I suppose you wish to know how I survived," Queen Mala said, pacing toward the duke. "You want to know how I was able to survive the wars that plagued the land that I once ruled."

"I want to know what's going on here," Duke Asmout demanded. "Mystic Seven, you'd better explain yourself."

"Nothing to explain, really," Mystic Seven said. "I was always working for Queen Mala. Since the very beginning. Every problem, every war, every threat that I saw for you was a creation of my own work. I played you like a predator playing with its prey. The best was what I did to you just a few days ago. I convinced you to send all your children, along with your top military advisors and troops, out into the wastelands of Cerrado on quests that will benefit the new queen."

"Benefit the new queen?" Asmout said, stupefied.

"The four quests," Queen Mala said. "The unicorn horn and the water of the Immortal River will allow me to live forever, strong and healthy, looking as young and as beautiful as I am now. The Knowledge of Cerrado contains curses that will ensure that no one tries to challenge me. I can curse them...destroy them. Just having the book will scare everyone away."

"And the sword of the Former Sword?" Asmout asked.

"The legend said that we would know the Former King by his sword," Queen Mala laughed. "If I have the sword and destroy it, there's no way to prove who the Former King truly is."

"But he destroyed you," Duke Asmout insisted. "You were dead and gone. How can you be standing here in front of me today?"

"The Former King was weak," Mystic Seven the Red said. "He couldn't destroy Queen Mala, he wasn't strong enough. Oh, he did damage her, and almost destroyed her, but Queen Mala is a survivor. She withstood the onslaught and through clever trickery, she came back."

"And where is your precious little king now, Duke Asmout?" Queen Mala scoffed. "He promised you so much, promised your family so much, but now you stand before me, you bow before me like a coward. You and the Former King are weak. I am strong. Bow before me, pig."

"I will never bow before you," Duke Asmout said, as he raised his blade toward Mala.

"You dare raise a blade to me?" Queen Mala screamed. "BOW!"

Queen Mala stepped toward Duke Asmout and summoned her magic to descend on him. Duke Asmout felt his knees go out from underneath him. His sword suddenly became increasingly heavier. He couldn't hold his sword anymore. He let it drop to the floor. Duke Asmout fought with everything he had, but he was no match for Queen Mala. Duke Asmout dropped to his knees and fell to the floor, bowing before her.

"I told you that you would bow to me, Duke Asmout," Queen Mala said. "You see…it isn't that hard. Now, you stay there while I look over my castle."

"This will never be your castle," Duke Asmout shouted. "The people will destroy you before cowering to you again. You destroyed Cerrado the last time you tried to rule here. The Former King used all his powers to unseat you and bring Cerrado back to glory."

"And where is he now?" Queen Mala asked. "Do you wish to fight me? Maybe your children will fight me. Maybe I can kill them all in front of your eyes before I kill you."

"Come to think of it," Mystic Seven the Red said. "I may have forgot to mention that when I saw your children gathered around your grave, they were already dead. That's right. They die before you. They die by our hands…one by one as they return home. And they never know who killed them or why. In fact, I bet your littlest pet Arctic will be back first. I may have a party with her before I slit her throat. What do you think about that, Duke Asmout?"

"You can kill me now but you will never have victory," Duke Asmout shouted.

"Kill you now?" Queen Mala scoffed. "Never. You need to be here to witness the delicious downfall of your family and Cerrado. Plus, killing you now wouldn't quite fit into my plans. I don't want people to know just yet that I'm in charge."

"Everything must play out the way I've seen it," Mystic Seven the Red said. "The Former King will try to return but he will be defeated when he sets foot in Cerrado. I know what he looks like and where he will come from. The Former King won't have time to mount a defense when he tries to come. It will be sweet."

"And now," Queen Mala said, moving toward Duke Asmout. "It's the dungeon for you."

Queen Mala was about to continue speaking but something caught her attention—a noise no louder than a mouse came from behind a tapestry on the wall. Both Mala and Seven looked at the heavy drapes, trying to figure out what the soft noise was. Both knew in an instant that the noise wasn't natural—wasn't from an animal. The tapestry swayed ever so gently against the wall even though there was no breeze in the chamber.

"What do you see, my mystic?" Queen Mala asked, walking toward the wall. "What was that?"

"There's something not right here," Mystic Seven the Red said. "Someone was spying on us."

"Impossible."

"No, it's not," Mystic Seven said.

Mystic Seven rushed to the wall and pulled the tapestry with all the force he could muster. The heavy blue blanket fell to the ground in a pile as both Mala and Seven gasped. There was a small hole in the wall, just big enough for a person to sit in while listening to everything that was said in the room. Mala used her magic to quickly float to the opening, put her arm inside, and created a light.

There was nothing in the six-foot deep hole. In the back half was a shaft that went upwards. Mala could see no way as to how someone got into and out of the space. She drifted herself back to the floor and grabbed Mystic Seven and shook him.

"There was someone there!" the queen roared. "I know it! You must find them before they leave the castle. No one can know that I am in charge yet."

"Impossible," Mystic Seven said. "There is no way that someone could have been there without us feeling their presence. It's simply not possible."

"There was someone there," Queen Mala said. "Find them."

Mystic Seven closed his eyes and let the natural forces of magic and energy fill him. Using his inner eye—his third eye—he let the magic be his guide as he allowed his consciousness to float around the castle. It didn't take him long to see a person dressed in black sneaking through the corridors of the castle.

In a suit of black leather, covered by a black duster, long black hair fell from beneath a wide brimmed black hat. The eyes of the figure were hidden behind the hair and the face was covered with a scruffy black beard. The person was short and stocky, not more than five feet tall with bulging muscles coming from under the heavy clothing. Mystic Seven was confused for a moment but as he studied the moving figure, he knew who it was and where he'd seen him before.

The man was by Prince Atin's side on the morning the children left the castle. Mystic Seven knew he'd seen this person around—he remembered thinking how strange the man looked. Bulging muscles and a puffed out chest, but the strangest walk from the short man. Now Mystic Seven knew what the truth was. The muscles were sewn into the clothing. The belly was nothing but stuffing. The large chest was real but the beard was fake. It was a woman posing as a man to gather information.

Mystic Seven scolded himself for not realizing the trick earlier. This woman could quickly shed the clothing and take the beard off and no one would ever know she had been posing as a man just moments earlier. It was an underhanded but sly intelligence-gathering technique. Mystic Seven quickly pushed his other thoughts aside, trying to track where the woman was.

"What is it, Mystic Seven?" Queen Mala asked. "Who do you see?"

"It is one of the men that stood by Prince Atin's side," Mystic Seven replied. "But it is no man. She is a woman, hiding in plain sight to gather information."

"And you never saw through this simple disguise?" Queen Mala asked, baffled. "How in the name of all that is evil didn't you see through that?"

"There was no reason to scrutinize him...her, I mean," Mystic Seven said. "We always thought she was a security guard for the prince."

"Where is she?" Queen Mala yelled. "I must kill her before she tells anyone what she saw."

"I see her walking toward the courtyard," Mystic Seven said. "There are few people out there right now. She could easily lose herself in the crowd."

"Send troops down there right now," Queen Mala said. "I will secure this room and detain the duke. Bring this girl to me. I will kill her in this room."

"I will, my Queen," Mystic Seven said, as he rushed out of the room.

Queen Mala watched as Mystic Seven rushed out of the room. She looked back to the duke who was still frozen on the floor in his bowing position. Queen Mala imagined all the things she could do to humiliate the duke but she wanted to wait until the children got there, before she unleashed her vengeance.

Mystic Seven rushed into the courtyard—normally a beehive of merchant carts peddling their produce and trinkets. The jesters juggling, storytelling, and performing magic tricks, and people out enjoying it.But on this cloudy, stormy day, the yard was almost empty. There was a cart with an old man peddling fruit, a pair of entertainers working on a juggling routine, a cart that had animal-hide clothing, and a few people milling around.

Mystic Seven couldn't see the bearded-man figure he'd seen in his vision. He began looking for a woman who would fit what he saw. There were very few women in the courtyard. He looked them over but they were all tall—none wearing high heels or lifts that would make them look taller than they were.

As he scanned the crowd, one woman with long white hair almost matched the height he was looking for. She was wearing boots with very high heels. The woman didn't move exactly like the figure did, but close. She was wearing a green dress that had a swooping low back, long sleeves, and was hemmed just above the knees. Mystic Seven didn't think she could have worn that dress underneath the men's clothing, but it was possible.

Mystic Seven began walking toward the woman. She didn't notice him as he got closer. As Mystic was almost to her, another woman caught his eyes. This woman was the right height and had the same hair as the men's figure had—choppy and black, covering part of the face. This woman walked the same as the figure and was wearing gray tights with a form-fitting gray sleeveless top—a perfect outfit to wear underneath the bulky men's clothing.

Mystic Seven turned toward the woman before he realized she already had her eyes fixed upon him and was walking up to him. In an instant, for reasons he couldn't understand, a moment of fear gripped his body. He couldn't explain it, but for that moment, he was frozen. The woman was getting closer, walking toward him with no fear whatsoever. She had a smile on her face that churned Mystic Seven's stomach. He started to tremble, not knowing what was going on. Mystic Seven the Red no more than blinked and the woman, who a moment ago was just a pace away from him—was gone. There was no trace of her anywhere.

"Mystic Seven the Red," a female voice said, next to him.

"Yes," Mystic Seven replied, turning to see the woman in the green dress next to him.

"You will never have victory," the woman said, as she disappeared before his eyes.

Chapter 10

The Blue Cerrado Forest was a harmonics of sound from all the animals that call the forest their home. On this bright and sunny day, when all the trees had a special blue gleam to them—a sign that they were healthy and happy—a shadow darted quickly between the trees. The shadow was moving as fast as it could, stopping by each tree—looking around and listening for something that was just outside of its grasp.

Another figure followed only two paces behind—a large white cat, moving with none of the urgency of the first form. The cat lazily made its way through the forest, tagging along with the figure as it checked all the corners around the trees. Hibit and Snowflake hadn't seen Princess Arctic for over a day now, and Hibit was worried that something had happened to her.

"Oh Snowflake," Hibit wailed. "Where did I go wrong? How could I have lost the princess? What am I going to tell her father? What will I tell the duke about how I lost his youngest little girl? He will throw me in the dungeon for the rest of my life."

Snowflake raised her eyebrows and yawned as the cat's long tail swayed back and forth in the air. Snowflake sniffed the air but couldn't pick up a scent. She scanned the ground but saw no prints that would have come from the princess. Hibit was a nervous wreck as he scanned the area.

"What do we do?" Hibit almost shouted. "The princess is missing and there's nothing we can do to find her." Hibit collapsed down on a log, burying his face into his hands as he sobbed. "I can't believe I failed the duke. I can't believe after so many long years of service this is how my tenure with the royal family will end. Losing the princess on a simple mission in the forest."

Snowflake tried to nuzzle with Hibit, purring loudly, hoping that he would calm down. Hibit cried as Snowflake licked his face. Nothing the cat did seemed to help. Snowflake stepped away and looked around the clearing they were in. The trees were gently swaying in the breeze, some birds were flying around, and a pair of green rabbits were peeking out behind a tree, investigating the noises that Hibit and Snowflake were making.

As Hibit was crying, he felt the cold sting of a steel blade being pressed against his throat. Snowflake hissed, realizing someone had snuck up on them. The person had cleverly used the trees Hibit had his back to, so the attacker couldn't be seen, let alone counter attacked. Hibit stopped sobbing, sat up straight, and prayed he would be able to find a way out of this situation.

"Don't get any funny ideas," a very powerful, and clearly female voice said, from behind the tree. "I have you...and there's nothing you can do to stop me."

"Please don't hurt me," Hibit begged. "I mean you no harm. I didn't mean to trespass. I have nothing of value on me. There's no reason to hurt or kill me."

"I have to be sure," the voice said. "Tell your cat to lay down out in front of you."

"Snowflake," Hibit said, commandingly. "Do what this person says. Lay down...out here in the light where we can see you."

Snowflake turned her head to the side, curiously looking at the sword held at Hibit's neck as she made her way out into the clearing. The standard European sword was a very shiny steel—a wide blade, with a teed hilt. The handle was made out of silver and bronze—held by a hand encased in a brown, leather, and fingerless glove. The glove extended halfway up the holder's forearm. Snowflake breathed somewhat of a sigh of relief that this was a straight wide blade, not the curved skinny blade the bandits had started carrying.

Snowflake sat in the middle of the clearing—hoping the owner of the sword would reveal themselves. The hand stayed steady though, not revealing any intent. Hibit was shaking like a leaf, waiting for the inevitable but praying for a peaceful solution. The tension mounted until the sword was pulled away from Hibit's throat.

From behind the tree came a gorgeous warrior princess. She stood tall, with her shoulders back and her head held high. Thick curly locks the color of ripened wheat were bound with a ring at the top of her head, causing her ponytail to cascade past her mid-back, bouncing as she moved into the opening. Her stunning hair swept the tops of her intense, big and wide set ocean-blue eyes, hovering above her button nose and pouty lips.

The warrior had a flat face, rounded with a powerful chin and defined planes.

She kept her sword trained on Hibit as she stalked her way into the center of the clearing. It was almost like she was keeping one eye on Hibit and the other on Snowflake. She wore a brown leather skirt, forming a 'V' at the top. The short skirt stopped just below her navel, and was designed with blue threads creating Celtic designs and different colored beads. Her top was of the same leather material—haltered and cropped—designed for fighting, with design patterns that matched her skirt.

The warrior wore brown flat-footed boots—tight around the calves, going to the bottom of the knees, with a cover that rose up out of the boot and protected the knee. She had brown fingerless gloves on each hand, with metal bracelets that covered her defined biceps. The woman had tattoos around her eyes—blue and black, forming Celtic symbols that matched the symbols sewn on her top and skirt. The warrior was well muscled, holding a large sword, and had a dagger at her waist and a knife in her boot.

Hibit was stunned by her beauty. She had the face of an angel and the body of a gladiator. Hibit thought the woman could rival the princesses in beauty, yet here she was, alone—wandering the forest, fighting. What surprised him the most was the silent stealth she approached with. He didn't even know she was there until the sword was at his throat. Her face was stone, although her lips were formed into a smile. Hibit couldn't wait to hear what she wanted. He was desperate to find the princess.

"My good lady," Hibit said, quickly. "Have you seen a young girl around here? She would be small but around eighteen years old. She was dressed all in white. Please, have you seen her?"

"I have not," the warrior said. "Although I have not been looking for a young girl. You are an old man. What are you doing chasing a young girl with a cat through the woods?"

"Please," Hibit begged. "The cat is hers. I was to help her on her journey. We got separated a day ago and I cannot find her. I must find her."

"You ask of my help freely although I held a blade at your neck?" the warrior asked. "You were moments away from being killed. I could have ended your life before you even knew that I was standing behind you."

"I have to find her or I am dead," Hibit said. "If I don't find her and help her along on her quest, the entire kingdom of Cerrado could be dead. There is an evil coming and she was key in stopping it. Please, my good lady. Please help me find her."

"I am not a good lady," the warrior said. "I am a fierce fighting warrior. I have trained constantly to be the best knight in the land. I am many things. A good lady is not one of them."

"You are not dressed in the garments of a knight," Hibit said. "Knights wear armor. Female knights are not allowed to have their stomachs exposed and they wear skirts designed from chainmail. You call yourself a knight, yet you say you are not a good lady. Who and what are you?"

"I am Lacey DuLake," Lacey said. "Ever since I was very young I have dreamed of being a knight, like my father and mother. They died in the wars fighting for the Former King twenty years ago. I was only ten at the time but I knew in that moment I would become a knight and defend this land against the evils that try to destroy it."

"Why didn't you come to the castle?" Hibit asked. "You could have pledged yourself to Duke Asmout, training and fighting along his best and brightest knights."

"My parents were loyal to the Former King," Lacey said. "I...was captured by an evil that's in the midst of returning. I was on my way to the castle when I was caught. I escaped because this evil has bigger plans than just me. I'm on my way to the castle to help Duke Asmout any way that I can."

"If you want to help the Duke then you can start by helping me," Hibit said. "Lacey, I am Hibit... advisor to the Duke and guard of the royal family. I was with Princess Arctic, helping her along on her first quest. We were separated a day ago and I haven't seen her since. Please, Lacey, you must help me."

"You freely give that information to me?" Lacey asked. "Not knowing at all if the story that I tell you is true or not?"

"I trust you," Hibit said. "There's something in your eyes that tells me that you are telling the truth. Either way, I've lost the princess and I will be thrown in the dungeon to rot for the rest of my life if I don't find her. I have to find her and will do anything to save her life."

"You say that you trust me," Lacey said, as she began to pace. "But what assurances do I have that you are who you say you are and you're actually looking for the princess to save her? How do I know you didn't kidnap her, if it's even the princess you are with?"

"A just question," Hibit said, reaching into his tunic and pulling out a piece of rolled parchment. He handed the scroll to Lacey who unrolled it and read it. "That is a decree order from the Duke, granting me certain powers and privileges as we trek through Cerrado."

"This gives you the power," Lacey said, stunned. "By order of the Duke, to conscript anyone you feel would be worthy to the cause. You can require anything you need to aid you and anyone in Cerrado is forced to follow this order."

"The Duke grants certain powers to people, yes," Hibit said. "Lacey, it also grants me the power to confirm rank and valor to those who are deserving. You help me on this quest, you help me find the princess, then help complete her quest, and I will make you a knight of Cerrado, with the Duke giving you proper armor...shield and sword, a horse, and squires and pages to assist you. You will be a high-ranking Knight in the order, Lacey. I promise you upon pain of death that if we succeed you will be a proper and respected knight."

"I accept," Lacey said, quickly.

"You don't ask what the quest that Princess Arctic has to complete is."

"I don't need to ask," Lacey said, proudly. "I am a knight defending my crown and its lands. If the princess needs help then I will lay down my life to protect her. I have accepted and entered into a binding agreement with you. Upon pain of death I will give everything that I am and everything that I have to help the princess accomplish her quest...once we find her. That being said, what is her quest?"

"She was tasked with coming to the Blue Cerrado Forest and finding the horn of a unicorn," Hibit said. "She was the only one of the children that a unicorn would appear to. Would one appear to you? If you found the horn before we found her that would make the quest easier."

"A unicorn would not appear before me."

"But you are a knight."

"I'm not a knight yet," Lacey said, with a sly grin. "I have experienced certain pleasures while I was working on becoming the best knight in the land. Why was the princess tasked with finding a unicorn horn?"

"There is a prophecy that within three months the duke will be killed," Hibit said. "His children were each tasked with finding something that would help protect or save him."

"Queen Mala is coming back," Lacey said.

"Impossible," Hibit stuttered. "Queen Mala was killed by the Former King. She will never return."

"There were doctors that saved her."

"Which doctors?"

"Exactly."

Hibit was confused. He tried to wrap his head around what Lacey had just told him. He was there when the Former King had defeated Queen Mala the first time and was certain that she wasn't coming back. He was pacing as he tried to believe what she said.

"Queen Mala was killed by the Former King before he left," Hibit said. "She couldn't return to this existence."

"But she did," Lacey said. "She's more powerful than ever and will crush Cerrado beneath her feet if she's not stopped before she reaches the Honor Throne.

"This would fit with what Mystic Seven the Red told the duke," Hibit said. "He said that a golden dagger would kill him and he couldn't see the hand that carried it."

"Mystic Seven the Red?" Lacey asked. "He works for Mala."

"Impossible."

"It's true."

"And how would you know this, living way out here in the forest?"

"I was captured by Mala when she killed my parents," Lacey said. "Not a full hour after she killed my parents the Former King thought he had defeated her. Her Mystics and Necromancers saved her and kept her hidden away while she regained her strength. I was captive there for ten years. I escaped when I was twenty and have been training myself ever since. I don't go to main tournaments or out in the public just in case they have people looking for me."

"How did you learn to fight?"

"In the dungeons," Lacey said. "Being a young girl there I had to learn to defend myself or I would have never survived. At first I did subtle things, when men would come to visit me I would give poisoned drinks. Once that trick was discovered I had to become handy with a concealed knife. It got to the point that when I was twelve they would no longer come to my cell at night. They were all afraid of me.

"I started training with Stanly, a farm boy who was my age and had also been captured and tortured in that dungeon. We had a pair of sticks and we would practice sword fighting all day. Older men would give us pointers. Once we were experts with swords we moved on to everything else...knives, daggers, maces, hand-to-hand, lances...anything that we could get our hands on.

"When I was getting close to twenty I decided that I was going to escape. Stanly was going to come with me and we were going to marry and train an order of knights to bring down Mala and all her plans. Everything was going perfect. We had killed many guards and troops. We were experts in stealth from sneaking around in the dungeons.

"Stanly and I were just about out when an arrow pierced his heart. He fell and I couldn't do anything to help him. Arrows were flying all around me. I could either hold him one more time and die, or make his life and death mean something. I escaped and that night I burned that castle to the ground. The main structure still stands but the innards were gutted. I slaughtered their livestock and killed most of the guards. They have had a hefty price on my head ever since..."

Lacey trailed off as she fought back tears. It was very painful for her to relive those days, the times when she and Stanly thought they might be able to have a life together. They had so many good memories in that evil place that at times it almost felt like a home. She looked to Hibit who gave her a sympathetic smile then to Snowflake who looked disinterested. She knew there was a job to do and that the time had come...her time had come, and a mission had fallen before her to prove that she was the best knight in the land.

"Where was the last place you saw Princess Arctic?" Lacey asked.

"Not far from here," Hibit said. "The princess was going to walk around a tree, hoping that the unicorn would appear to her."

"Anything else?" Lacey asked. "Anything strange happen?"

"There was a bolt of thunder and a crack of lightning," Hibit said. "Strange that it was a clear day and no rain followed."

"Then we have big problems," Lacey said. "You know the story of the arches?"

"Those are children's bedtime stories to keep kids from wandering in the woods," Hibit said. "There are no magical arches that can transport people around Cerrado. Princess Arctic didn't go to another land."

"They are not stories," Lacey said. "I have seen the arches with my own eyes. I've never walked through one but they are there, and the stories are real."

"I still don't believe," Hibit said. "But for argument's sake, if they were real, how would we find one and should we go through it?"

"The thing of the arches is," Lacey said. "They do always appear in the same place, but they don't always appear. If you walk through one it will always take you to the same place but if you walk through the arch on that side it's not guaranteed that it will take you to the arch you walked through on this side, but it will take you to the same place each time."

"So there's no guaranteed home trip?" Hibit asked.

"Right," Lacey said.

"So, what's our best course of action?" Hibit asked.

"We search the area that you last saw the princess in," Lacey said. "If we find an arch in that area we go through it and hope the princess is there."

"Is there a better option?" Hibit asked.

"I don't believe so," Lacey said.

"Okay," Hibit said. "Follow me. I will lead us to where I last saw Princess Arctic."

Lacey and Snowflake followed Hibit as he began to walk a narrow trail in the forest. Lacey was concerned from all the stories that she'd heard about the arches and some of the dangers that followed, but she was finally on her knight's quest—on her way to becoming a knight in the king's court.

After three days of searching, the group was ready to give up. Hibit had brought Lacey to the exact spot that Arctic had told him to wait. They searched every tree, every nook, every hiding spot that she possibly could have gone to and they didn't find a single trace of the young princess anywhere. Snowflake couldn't pick up any scent of Princess Arctic. The group was dejected and ready to give up when they saw two trees, leaning toward each other, forming an arch.

"There," Lacey said, pointing to the arch. "That is an arch. We go through it and we could find Princess Arctic."

"Or it could lead us somewhere entirely different," Hibit said.

"We don't have a choice," Lacey said. "Follow me."

Hibit and Snowflake followed Lacey into the arch. The trio rushed through the arch at the same time. From the clear sky came three bolts of lightning and three cracks of thunder before the sky returned to its clear, calm self. Where three people had stood was now nothing as the trees moved away from each other, removing the arch that they'd come through.

Chapter 11

The midday's sun was high in the sky—bright and powerful, with not a single cloud obstructing the sun's view of the earth. It was one of those magical summer days—hot and muggy, but the world was so alive—bright and shiny. The air was so crisp and clean, laden with a humid flower fragrance. A light breeze barely made the trees and grass dance as it lazily brushed by. During a day like this the last thing anyone expected was two bolts of lightning that made the day even brighter and two cracks of thunder that shook the ground—but that's exactly what happened, disrupting the perfect day for just a moment before the sky returned to its peaceful warmth.

Krispin and Arctic were holding hands as they walked through the forest. In the distance they could hear the sounds of people and horses, but they couldn't see anybody yet. They both seemed confused, unsure of their surroundings. Neither said anything as they walked along a small dirt trail. Krispin looked at the trees, realizing that he'd never seen trees like these before. They had a reddish tint to their bark, with dark red veins in the green leaves. He stopped to look the tree over. All the trees were like that, nothing like he'd ever seen before.

"This is so odd," Krispin said, as he investigated the tree further. "I've never seen anything like this. I didn't know that a tree like this existed in the Moon Forest."

"I still wish you would tell me what this Moon Forest is," Arctic said. "Krispin, you are a very strange person."

"Oh, right," Krispin said, mockingly. "I'm the strange one here, Miss Eighteen-year-old-on-a-unicorn-hunt? I've never heard of Cerrado...and my father's been many places. If somewhere called Cerrado did exist, he would have told me about it."

"I live in Cerrado," Arctic said. "Why are you being like this? Just listen to everything I say and do exactly what I tell you and we will get along just fine."

"I'm not big on taking orders," Krispin said. "I thought we agreed to be equal partners in this endeavor."

"I know what I'm talking about," Arctic said. "We need to be in the Blue Cerrado Forest to find a unicorn. That's where the unicorns live. There are other things in that forest that people have to be careful for. That's why I had others with me who were to protect me, but the Blue Cerrado Forest is generally a safe place."

"I just wish I knew where it was," Krispin said. "I've never heard of it before. I've never seen a place like this before. Come on, we need to keep moving. I hear people somewhere."

Krispin took Arctic by the hand and they started walking again. Krispin kept his eyes on the trees and plants that they were passing. He couldn't figure them out. Everything was different from what he was used to. As the pair walked along, Krispin began to realize that something wasn't right. He couldn't place it, but there was something amiss about what was going on.

"Where are we?" Krispin asked as he noticed that he was again holding Arctic's hand. "I don't recognize this place."

"At first I thought we were still in your forest," Arctic said. "The Moon Forest? Is that what you called it? I don't know where we are now. This looks familiar but I can't be sure."

The pair walked around a bend in the trail and stopped in their tracks, stunned at what they saw. In front of them was a massive red stone castle. The castle was sprawling, with tall towers and spires that extended high into the air. The red stone was partially covered with a black ivy, and the lawns around the castle were perfectly manicured.

There was a larger trail near the small walking trail they were on. Horse drawn carts were making their way through the massive stone gates. Past the gates Krispin could see that there was some kind of market or bazaar going on. There were people and carts everywhere. It looked like a busy place and all the people looked to be in some form of a hurry.

"I know where we are now," Arctic exclaimed. "This is the Century Castle on the southern plains. I've seen paintings and heard descriptions of this place. The bazaar in its courtyard is one of the oldest markets in all of Cerrado. The Century Castle sits on the boarders between the southern grassland plains and the midland forests."

"Southern grassland plains?" Krispin asked, skeptically. "You're not making any sense. I've never heard of any Century Castle to the south or any of the other things you are talking about."

"Well, it's where we are," Arctic said. "I don't understand why you don't believe me. We are at the Century Castle in the south."

"How do we get back to the Moon Forest?" Krispin asked. "That's where we should be right now. Why aren't we in the Moon Forest?"

"HALT!" a powerful voice said, from behind them.

Krispin and Arctic turned to see four foot-soldier guards had come upon them. The guards were in shiny armor adorned with red and black markings. The guards had their swords drawn and didn't look to be in good moods.

"What are you doing here?" the lead guard barked.

"We were walking in the forest," Krispin said.

"Likely," the guard barked. "There are reports of bandits in the forest, making their way toward the rich bazaar. The Century Baron Robert the Brave has decreed that anyone found in the forest without parchments is to be thrown in the dungeon. Do you have parchments?"

"We do not," Arctic said. "But we are not with the bandits."

"Likely," the guard said. "To the dungeon with them."

The guards sheathed their swords and grabbed both Krispin and Arctic. The guards rushed them into the courtyard where all the buyers and sellers began gawking at the pair that was under arrest from the castle guards. Krispin felt a level of embarrassment that he'd never felt before. Every eye in the bazaar was on him, mocking and judging him for some imagined crime. Krispin was sure most people would think he and Arctic were thieves—stealing bread and fruit to survive.

Krispin's embarrassment was replaced with a sense of dread when the guards shoved them into the castle. The interior hallways were of the same dark red stone as the exterior. As they made their way deeper into the castle, any natural light was replaced by candles hanging on the walls.

Krispin guessed they took them deep into the earth before they emerged into a dim, dank dungeon area.

Water was dripping from the ceiling and pooling in puddles on the dirt floor while rats and other shadows moved about along the sidewalls. In the dim candlelight Krispin could see holding cells but couldn't make out the figures that were in them. The entire area reeked of death and decay—a stench that was so powerful he could taste it—gag on it.

The guards opened a door and shoved Arctic to the ground inside. Krispin watched her hit the ground and saw the mud splatter around her. Her snow white clothing was covered in mud. The guards shoved Krispin in next. He was able to keep his balance and stay on his feet despite the way they threw him in. Arctic didn't attempt to stand until the door was closed and locked.

When Arctic stood, she was dripping with mud and water. Krispin felt bad for her, but he didn't have any clothes that she could change into. The cell was cold, even though it was a very hot day outside. Krispin helped Arctic to her feet and tried to brush some of the mud off of her. When his hand brushed over her back and lower, Arctic squirmed— looking Krispin in the eyes. For a brief moment, there was an electrical spark between them. Krispin thought he should kiss her right there, but the thought of Holly and his wedding to her was still in the front of his mind.

"Sorry," Krispin said, pulling his hands away. "I was trying to get the mud off of you."

"Don't worry," Arctic said. "You're intent was noble, that's what matters. For some reason I trust you. Many men would try to take advantage of me in here."

"I have to remain true and pure for my Holly," Krispin said.

"That's the girl you need to have an adventure to marry?" Arctic asked.

"Yes."

"That's so strange. I've read about love often, but I've never heard of someone needing an adventure to win love. I've heard of people going on adventures and falling in love, but not the other way. I think everyone should have the chance to find love on their own terms. I have to stay single for certain reasons but I hope that one day I will find my true love."

"You don't understand, Arctic," Krispin said. "The problem is that everyone in my little village thinks that Chester is this amazing man. He drinks all night and works all day. He's won strength contests, fights, and races. Mark my words, he'll never win an intelligence contest, nor could he even spell 'contest', but according to all the girls in the village, he's dreamy, mysterious—untamable. All the girls want to be the one to tame him, to make him settle down. He has a list of women whose hearts he broke that extends from one village to the next, but yet they all line up to have a fling with him and have their name added to the list of broken hearts. I doubt that this marriage will last very long."

"Why does he want Holly then?"

"Holly is the most beautiful girl in all the land," Krispin said, with a smile on his face. "She's got this hair...and these eyes...and that look on her face...it drives men wild. All the men in the village want to marry her. She'd make a fine wife. But I know that I'd be the only man who could make her truly happy."

"Other than her looks," Arctic asked. "What does she have to offer?"

"What do you mean?"

"I mean, other than her looks, what else does Holly have to offer? Name one other feature about her that would make her worthy of all this attention."

"Well...there's...look kid, you just don't understand," Krispin said. "Holly and I used to walk home from school together when we were young. We'd talk the whole way—laughing, and having a great time. Once she got older, more men started noticing her and she didn't spend time with me, but we still have our walks...there's still those conversations we once had. When you get done hunting unicorns and find love, you'll know what I'm talking about."

"How long's it been since you've had those talks?"

"About ten years."

Arctic smiled a knowing smile while giggling. Krispin ignored her and began looking over the cell. He couldn't figure out how things had gotten so upset so quickly. Krispin couldn't understand why the guards arrested them so fast. As he was replaying the incident in his head, a thought crossed his mind.

"Arctic?" Krispin asked.

"Yes, Krispin?"

"How did we get to the Century Castle?" Krispin asked.

"We walked here...right?" Arctic replied.

"No," Krispin said, thinking. "Hang on a minute. I met that woman I thought was your mother...then I met you, and we talked...then we were arrested."

"We met in the Moon Forest," Arctic said. "As you kept calling it, although I've never heard of the Moon Forest."

"Then how did we get here?" Krispin asked.

Arctic thought about it for a moment. She realized that there was a moment in time that she couldn't remember. She could see the image of Krispin and her speaking in the Moon Forest, then they were arrested outside the Century Castle. No matter how hard she tried, there was a fog—a gray mist in her mind that separated the two events.

"I don't know how we got here," Arctic said. "I have no memory of it."

"Neither do I," Krispin said. "Oh, this will make a good start to my adventure for Holly. When she hears that I met some strange little girl who was hunting a unicorn and we ended up in the dungeon of a mystery castle that no one from my village knows about, she will surely choose me over Chester. This is good, Arctic."

"And you call me the strange one," Arctic laughed. "Well, lover boy, we have one simple problem...we're in a dungeon."

"That does pose a slight problem," Krispin said. "You seem to know something about this area. How long will they hold us for?"

"No idea," Arctic said. "They could release us or kill us anytime they want, Krispin. Remember when the guard said that there were bandits about?"

"Yes," Krispin said. "Who are the bandits?"

"They are an outlaw group led by a cunning, evil man named Ornthal," Arctic said. "They steal whatever they want. They live in a massive pleasure palace that's hidden away. They are killers…expertly trained…and they rarely take prisoners."

"You'd think that the king of this land would have dealt with them," Krispin said.

"He's got other things to worry about," Arctic snapped.

"Sorry," Krispin said. "Look Arctic…we're still trapped in this dungeon and there may be bandits on the way. I have to finish out my adventure and you have your quest that you're on."

"To find a unicorn horn and bring it to my father," Arctic said.

"Right," Krispin replied. "Let's make a bargain. I will help you find the unicorn horn and once we have it you will return to my land with me and confirm my adventure to Holly. When she hears of it she will surely fall into my arms with love."

"Although, I think you're delusional," Arctic said. "Okay, I agree." The pair shook hands. "Now, how do we get out of here? I order you to get us out of this dungeon."

"Hang on one second," Krispin said. "You will not order me to do anything. We work as equals here. We will plan our escape together."

"Listen to me," Arctic said, as she raised her tone and put her hands on her hips, "I know this place and you don't. I know this land. You will follow my orders as I command them and I order you to get me out of here."

"What do you think you are, a princess?" Krispin asked.

"I…" Arctic trailed off. She'd always ordered people around in the castle, but this was different. She didn't want to give away that she was royal but she needed Krispin to follow her commands. Arctic wished she had more experience in this sort of business. She didn't know how to get Krispin to follow her orders. "I'm used to people doing what I tell them. Sorry. I'll try to work with you, Krispin. This is my first time away from my father and out of our house. I'm not sure how all this works."

"This is my first time away as well," Krispin said. "We can work this through together. Trust me Arctic, we will find your unicorn horn and have an adventure."

Arctic smiled at Krispin and he smiled back at her. Had the pair known what was heading for the Century Castle at that moment, they would not have been smiling. The bandits were coming. A line of horsemen were coming from the east, footmen from the north, archers from the west. As for the forest that Krispin and Arctic had been caught in, if the guards would have looked up, they would have seen the tops of the trees crawling with the legendary bandit stealth troops, all looking to sack the rich bazaar at the Century Castle.

Chapter 12

The Windswept Castle sat high on a swell, on land, in the center of an ever-expanding prairie that was full of green grass—a mosaic of flowers, and herds of cattle. Horse masters drove the cattle through the Windswept Plains, which gave the rulers of the Plains vast amounts of money and power. People from every corner of Cerrado would come to the Windswept Castle to buy the grass-fed cattle—the highest quality meat in all the land.

From this castle is where Princess Ashlynn ruled. Being a young princess, of only twenty years old, the princess couldn't take the title of 'Queen of the Windswept Plains' until two things happened—Princess Ashlynn must get married, and the feud with the Ryder Family must come to an amicable resolution. Many have proposed that Princess Ashlynn and Prince Tobin Ryder get married, but the deep hatred between the families runs great—neither side will advocate to the other.

Prince Alos brought his foot soldiers to the gates of the Windswept Castle. The prince had heard rumors that Ashlynn was practicing necromancy in an effort to turn the war for her homeland in her favor. Prince Alos thought that the best place to start looking for Necromancer Oliver's 'Knowledge of Cerrado' would be with the princess herself. The prince instructed his men to wait outside the castle walls until he signaled them. The soldiers obeyed his commands to the letter.

Prince Alos was brought before Princess Ashlynn in the grand throne room. Like the castle itself, the throne room was larger than necessary—immense with high ceilings, vaulted roofs, stunning pillars, and decorations everywhere. The room was made of a sandstone-colored granite. Carved into the walls and adorned with the most magnificent paints and colors, was the story of how Princess Ashlynn and her family had come to rule the Windswept Plains. Nowhere in the story was conflict with the Ryder Family, or who was to blame for the bloodshed that had befallen both sides.

Standing before her ornate throne, was the princess herself. Alos studied the princess. She was tall and skinny—regal, yet she had an air about her that said she didn't cling to the staunchly traditions a princess would be required to follow. Princess Ashlynn wore a dark red dress cut from the finest silks in all Cerrado. The strapless dress was tight from her bust to where it stopped just above her knees. The princess had black leather boots with shimmering silver buckles that came up and almost touched the bottom of the dress.

Over the dress and boots Ashlynn wore a black leather duster that was trimmed with red threads. On her head, the princess's long black hair had been styled to look like a tiara with red highlights alongside silver and gold jeweled accessories. The princess wore a smile on her red painted lips. Her owl eyes, behind their mask of black makeup, seemed to glow as she looked over the prince before her.

The only other people in the room were two knights—Sir Wayne and Sir Bromas. Both knights were in full armor, complete with shield and sword at their side. Both knights were watching the two royals in the room with hawk eyes, making sure neither made a move on the other. Sir Wayne had white and blue markings on his shield, signifying he was loyal to Prince Alos while Sir Bromas had black and red markings on his shield, showing his loyalty to Princess Ashlynn.

"Prince Alos," Princess Ashlynn said, in her high pitched, scratchy voice. "Oh my, the rumors about how handsome you are don't do you justice. You are indeed the most handsome man that I've ever seen within Cerrado."

"Princess Ashlynn," Prince Alos said, bowing. "Your beauty proceeds you. I'm honored to be able to stand before you in your court."

"Thank you, kind sir," Princess Ashlynn said, as she sat on her throne. "My good knight Sir Bromas tells me that you are here on some kind of business. I hope that before this business takes place there might be time for us to get to know one another. I would think that you and I could be good friends...if not more."

"You have aspirations to sit at the right hand of the Honor Throne as my mother did?" Prince Alos asked. "You wish to marry into the ruling family?"

"There are worse matches than you and I, Prince Alos," Princess Ashlynn said. "Together we could take Cerrado to levels never thought possible. Once your father passes away from natural causes of course."

"Of course," Prince Alos said. "Tell me, Princess Ashlynn...if you and I were to enter into a marriage together, what would become of your Windswept Plains?"

"I would rule the plains from the main Cerrado Castle," Princess Ashlynn said. "I would have a proxy who would sit in this throne, carrying out my orders. Think of the money and power Windswept Plains could bring to the ruling family of Cerrado. You would be the most powerful ruler that Cerrado has ever seen. Even the bandits would have no choice but to bow before you. The people would love us and we could be happy since there would be peace throughout the land."

"You make an interesting proposal," Prince Alos said. "But what of the Ryder Family and Tobin Ryder?"

"They would submit once they learned of our union," Princess Ashlynn said. "They would not dare stand before us, defying our rule. They would submit and we could give them something...a token for being peaceful."

"Young Master, I must protest," Sir Wayne said. "We should do what we set out to do. Talk of this can come after we have saved the kingdom."

"Saved the kingdom?" Ashlynn asked. "Is it in trouble?"

"Mystic Seven the Red has had a terrible vision," Alos said. "Cerrado could be destroyed if we don't act quickly. My father, your duke, is in mortal danger and we must do all we can to save him. Princess Ashlynn, I have heard much about you and I know that you can help us."

"You have heard much about me?" Ashlynn asked, with a crooked smile. "And how may I be of help to you?"

"Let us have our guards leave," Prince Alos said. "This is to be discussed between you and me."

"So be it," Princess Ashlynn said. "Sir Bromas, leave us."

"You too, Sir Wayne," Prince Alos said.

Slowly, reluctantly, both knights left the room. Once the doors were closed, Princess Ashlynn stood and removed her duster jacket, tossing it sloppily on the floor next to the throne. Prince Alos was quick to notice the bangle that Princess Ashlynn wore around her left bicep. It was big, about four inches wide, black with red markings, outlined with gold and silver—and had the sign of an enchantress, a female necromancer.

On Princess Ashlynn's right arm, Prince Alos noticed a solid gold snake wrapping around the princess's narrow arm, starting at the elbow with the head of the cobra almost touching her shoulder, looking out with milky-white stone eyes. Prince Alos had heard of women that wore snakes like this on their right arm, but he'd never met one—never knew that one still existed. A snake around the right arm signified that the wearer was a leader of a coven, a trainer of Mystics, a master of necromancy. Prince Alos swallowed in a throat that was suddenly dry, realizing that Princess Ashlynn might be far more powerful than he'd ever imagined.

"What did you wish to ask me that was too hot to lay before our knights?" Princess Ashlynn asked, sitting back in her throne. "Do you wish to proposition me?"

"Our Mystic has sent myself and my other three siblings out on quests," Prince Alos said, mustering as much courage as he could. "We will not allow Cerrado to fall into the wrong hands. My quest is to obtain a copy of Necromancer Oliver's 'Knowledge of Cerrado.' Princess Ashlynn, I've heard the rumors and looking at your arms I see they are confirmed. You practice necromancy and sorcery. You are a trainer of witches. You must have a copy of the book that I can claim for my own."

"Brave boy," Ashlynn said, with a crooked smile. "You openly speak of such things? You must have courage that runs very deep. I've heard the rumors that you are a true man, powerful and brave. You speak of my armlet and little snake? They are trinkets that I bought in the bazaar at the Century Castle. Many strange things there. I wear them because they look good on me."

"I noticed that you didn't reveal your arms until my knight was out of the room," Prince Alos said.

"I was hot," Ashlynn replied. "Nothing more. You accuse of things that aren't there. I must accuse of something as well. You seem to know a lot about necromancy and the rules governing it...do you practice the dark art?"

96

"As a possible future leader of Cerrado, I have educated myself," Alos said. "I know enough to defend myself. I know enough to see the signs."

"Then you would also know that if I was as powerful as these symbols say, that you would have no chance of defeating me," Princess Ashlynn said. "Unless you've practiced yourself."

"To know true light one must walk in pure darkness," Prince Alos replied.

Princess Ashlynn smiled and stood from her throne. She seductively walked toward Alos, stepping right up to him. She licked her lips as she pulled his sword from its sheath at his waist. Ashlynn tossed the sword across the room and motioned for Alos to back up. Prince Alos took two steps backwards, into the main chamber of the throne room. Alos tried to control his breathing, tried not to show fear, but he realized he was in the process of being called into a magical battle with a very powerful sorcerer.

Ashlynn twirled her fingers and a strange light seemed to encompass the princess. When the light subsided, Ashlynn had changed from her dress. She was in the garb that Prince Alos had heard was battle gear for the witches—black pants that danced around her legs with a black top. It was something Alos had never seen before. The top exposed Ashlynn's arms and was tight, but the material was something strange, a glowing black that almost appeared to be liquid.

Prince Alos stared at the top. There were flecks of red in the black that seemed to be moving—up and down, up and down. The fox prince couldn't figure it out. As his eyes were fixated on the top he didn't realize that Ashlynn was moving toward him. Something in the back of Alos's mind, a training that was long ago forgotten, started screaming at him and telling him to wake up. In that moment Prince Alos realized that Ashlynn was almost to him.

The prince acted in the blink of an eye, taking a quick step toward the princess, lifting her up and gently putting her to the ground on her back. The prince got on top of her and quickly pulled his dagger out of his waist sash, holding it right at Ashlynn's throat.

"Clever girl," Prince Alos said. "I remember that witches wear trick clothing or jewelry that can hypnotize a man, forcing him to submit to your will. You dared to try and take me?"

"I dare a many things," Princess Ashlynn said.

In the blink of an eye, Prince Alos felt a warmth rush through the room. It was like nothing he'd ever experienced before. When he got his wits about him, the prince realized that he and the princess had switched positions—he was on his back and she was on top of him with the dagger pointed to his neck. Prince Alos tried to move but found that his arms and legs didn't respond with the strength and speed they normally did.

"Don't try and move," Princess Ashlynn said. "I have a spell on you. It will hurt too much for you to move."

"What do you want from me?" Prince Alos asked, struggling under the magic of her spells.

"I want what's mine," Princess Ashlynn said. "I want the Windswept Plains. I'm sick of sharing it with the Ryder Family. My family controlled these plains for generations then they came along and took over. They gained enough power and influence that they got the king to allow a dual rule of the lands...but that will never work. They keep trying to gain more and more. You think I wanted to make the sacrifices that it took to become this powerful? I hate what I have become but it's the only way I can defeat them."

"Give me what I want and I will grant you full control over the Windswept Plains," Prince Alos said. "My family has the power and we will make you the sole ruler here, under one condition."

"What's that?"

"You must give up all your dark powers," Alos said. "We cannot allow one such as yourself to sit in a seat of power."

"I would require something then," Ashlynn said.

"What?"

"You...for one night."

Prince Alos smiled as he looked into Ashlynn's eyes. There was something there in those eyes—something evil. The prince wasn't sure what he was looking at. It was almost as if he was looking past Ashlynn and seeing someone else in her place. The front of her eyes were empty, but the backs—the souls—contained something that didn't feel right. Prince Alos kept testing the powers that were pinning him to the floor but he couldn't counter them, didn't have the ability to mount a fight in the position he was in.

"Interesting," Prince Alos said.

"As I said before," Princess Ashlynn said, "there are many worse matches than you and I."

"And it just so happens that if a witch of your power would get a willing partner…a partner who also practiced necromancy…then you would be able to gain his powers through the act of intercourse. But he has to be a willing participant, correct?"

"You are most wise, Prince Alos," Ashlynn said, standing up.

Ashlynn stood and snapped her fingers, changing back into the dress she'd been in before. Ashlynn extended a hand to help Alos up. The pair stood close to each other—almost touching, glaring into the other's eyes. They were still holding hands as neither was willing to let go first. Prince Alos knew that he could defeat the princess if it came to that, but he wasn't sure he wanted to pay the cost that defeating her would entail.

"We stand at a crossroads," Prince Alos said. "I need the book, you want your homelands, and I have a feeling that there's nothing that would make you give up the sorcery that you practice."

"Why do I have to give it up?" Ashlynn asked.

"We can't have you trying to hypnotize others," Alos said. "You can't be allowed to go after the Honor Throne. Necromancy was banished many years ago and we follow that decree."

"Then what do you propose that we do?"

"Give me the book," Prince Alos said. "Show me how to use it and I will protect my father. Once the dangers for him have subsided, you will

99

give up your powers and we will put you on the throne of the Windswept Plains. The Ryder family will be forced to give up their claim."

"And if I don't give up my power?" Ashlynn asked.

"I think you'll give them up without a struggle," Alos said.

Ashlynn snapped her fingers and was back in her battle gear. Alos draped himself in magic and was wearing tight blue pants and no top, showing off his chiseled abs and chest. Ashlynn hesitated for a split second, gazing upon his physique as much as she was stunned that he was so powerful with magic. In that split second of hesitation, Alos put Ashlynn on the floor and stood up. Ashlynn tried to stand but the magic was holding her down. No matter what she tried she couldn't break it.

Alos waved his hand in the air and Ashlynn was brought to her feet. She was dumbfounded by what had just happened. Ashlynn tried to conjure a spell but Alos prevented her from doing so. No matter what she tried, Alos was one step ahead and a few degrees stronger. Ashlynn frantically tried everything that she knew, exhausting herself in the process, but nothing had an effect on Prince Alos. Alos just kept pacing around the princess.

Finally, after a minute of trying spells, Ashlynn collapsed to the floor—exhausted, drenched in sweat, and trying to catch her breath. Alos walked up to her cautiously, stood over her, and looked down. Ashlynn was hysterical, the powers she'd used were draining her so. Ashlynn brought a dagger to her hand and used it to cut her top off. She ripped the material away, exposing her chest and stomach to the fox prince before offering him the dagger.

"Take this blade," Ashlynn wailed. "Have its tip find my heart. To be bested in this manner is death for me. If my order or students ever found out that I was on the floor, helpless before another, they would tear me apart. Prince Alos, you know this to be true. I cannot give up my powers. Those who follow me will not allow it. Please kill me."

"I will not," Prince Alos said.

The prince waved his hand and in an instant both were back in their original outfits—Ashlynn sitting in her throne. The princess looked over her garments and her position, not believing how easy it was for Alos to control her. The princess looked to the prince with longing eyes.

"They will kill me," Ashlynn said. "You know they will. If any of my followers get word that I was defenseless on the floor, then my life is forfeit. You know that to be true."

"I promise you this, Ashlynn," Prince Alos said, adjusting his robe. "You give me the book and show me how to use it, you help me defend my father and family, and I will personally help you defeat your followers and keep you safe."

"Will you make me your wife?" Ashlynn asked. "If I marry you, then the defeat is part of a conquest and they would have to challenge you…something that none of them would do."

"That will be decided later," Prince Alos said. "For now, we need the book."

Ashlynn nodded and waved her hands. A swirl of air formed in the middle of the room and began to take the shape of a pedestal with a large book on it. It took a minute, but Alos saw the pedestal form into the shape of a large raven's claw, with an obsidian stone cover. The book that formed on top looked to be bound with flesh—human flesh. Upon it, were written horrible curses. When the book was fully formed, Ashlynn prevented Alos from approaching it, signifying they had to remove curses before they could open it. Alos smiled, knowing he had completed his portion of the quest. And now, with the book in hand, he might be able to help his other siblings complete theirs.

Chapter 13

Krispin had looked over every inch of the cell as Arctic was looking on. Krispin knew there had to be something that they could do to get out of the dungeon. He wanted to move quickly, not knowing how long it would take them to get back to the Blue Cerrado Forest to find the unicorn before making their way back to the Moon Forest. Krispin kept thinking about how they were going to do that, but he would always push those thoughts out of his mind. He figured if they didn't get out of the cell there would be no point in planning out the next leg of the journey.

Krispin returned to the gate of the cell. He knew from herding sheep so many years that whether the sheep wanted to get out or a wolf wanted to get in, gates were relatively easy to break through. He'd looked the gate over before but hadn't seen anything, so he looked over other things, hoping an idea would come to him. Nothing did. Arctic looked on with excited anticipation. She didn't say a word so as to let Krispin think. Arctic hoped they would be out of there soon.

"I know there has to be a way to get through this gate," Krispin said. "The sheep and wolves do it so often that it can't be that hard."

"Do you like being a shepherd?" Arctic asked.

"I do, I think," Krispin said. "It's hard to honestly answer that."

"What do you mean?" Arctic asked. "You've been a shepherd your entire life. Either you enjoy it or you don't."

"Therein lies the problem, Arctic," Krispin said. "I've been a shepherd my entire life. I don't know anything else. I have no other reference points to compare it to. Everyone in my family has been shepherds, although dad did leave for university to study the stars for a few years before returning. I often look up at the stars and wonder if there are other worlds up there...you know, other worlds that have people like us on them."

"What a curious thought," Arctic said. "I've never heard of anyone looking up at the stars and wondering if there are other worlds. Why would you need another world? There's so much here to be explored and explained that you could spend your lifetime and not see even a tenth-of-a-tenth of it all."

"That's an interesting way of looking at it," Krispin said. "And I think I have it figured out."

"The gate?"

"Yes. Look here...these hinges are constructed with interlocking barrels held with pins. The gate itself is so heavy that to swing into the cell, the barrels have to be on the inside. If we could pop the pins out, the gate would open from this side. We wouldn't have to worry about the locks."

"But how can we get that out?" Arctic asked, looking to where Krispin was pointing. "We would need tools."

"A hammer and a thin, but strong piece of metal," Krispin said. "There are loose stones here that would work for a hammer, but nothing skinny enough to slide into the hole. It was a good idea."

Arctic was about to speak when a blast rocked the entire castle. Everything in the dungeon shook with violent force. Arctic started to fall toward the mud but Krispin, moving quickly, grabbed her and allowed her to fall into his arms. This threw Krispin off balance, dropping him in the mud. Arctic stayed clean this time, landing on top of him.

Arctic looked Krispin in the eyes before quickly standing and helping Krispin up. Krispin brushed the mud off while they listened to smaller blasts and explosions that were taking place all over the castle. They could hear a great deal of yelling and shouting coming from above them. There seemed to be general panic in all directions.

"Bandits," Arctic said. "That's the only group who could cause problems like this. Remember they said that bandits were coming this way."

"We'll be safe here, right?"

"Not a chance," Arctic said, coldly. "The bandits win...they always win. They will ransack the castle, taking anything worth value. They will steal everything they can from the bazaar and the people in it. Once they have finished, they will come to the dungeons. They will take all of us, either making us slaves or holding us for ransom."

"What do you think we should do?" Krispin asked.

"Figure a way out of here as quickly as we can," Arctic said. "The guards will all be out fighting the bandits so no one will stop us from leaving. The hallways of the castle will be empty."

"We hide somewhere here?"

"They will search everything," Arctic said. "Our best bet is to flee this castle and hide in the forests. The bandits won't bother with two young travelers...not worth their time."

"The fact still remains that I need something to break these hinges apart," Krispin said, as he looked over the cell.

In the corner of the cell something caught Krispin's eye. There was a stone that was broken apart into many long pieces. Krispin looked the broken stones over and saw one he thought might work. Krispin took a larger stone to use as a hammer and approached the hinges of the cell. The castle was still shaking and there was still pandemonium all about as Krispin used the rocks to try and push out the pins.

The first few times, the pin didn't even move. Krispin hit the stone harder, shattering it. He went back to the corner and found a bigger piece of stone and started again. He slowly increased how hard he was hitting the pins, and to his amazement, the pin started moving up. It took a quarter of an hour, and four more pieces of stone, but Krispin knocked all three pins out of the hinges and the cell gate fell to the floor with an ear-piercing bang.

"My hero!" Arctic exclaimed, giving Krispin a big hug.

"That's twice I've saved you now, Arctic," Krispin said, with a smile.

Krispin took Arctic's hand and the pair began to rush through the dungeon. The hallways were dark and dank with no indications as to where they should be going. Krispin tried to remember the way they came but everything looked identical there. The massive labyrinth of hallways twisted and turned underneath all the excitement that was going on

104

above them. After a few twists and turns, Krispin and Arctic found themselves at a dead end.

"Now what?" Arctic asked.

"I have no idea," Krispin said. "This dungeon is huge. Do they really need all this space?"

"There was a time when it was required, yes," Arctic said. "There were a lot of war prisoners here. Most of these cells are used for storage now. Sometimes people live down here during the depths of winter when it's unbearably cold outside."

"I don't remember the way," Krispin said. "We could wander down here forever and not find our way out. They moved us so quickly when we came here. You're supposed to be the expert on these places...you have any ideas?"

"Now it's my fault we're trapped?" Arctic said, putting her hands on her hips.

"That's not what I said," Krispin replied, quickly. "I said, you know this place better than I do and I asked if you had an idea. Don't jump to conclusions."

"You're the one who's been rescuing me," Arctic said. "I'm not sure what we should do."

"I have an idea," Krispin said, walking back the way they came.

Krispin got to a junction in the hallways and stopped. He turned his ear to the ceiling and listened. Arctic tried to say something but he motioned for her to be quiet. It took a moment but Krispin thought he could tell what direction the voices were coming from. Krispin led Arctic until they got to another junction. He listened again and found a heading. The pair did this a few more times, each time the noises got louder. Finally they saw a flight of stairs that would take them back to the castle.

"There's our way out," Krispin said. "But the question is, should we go out there right now? It sounds pretty bad."

"The fighting will come here," Arctic said. "There's no question about that. We are safer to try and run. We have a chance that way, there's no chance down here."

"Okay," Krispin said. "When we get out, hold my hand tight and keep up. We will run for the forests as fast as we can."

"Agreed," Arctic said.

The pair looked each other in the eyes. There was a moment where Krispin thought that he should kiss Arctic. A feeling flooded him, a wave rushed over him, and in that moment he felt like kissing her was the thing to do and thought it was what she wanted, but Krispin kept Holly in the front of his mind. No matter how inviting Arctic's eyes looked, he had to remember Holly and why he was on this adventure.

Krispin squeezed Arctic's hand and he took off running with her in tow. The pair burst through the doors to see bandits everywhere, harassing the people of the Century Castle. The bandits wore black trousers, dark colored shirts, bandanas, and carried swords larger than anything Krispin had ever seen before. The swords were a narrow blade, curved, and the bandits could swing them with lightning speed. Even the females who were with the bandits looked to be experts at swordplay.

Krispin and Arctic ran as fast as they could through the courtyard, jumping over the disaster of the bazaar that was there just moments before. There were carts overturned, wagons broken, and merchandise spread all over the ground. Krispin noticed that there was a pile of bodies in the middle of the courtyard—and the bandits were adding more people to the pile. He tried to keep Arctic from seeing the dead, not wanting to scare her more than she already was.

The pair could see through the main gates of the castle that the forest was just beyond. It appeared that none of the bandits were watching the gates anymore, being occupied with rounding up all the loot they had won. The king of the castle was on his knees, begging the leader for mercy but the leader looked to be ordering the king to hand over all the money. Krispin couldn't believe that the castle would be that vulnerable to an attack like this.

Just when he thought the king was going to surrender, the king made a motion. Archers started raining down arrows from upper levels of

106

the castle walls. The bandits started to scurry like roaches in the light, every one of them ducking for cover from the hardwood arrows. Krispin used every ounce of energy he had to run like the wind for the castle gates. He was almost dragging Arctic behind him, her short legs doing everything they could to keep up with him.

The pair made it through the gates and into the trees without incident. They collapsed in the forest, Krispin on his back, Arctic on top of him, the pair hugging and laughing that they made it safely.

"I thought we were dead for sure," Arctic said.

"Me too," Krispin replied. "Now that's three times I saved your life Arctic."

"No," Arctic said, with a mischievous smile. "It's only two. That whole incident, the dungeon and the courtyard, counts as one. Maybe a big one, but it's still one."

"You think so?" Krispin asked.

"I do."

"You know, maybe I'll get tired of saving you, if you're going to argue the numbers with me."

"You'll never get tired of saving me," Arctic said, with a grin. "You'll want to save me for the rest of your life."

Krispin looked Arctic in the eyes again. In his eyes she was so incredible. And there was that spark again, something that told him he should kiss her right then and there. The image he had of Holly was getting smaller in his mind, being replaced by an image of Arctic. Before Krispin could think, a voice rang out behind them.

"Don't even think about running any farther," a powerful female voice said.

Krispin and Arctic looked to see they were being held at sword point by a female bandit. The woman wore all black, including a mask that allowed just her eyes to be seen. The woman was short, yet taller than Arctic, and moved with a feline quickness and grace as she bounced between her feet, passing her sword back and forth between her hands.

Krispin and Arctic stood with their hands in the air. As the woman kept staring at Arctic, a quizzical look flashed through her eyes.

"Well, who are you, little one?" the woman asked in a sultry voice. "I think I know you."

"You do not," Arctic said, firmly. "I am no one."

"Everyone is someone," the woman said, moving closer. "I think I know who you are. Even under all that mud and muck, I know you. This is not one of your brothers. Is he your knight? Your protector, perhaps?"

"He is my friend," Arctic said. "You do not know me."

"If I were you," Krispin said. "I would be more concerned about the damages being done to the bandits inside the courtyard. You are losing."

"Bandits don't lose boy," the woman said. "I know who you are, and this raid just got a lot more valuable."

The woman moved in quickly. She put her hand under her black clothing and pulled something out. The woman tossed an object toward Krispin and Arctic and then she quickly backed away. Krispin saw Arctic cover her mouth and nose with her hand so he did the same as the object began to spew a mist. When the mist got near Krispin's nose he could feel himself getting lightheaded. Arctic fell to the ground in a pile. Krispin tried to catch her but he fell too. Krispin tried to stand as he felt a blanket of unconsciousness encompass him.

Chapter 14

The Hammerbrite Castle stood tall in the morning sun. The castle was smaller, made from light colored granite that looked green from the ivy and algae that grew on the castle. Hammerbrite Castle sat on a low bluff that looked over a large lake. Strong winds off the lake and crashing waves on the rocks below kept the north and west walls of the castle dripping wet for three seasons of the year and ice-covered for the fourth.

Prince Atin and Princess Ambriss led their teams to the open field that was in front of the castle. The amount of flowers and decorations that adorned the greeting exterior of the castle melted the women's hearts, but Atin was unmoved by the display. He held his hand up, signaling that the teams needed to stop.

"Sister Princess," Atin said. "You and I will enter the castle and negotiate for the maps. Your team must wait out here. Leave them with a top commander and instruct them to do nothing without our instructions."

"The princess will not enter alone," January said, firmly. "I will attend her."

"Very well," Atin said. "But just know this...I'm bringing my companion then, and she will have instructions to deal with you very quickly if you do anything without my permission. I know the princess here, I know what she will and will not allow. You must follow my lead."

"We will follow, Brother," Ambriss said. "Rose, you will be in command of the troops and horses while I am inside. Watch for any signals and be prepared to act."

"I will, my Princess," Rose said, bowing in her saddle to Ambriss.

"Now, follow me and try to not do anything stupid," Atin said. "In fact, just don't do anything at all. Let me do the talking and everything will be fine."

"I don't know if I like this," January said.

"Then stay here," Atin said. "It would make everything go so much better."

"I will not leave Princess Ambriss's side," January said. "I will go with her and defend the princess until my last breath."

"Splendid," Atin said, getting off his horse. "Follow me."

Princess Ambriss, January, and Atin's companion dismounted their horses as Rose gave instructions to the troops. The group, following behind Prince Atin in a single-file line, made their way through the rest of the field, up to the main gate of the castle. Atin lead, followed by Ambriss, January, and Atin's companion. January and the companion kept exchanging glances. January was ready for any trickery that might happen.

When the group reached the gate, a pair of guards, clad in shiny armor, blocked the way. Their steel lances were crossed and they didn't look like they were interested in hearing anything from the man and his three women that were walking up the trail. Prince Atin motioned for the others to stop further back as he walked up to the knights.

"Halt!" the guard on the right said. "State your business."

"I am the wolf prince," Atin said. "My travel companions and I have business with the Hammerbrite princess. Although she is not expecting us, we must speak with her."

"The princess is not holding court with anyone on this day," the knight said. "Be gone with you. We have no desire to discuss this matter any further."

"Do you now?" Atin said, with a wolfish grin. "The wheat in the southlands grows best with a northern rain."

"I'm so sorry, sir," the knight said, as they both moved out of the way. "Please, the princess is in her chambers. We will send for her if you would be so kind as to wait in the grand audience chamber. Is there anything else we can get for you?"

"The princess will do just fine," Atin said, as he walked by the guards. "She'll do just fine indeed."

Princess Ambriss followed her brother as he walked into the castle. She couldn't help but raise her eyebrow at how smoothly her brother got them past the guards. She'd often heard rumors that her brother was a trickster—someone who had many shady dealings

110

throughout Cerrado—and this situation was confirming it. Ambriss was staring at her brother when January leaned in and whispered to her.

"There's something not right here," January said. "I can't put my finger on it."

"I think I know what's bothering you, January," Ambriss whispered back. "Up to this point, no one has mentioned the name of the Hammerbrite Princess. I confess that I don't know what her name is either."

"Strange," January said. "Both your brother and the guards talked about her. Why wouldn't they use her name?"

"Because her name is impossible to pronounce," Atin's female companion said, leaning in toward the pair.

"Is that the same reason we don't know your name?" January asked.

"Not at all," the woman said. "My name is hidden because I am hidden. Atin saved me from a death sentence and I owe him my life. If my name were known then it would be possible the person who gave me the death sentence could come after me."

"And you are my brother's lover, correct?" Ambriss asked.

"Love has nothing to do with what we do," the woman said. "It's lust and enjoyment. I wouldn't expect someone like you to understand."

"Someone like me?"

"You've been pampered and privileged your entire life," the woman said. "I was born in a dungeon, and my luck went down from there…until Atin saved me."

"I confess that I've lived a good life," Ambriss said. "But I wish to know you, I wish to know those who are important to my family."

"We are just about to the chamber," the woman said. "Quiet."

The group went from an oversized stone hallway to a large chamber. The chamber had vaulted ceilings with skylights, a stage on one side and open throughout the rest. The guard that was leading them took them through the chamber, past an arch, and into an antechamber on the far side of the room.

The antechamber was cozy and comfortable on the hot morning. There was a table with wooden chairs around. The guard motioned for the group to sit down as an attendant rushed in with goblets and a flagon full of wine. The attendant filled all the goblets before setting the flagon in the center of the table. Atin sipped the wine and smiled.

"Is it to your liking, good sir?" the guard asked.

"It is," Atin replied.

"Is there anything else that you require?" the guard asked. "Food, perhaps?"

"We are content here," Atin replied. "Thank you, knight."

The knight bowed and rushed out of the room, leaving the group by themselves. Atin and his companion both sipped at their wine while Ambriss crossed her arms, sitting back in her chair with a glare toward Atin. It didn't take Atin long to realize that his sister was upset with him.

"What is it, dear sister?" Atin asked.

"I can use my power to get special treatment at certain places," Ambriss said. "But the knights didn't know you, and you never gave them your name. We are getting royal treatment but Hammerbrite is a fringe castle, and the princess doesn't pledge loyalty to us although she does support us. What sort of agreement do you have with her?"

"A fun one," Atin said, winking as he took another drink of wine.

Ambriss was going to press the issue when the princess walked into the antechamber. Everyone quickly stood when she walked in. The princess was hauntingly beautiful—brunette hair falling to her waist, and big doughy eyes that seemed to hide a sadness no one knew about. The princess wore a green and gray dress, elegant and formal. She was adorned with many pieces of gold jewelry, including the crown she wore on her head.

Atin approached the princess and bowed, kissing the woman's hand. Ambriss figured, based on historical information that this woman had to be in her early fifties, although she could pass for a much younger woman based off her looks.

The princess smiled a bored smile as Atin held her hand and looked her in the eyes. Atin moved in, whispering something into the princess's ear, causing her to light up like a fire. There was a glow about her as she began to giggle. Ambriss couldn't help but notice that the woman with Atin didn't look happy with the actions that Atin was making. There was tension between the princess and the woman.

"Mister Atin," the princess said, smiling. "You bring friends."

"We are on a quest," Atin said, as everyone sat down. "We need information."

"You wish to use my maps?"

"We do."

"And what coin did you bring to bargain with?"

"What coin would you like?" Atin asked.

"I could think of a number of things," the princess said. "But then again, I suppose that I still own you for a number of things that you've done for me in the past."

"And what would those things be?" January asked. "If we are to trust you, we should know the history of what brought you two together."

"She's an interesting one," the princess said.

"She was told to keep her mouth silent," Atin said, glaring.

"I wish she would," the princess said. "I'm surprised, normally when you arrive it's just you and your companion here. I've never seen you with these other two."

"One is my sister," Atin said. "The noisy one is her attendant."

"I'm so much more than an attendant," January shot back.

"And that's not what we're here for," Atin said. "We have something that we need to get and we should be sticking to the plan.

There's no reason to get up in arms here, January. Now, princess, we seek knowledge."

"Then you are in the right place," the princess said. "I've heard that your father is in trouble."

"Word has reached here then?"

"In a form, yes," the princess said. "I've heard that Queen Mala has returned."

"Impossible," Ambriss said. "Mala was killed by the Former King."

"Not fully," Atin said. "I had a feeling that she would return. Let me guess, Mystic Seven the Red was working for her the entire time."

"You were duped," the princess said. "He sent you away so that Duke Asmout would be vulnerable for her return. The tasks were all things that she needs to take over Cerrado and hold it without being challenged."

"There's no way that is possible," Ambriss said. "Mystic Seven was loyal to us. Look at how many times he's saved us."

"They were all setups," the princess said.

"Why haven't you told us that before?" January asked. "Why do you spring this on them now, when events have already been placed into motion?"

"It is the way of things," the princess said. "I wasn't aware of this plot until events were put into motion. Had I known, I would have alerted Atin to try and prevent it. Cerrado has a funny way of revealing information across the lands."

"If you are correct," Ambriss said. "That would mean that our actions to acquire the items of our quest won't help us. Are we to forgo our quests and return to the castle to help father?"

"That would be unwise," the princess said. "She will not kill him, not until the children have returned. I guess that Mala has plans for Asmout."

"Then what are we to do?" January asked.

"Bandits," Atin said.

"Yes," the princess agreed. "The bandits. They are your ticket."

"Ornthal controls the bandits," Ambriss said. "What can we gain with them?"

"What you will gain is the safety of other family members," the princess said. "I foresee that your little sister is in great danger. She has befriended a strange boy that I cannot understand. He serves a strange purpose. They have been captured by the bandits and very soon will be held for ransom. If you do not work quickly to save them there might not be a chance to get Arctic back."

"How do you know this?" Ambriss asked. "Who are you?"

"I am older than I look," the princess said. "I am here to watch over the maps of Cerrado. I know all that has ever been in Cerrado."

"Where is the Immortal River?" Ambriss asked.

"I have seen people use the waters of the Immortal River," the princess said. "My friend, Captain Creature, has spoken before of sailing between her banks. There are many rumors about it but I can assure you that no map of Cerrado contains the location of the Immortal River."

"How is that possible?" Ambriss asked.

"Because the river is not in Cerrado," the princess said. "It is somewhere else."

"How would you get to it?"

"Have you heard the legends of the arches?" the princess asked.

"I have."

"That is how you would get to them." The princess said. "Captain Creature has maps of the arches. He sails through them, involving himself in many worlds."

Ambriss looked at the princess. She didn't know what to make of all this. Ambriss was very concerned for her father but was even more concerned for what was said about Arctic. Ambriss knew that her father

115

would be able to take care of himself but her little sister had never experienced things like this. Ambriss knew that Arctic had been sheltered her entire life and had yet to experience the real world. Ambriss also wanted to push further about the Immortal River but decided to inquire about what seemed the most pressing at the moment.

"What must we do to save Arctic?" Ambriss asked.

"You must go to Yorehill Manor," the princess said. "You must go there in the clothing of the bandits. There you will join with them. Your sister will be taken to Yorehill where Ornthal himself lives. There you will have to save her and the man with her."

"Why do we save him?" Ambriss asked.

"I don't know," the princess said. "All I know is that you have to save him. He will be important to your cause. He has entered into a bargain with Arctic. They are helping each other out and they both need to complete their tasks."

"But you cannot walk into Yorehill Manor with a division of riders," January said. "The four of us will go there but what will the rest of the women do?"

"Only two will go to Yorehill," the princess said. "Atin and Ambriss. The rest of you will rush back to Cerrado Castle. The duke is still in power but Mala is behind the scenes, pulling the strings. You will have to make contact with Atin's other companions to figure out a plan that will help hold the castle. You cannot strike too soon, otherwise there will be more evil in the land."

"We are to wait, in hiding, for the proper moment?" January asked.

"That is what I am saying," the princess said. "Every step must be taken with caution. There are so many ways that you could lose everything now. Every step must be planned out and taken with caution."

"You are trying to scare us," Ambriss said. "Atin, what assurances can you give us that her words are true? We know nothing of what she says. I want something...anything that can give me rest that she is not leading us down the prim roads past."

"Ambriss," Atin said. "Have I ever lied to you?"

"No."

"Have I ever hurt you?"

"No."

"Have I ever tricked you?"

"No."

"And I am not doing any of those things now," Atin said, looking his sister in the eye. "I know that I may seem shady, and on the outside of the family, but now more than ever, you need to trust me. We will not allow our family to be destroyed."

"I still don't know," Ambriss said. "There are so many unknowns right now. I just wish there was something more to go on."

"In time there will be," Atin said. "Right now we don't have the time to sit and debate this. I trust this woman with my life and she knows what would happen to her if she lied to me. We need to move...and move fast."

"January," Ambriss said, after a tense moment of silence. "Take the women and ride back to the castle. Take Atin's companion with you and make contact with the others. Use your judgment on what to do. I will return to you."

"I know you will," January said, standing to follow the companion out of the room.

"Now," the princess said. "We need to conceal you in the garments of the bandits."

Ambriss gave her brother a concerned look—he simply smiled a smile that said he was confident in what they were doing. Ambriss wished she could find his confidence as the pair followed the princess toward a different part of the castle to an unknown that Ambriss didn't know if they could overcome.

Chapter 15

Prince Alos stood in the center of the throne room of the Windswept castle, sweating profusely in his fighting gear. He looked at Princess Ashlynn, on her knees across from him. Ashlynn was also in her battle gear and sweating heavily. The pair had been sparring with the magical incantations contained within the 'Knowledge of Cerrado.'

Prince Alos waved his hands, moving forward, and sent magic toward Ashlynn. She let out a scream as she was sent flying across the floor, being pinned and held against the far wall. Ashlynn tried to fight, tried to escape the magic, but Alos had picked up the subtleties of the magic very quickly and was already very good with the magic. The pair had spent the entire day working on the magic—Ashlynn showing the prince different tricks that could be done with the magic. Now, he had defeated her again.

"I surrender to you," Princess Ashlynn called out. "Please stop."

"As you wish," Prince Alos said.

Alos waved his hands and Ashlynn was set on the floor. She remained spread on the floor, breathing heavily, trying to compose herself. The magic had drained her so hard that she was not only having trouble standing, but having trouble breathing. Ashlynn took a moment to compose herself. She stood and used her magic to change back into her dress and duster as she walked to her throne and sat down. Alos changed back into his clothes and stood before the princess, next to the pedestal with the cursed book sitting upon it.

"You have mastered much of the magic before you discovered this book," Ashlynn said. "I wonder, why do you need this when you could stand against powerful wizards?"

"The book would serve as a symbol," Prince Alos said. "It would show that we have the power without me having to demonstrate what I can do."

"An interesting ploy," Ashlynn said. "With your power, I doubt there is a necromancer in the land that could stand with you. I have fought many and this is the first time I've ever lost."

"You have strong powers," Prince Alos said. "How many people have you trained? How big is your coven?"

"There are six women," Ashlynn said. "And four men. They are all strong and well trained."

"How did you learn the dark arts?" Alos asked.

"After I saw how my family had to share power with the Ryder family, I began to train," Ashlynn said. "I was only twelve years old when I started. I knew I needed to be more powerful than anyone who'd ever come before me, so I made sacrifices that no one should ever have to make."

"You're parents died right around that time, correct?" Alos asked. "You had to sacrifice your parents to gain the powers that you have."

"I killed them in their sleep," Ashlynn said. "That was part of the price I had to pay. I killed others to gain powers. I started training others in the magic. I even killed my trainer."

"Who was she?" Alos asked.

"That's not important," Ashlynn said. "What matters is that the Ryder Family is utterly and completely destroyed. They must all be destroyed. I must be the one to kill that rat Tobin. I cannot believe that some have suggested that I marry him to unite the land. I would never submit to that poor fool."

"Then we are ready to take the book back to the Cerrado Castle and defeat those who are coming for my father," Alos said. "It is time for us to leave here."

"First you must declare me the ruler of the Windswept Plains," Ashlynn said. "You must declare me the sole ruler of this land."

"We don't have time to deal with the Ryder Family right now," Alos said. "We will defeat this evil that comes for my family, then we will return here and defeat those that are trying to take from you. We must get to my father as soon as possible."

"I want my land," Ashlynn said, firmly. "I want it now."

"If the book works like you said it would," Alos began. "And we survive the fight, then you will be the leader of the Windswept Plains. There's no time to waste though, we must get to my father and make sure that he's safe."

"I'm changing the agreement that we had," Ashlynn said. "I want to kill the Ryder family right now. We must go there and destroy them. Once we do that we can go to your castle."

"We will stick to the original agreement," Alos said. "There's nothing you can say or do to change it."

"That's what you think," Ashlynn said, standing.

Ashlynn took a step forward, instantly changing into her battle gear. She waved her hand and Alos was thrown against the far wall, crashing into a pile on the floor. Alos tried to stand and mount a defense but Ashlynn was able to deflect everything that Alos threw at her. Ashlynn sent Alos spinning across the floor, slamming into a wall before bringing him back to the center of the room.

Alos was trying to fight with everything he had but he was defenseless against the powerful necromancer. Ashlynn had a coy smile on her face as she tossed Alos around the room, hurting him in ways he had never imagined. Finally, after a few moments of being throttled, Ashlynn brought Alos to the middle of the room, using magic to keep him pinned to the floor.

"You think," Ashlynn said, with a laugh. "In your feeble little mind, that you can actually defeat me? You think for one moment that you are more powerful than me?"

"But before," Alos struggled to speak every word. "You wanted me to kill you. I bested you twice."

"Because I allowed you to," Ashlynn said. "I needed to know your full abilities and where your heart lies. You have a good heart...a true heart...but I do not. I am black-hearted and I have designs on things that you couldn't possibly imagine. I care not for your pathetic father or your little quests. I will destroy the Ryder family and take what is mine."

"Why did you make the bargain with me?" Alos asked. "Why did you promise to help?"

"Because I wanted to know what you were truly about," Ashlynn said. "I needed to know exactly what you were after. I've seen what Mystic Seven the Red has seen. I know who comes for your father. And incidentally, you and I have an aligned goal."

"What do you mean?"

"I have seen who is coming to kill your father," Ashlynn said. "Queen Mala."

"Impossible..."

"It is Mala," Ashlynn interrupted. "Don't try to convince yourself that it isn't. Mala has returned. What most people don't understand is that Mala wasn't the person who was in line for the Honor Throne. Mala had two older sisters, Tala and Bala. When Mala decided that she was going to take power for herself, she first killed her parents. Tala wasn't old enough for the throne, so the Former King, a distant relative, was placed on the throne to hold it for her."

"Mala killed her parents?" Alos asked. "How do you know that?"

"I know because I've seen things," Ashlynn said. "There are things that were only known to certain people, and I was able to learn how all this happened. I used all my powers to discover these facts."

"What's your game in all of it then?" Prince Alos asked. "I have a feeling that you are after more than just the Windswept Plains. There's more to your game than you let on, Princess Ashlynn."

"Of course there's more than I let on, fool," Ashlynn said. "I have developed my powers to the point where no one in all of Cerrado can stand before me. I will destroy anyone who tries to stop me. You think I'm after more than just Windswept? You're right. You have no idea the plans that I have. There is so much that you think that you know. But poor Prince Alos, you have no idea. In a very short amount of time all your siblings will be destroyed and there will be no one to stop either Mala or myself."

"You plan to allow Mala to take us," Prince Alos said. "Then you will make a move against her when's she weakened from fighting us."

"Either Mala or you," Ashlynn replied. "Whoever wins will have me standing there ready to strike. The winner will have no rest before I attack. I will have my entire coven at the Cerrado Castle and there will be nothing that will stand in our way. Now I need to gain more power. Tobin Ryder's younger brother Tybin Has begun learning the dark arts. You will arrange a wedding between Tybin and myself. He will be a willing partner and I will be able to assume all his powers while I destroy his family. I will have everything that I want."

"You deserve nothing," Alos said.

"You have no idea what I deserve," Ashlynn said. "There's so much you don't know you pathetic fool. Now, send word that you are arranging the marriage. I want to marry him within a fortnight. We have to do this."

"I refuse," Alos said.

Ashlynn summoned all her hatred, all her anger, and all her malice, and directed it toward Alos. She threw him around the room while using powerful magic to torment him as she punished him. Prince Alos tried with all his might and magic to fight Ashlynn off but she was far too advanced magically for him to defend against. Alos was stunned that Ashlynn was able to play so well when he had her down. He thought she was weak and would be an easy person to defeat.

Ashlynn showed no signs of stopping as she destroyed Alos. She paused for a moment with him in the middle of the room. Alos was struggling to even get up off the floor, trying to get on his hands and knees, but Ashlynn had him right where she wanted him. Ashlynn stood over Alos and laughed as four women, dressed all in black, came into the room. The women used magic to bind Alos to a board, and carried him out of the room.

When they were out of the room another woman entered the room. This woman was big—tall and thick, skin and hair black as night, and was wearing a red cloak. The woman stopped in the middle of the room and bowed before Ashlynn. The woman got on her knees and postured herself before Ashlynn.

"Rise up, dearest Rishi," Ashlynn said, offering the bowing woman her hand. "I have made sure the unbeliever will think twice before trying anything again."

"Events are moving faster than we'd anticipated," Rishi said, in a deep and breathy voice. "I never envisioned Mala moving this quickly…this boldly. Surely she cannot be at full power yet."

"Don't be too sure of that," Ashlynn said. "We do not know where she has hidden these past twenty years. My guess is she looks the same age as when she was defeated. There is much magic in this land that we don't know about."

"Then what is our play?" Rishi asked. "If his siblings find out about his imprisonment here they are sure to come for a rescue. Do we have the resources to battle them all?"

"We do," Ashlynn replied. "It is part of my play now. We have the eldest of the children. They will have to come here. Once we have them all then we can use them to control the royal armies. Using mind melds we can let them defend against Mala before we fight her."

"She will defeat them?" Rishi asked.

"After what she was put through there is nothing that will stop Mala," Ashlynn said. "I'm sure she has everything moving in her direction. She has planned for everything, but she hasn't planned for me. She hasn't planned for what I've got coming."

Ashlynn moved to her throne, snapping her fingers, changing back into her dress before sitting down. Rishi moved and sat on the floor to the right of the throne. Rishi watched as Ashlynn brought the 'Knowledge of Cerrado' back into the room and started reading through its pages. Ashlynn smiled, knowing that there was nothing that Mala, or anyone else for that matter, could do to stop them.

Chapter 16

Thoughts began to make their way back into Krispin's mind. Like a mist rolling off a pond in the first rays of the morning's sun, a fog was lifted from his brain. Krispin's body was in pain, like nothing he'd ever felt before. There were strange sensations he tried to identify, but it was like his mind was still searching for a point of reference to latch onto. Nothing seemed to make sense, least of all where he was and what he was doing.

Krispin tried to open his eyes. His heart skipped a beat when his eyes opened just enough to begin to see, but there was nothing there—complete darkness. The thought that he was blind disappeared when he noticed a slit of light to his left. Krispin realized he was in a box—a box that was moving. He could feel the trail beneath him—every bump, every rut, bounced him around in the box. There was a small amount of padding beneath him and from the odors that were penetrating his nostrils, Krispin figured that it was straw.

Krispin felt a weight on top of him. It was heavy, yet light, and the weight seemed to be moving in a rhythmic fashion. It took Krispin a moment to understand that the weight was Arctic. They had placed her on top of him in this box that was in some kind of cart being pulled by a horse who was racing down a bumpy trail. Krispin tried to figure out how they got in this situation but the last image he could remember was the carnage that was in the bazaar.

"Krispin?" Arctic's voice was soft, only a whisper. "Krispin, are you awake?"

"I am, Arctic," Krispin said. "Are you hurt?"

"I feel strange," Arctic said. "But I remember hearing stories of the bandits and the weapons they use to catch people. The effects should wear off soon."

The Bandits. Krispin remembered now. They had left the courtyard and raced into the forest where they had been captured by the bandits. He remembered the strange woman throwing something at them and the cloud of smoke that it produced.

"Where are they taking us?" Krispin asked.

"To a place called Raven's Head," Arctic said. "From there, Ornthal, the leader of the bandits, rules in a massive pleasure palace. It is where the bandits keep all of their treasure. I've heard horrible stories about that place."

"What kind of stories?" Krispin asked.

"Girls such as myself are forced into all kinds of horrible positions," Arctic said. "For the pleasure of the bandits. Men like you are forced to serve the bandits. To clean and care for them. If you refuse, you are beaten and killed."

"I will not allow them to take you in that manner, Arctic," Krispin said. "I will do everything that I can, including laying my life down, to prevent that."

"Why do you do that for me?" Arctic asked. "We hardly know each other...and you have your Holly to get to."

"It's what's right and wrong, Arctic," Krispin said. "No one should ever have to live under conditions such as that. When we are released, just follow my lead and we will escape that awful place."

"I love that you would protect me in such a way, Krispin," Arctic said. "But I suspect that they have something different in mind for us."

"Different?"

"Did I ever mention that I'm the youngest daughter of the ruling Duke of Cerrado?" Arctic asked, sheepishly.

"No," Krispin replied, flatly.

"You sure I didn't mention that?"

"Positive," Krispin said. "That's the type of thing that I'd remember."

"Well, I am," Arctic said. "My prince brothers and princess sister and I were all sent on different quests to help save our father. My task was supposed to be the simplest...find a unicorn horn and return to my father. I had Hibit...an old family advisor and educator...and my pet cat and best friend, Snowflake. I was only going to be gone from the castle for a couple days at most. This is my first time away from my home."

"This is my first time away from my home as well, Arctic," Krispin said. "I wanted to have an adventure and I think I've found a good one...if I can ever get home to tell anyone."

"We will have our victory," Arctic said.

"But you're a princess?" Krispin asked. "Should I start referring to you as Princess?"

"Please don't," Arctic said. "I don't need any more attention out here than we already have."

"I understand that," Krispin said. "I don't get what kind of transport we're in though. Why do they have us in this box?"

"It's not a box, per se," Arctic said. "It's a casket. The cart we are riding in is a hearse."

"WHAT?" Krispin exclaimed.

"It has its advantages," Arctic said. "Any other cart will give way to us. They can pass any toll road without paying. There is an undertaker driving the cart. He is allowed certain leeway when it comes to inspections and guards. Yes, a hearse will garner attention, but it's the right kind of attention for what they are doing."

"This world still seems so strange to me," Krispin said. "How long do you think we've been in here?"

"The travel time from the Century Castle to Raven's Head would take days," Arctic said. "And I don't know how long we've been out from the weapon."

"What do you think they'll do to us?" Krispin asked.

"The woman must have recognized me," Arctic said. "Even though I'm dirty and muddy, I'm in my royal outfit. They will take us to Raven's Head and from there a message will be sent to my father. Hopefully the message will say that I was taken with a male companion and that we are being held for ransom."

"Your father will think it's your friend, Hibit," Krispin said. "Will he pay the ransom for both of us?"

"I'm his youngest daughter," Arctic said. "He will pay any price...for both of us."

"That's good to know," Krispin said. "I'm so hungry though. It feels like I haven't eaten in days."

"I was thinking the same thing," Arctic said. "If we haven't eaten in a couple days, I'm sure we are close to Raven's Head. The weapon they used to make us sleep makes it so we don't need to eat during the time we are out. They will have food for us when we arrive."

"I hope so," Krispin said.

As Krispin was about to continue speaking, the hearse came to an abrupt stop. Krispin could hear horses and people outside the casket. He worried about what they would find when they were pulled out of the casket. Krispin didn't have to wonder long as the lid to the casket was thrown open and bandits pulled Arctic off of him, then pulled him out.

The bright light of a midday sun hurt Krispin's eyes that had become accustomed to the dark of the box. Krispin squinted and blinked to try and see where he was at. They were in the courtyard of a large castle that was built with dark stone. Stone statues of ravens were everywhere. The courtyard was adorned with dark flowers and plants.

Around the courtyard, the bandits were drinking wine and counting loot. There were carts and hearses everywhere that were overflowing with the most amazing amounts of treasure Krispin had ever seen. There were two women who looked to be counting the swag, entering each piece into ledgers before the items were being taken into the castle.

Krispin felt big hands holding him in place. He looked to see two big men holding him. There were two similar men, both towering over little Arctic, holding her where she stood. The men were dressed in black, with curved, thin blade swords strapped to their backs.

Krispin could now see the hearse they had been brought in. It was black as night and large, being drawn by four great horses. The casket they'd been stuffed in was ornate, imbedded with gold, silver, and jewels, looking for all the world like the final resting place of some important person—more reasons to let the hearse pass without notice.

As they were being held, a big man emerged from the castle. He had a full red beard that matched his long red hair, cascading over his broad shoulders. The man's belly protruded out, a strange sight amongst the others since all the other bandits were very fit. The man had a fat baby face, with a snake smile showing crooked yellow teeth. The man held a golden goblet that was full of wine. As he made his way toward Krispin and Arctic, the other bandits stepped aside.

The man was wearing black pants with a fox fur jacket that was open. His thick fingers were covered with rings of gold, silver, and diamonds. The man stepped in front of Krispin and took a large gulp of his wine. He looked over Krispin and Arctic, before turning to the tall, skinny, pale undertaker who was in a formal suit of all black.

"What do we have here?" the big man asked.

"I was given instructions to bring them directly to you, Ornthal," the undertaker said. "I know not who they are."

"I think I know who this little one is," Ornthal said. "My, you are pretty. I've heard rumors of your beauty, Princess Arctic. Now the question is, what do we do with you?"

"Release us at once," Arctic commanded.

"I don't think that we'll be doing that," Ornthal laughed. "The real question should be, how much will your father pay for your life?"

"He will attack you with all the might of the armies of Cerrado," Arctic said. "You will be crushed and erased from history."

"I think not, little one," Ornthal said. "Take them to the dungeon."

The guards that were holding them roughly shoved both Krispin and Arctic toward the castle as Ornthal watched. Ornthal and the undertaker watched as the pair disappeared into the castle.

"Holding her here is dangerous," the undertaker said. "If word got out that she was here, the duke would send his armies here to level us."

"That's something we can't let happen," Ornthal said. "We have an opportunity here to garner more treasure in one haul than we could in a lifetime of stealing. We need to make sure that he knows we have her and her companion. I have a plan. We will tell the duke that they are being held at Lancer."

"Lancer has been abandoned for years," the undertaker said. "He may know that."

"Even if he does it will keep them from looking here," Ornthal said. "We can't allow them to know how many members we have...and how much loot we have. We will ask for a large amount of gold and silver. We will ask for treasure. This ransom will be our biggest haul ever."

"And the pair?" the undertaker asked. "We hold them here?"

"No," Ornthal said. "Take them to Yorehill Manor, in the steppes to the west. That place is out of the way and well hidden. I've heard that two people, a man and a woman, came and have joined with us. Something doesn't feel right about them. Load the pair in the casket in the morning and have the new pair transport them. Send word to Yorehill that upon their arrival the new pair is to be given a meal in thanks of their work."

"Poison in the drink?" the undertaker asked.

"In the drink, in the food," Ornthal said, "kill them in their sleep. I don't care what. Let them use their imagination. I don't trust them and I don't want them in the bandits. Make sure the pair leaves here before first light."

"It will be done Ornthal," the undertaker said.

The undertaker rushed inside the castle while Ornthal looked over his bandits work. There were people rushing everywhere, handling the treasures that had been stolen. Ornthal smiled as he watched his people work efficiently and quickly. As he watched, Ornthal noticed two pleasure women walking through the courtyard. He signaled the women to approach him. As the women walked up to him, Ornthal knew the bandits were about to become wealthier than they had ever imagined.

Krispin and Arctic were thrown roughly into another cell. This time, both of them were shoved into the mud as the cell gate was slammed behind them. Krispin stood quickly before helping Arctic up. They brushed the mud off each other as their eyes met—almost enough electricity in the air to warrant a kiss, but the pair held back because of Krispin having thoughts of Holly in his mind.

"We're in a dungeon again," Krispin said, as he looked around.

The dungeon was dank and wet, the stone walls bore a sweat that came with the heat of the area. The floor was solid mud with pools of water. The area was silent except for the falling drops of water hitting the puddles on the floor. Krispin looked over the gate but realized that this time there was no way he could break the hinges.

"I think we're stuck here this time, Arctic," Krispin said. "This gate is built much stronger than the other."

"At least they won't kill us," Arctic said. "We're worth far more alive. They know what would happen to them if they killed us."

"That's comforting to know," Krispin said. "I wish they would have brought us some food. I'm still starving."

"Me too," Arctic said. "Do you think Holly is going to like your adventure?"

"Let's see," Krispin said. "So far, I've met a strange girl, ended up in a different forest, been thrown in dungeon for being accused of being a bandit, and been taken by the bandits in a casket and thrown in their dungeon, all the while trying to figure out where to find your unicorn. It seems almost too good to be true. Chester has never been through an adventure like this."

"She will fall into your arms for sure," Arctic said, laughing.

"You don't think this adventure will win her heart?"

"It's not that, Krispin," Arctic said. "I don't think a heart can be won in that manner. Even if she enjoys this story and marries you, it still isn't love."

"What do you know about love?"

"I know that it doesn't cost anything," Arctic said. "And that it's freely given between two people who are in love. And that love is messy, strange, and sometimes looks a lot like anger or pain. But then there are the times when love is the most magical thing that anyone has ever been through."

"Have you ever been in love?" Krispin asked.

"I love my cat, Snowflake," Arctic said. "But the kind of love you're asking about, no. I've never been allowed to be around other people. I've been kept sheltered away from people."

"How come?"

"I was the youngest," Arctic said. "And mother died shortly after I was born. All of my siblings spent time outside the castle growing up. My sister was with horse masters. My brothers with fighters and military men. They learned so much from their time away from the castle. I wish I could have gotten out and explored Cerrado."

"You're exploring now," Krispin said. "You're having an amazing adventure as well. You will have a great story to tell your siblings and father."

"You're right there," Arctic said. "This has been a great time. I've been away from my friends for weeks, and away from the castle for longer. I'm learning more than I ever thought I could. I feel that I am really growing up now. I have a thought, Krispin. You want an adventure and I want to find the unicorn horn."

"You're not giving up on that quest, are you?" Krispin asked.

"I cannot fail my father," Arctic said. "But it would be easier if I had a knight to guide me."

"A knight?"

"You can be my knight, Krispin," Arctic said. "Sir Krispin, the honorable and brave. That is what I would call you. I can knight you now if you wish."

"You can knight me?" Krispin asked. "Do it."

"Get on one knee."

Krispin dropped down to one knee as Arctic stood in front of him. She tapped both of his shoulders as she spoke.

"Under pain of death," Arctic said. "Do you swear to uphold the honors and traditions of your king and his kinsmen?"

"I do," Krispin said.

"Under pain of death," Arctic said. "Do you swear to protect the needy and weak, defeat the wicked, and help all those in need?"

"I do," Krispin said.

"Under pain of death," Arctic said. "Do you swear to be brave in the face of danger, honorable in times of temptation, and strong in the face of fear?"

"I do," Krispin said.

"Then I dub you, Sir Krispin the Honorable and Brave," Arctic said. "May you uphold the chivalric code and be honest and true to your king."

"Thank you, my good lady," Krispin said. "I will make my king and his kinsmen proud."

"That's good," Arctic said. "Now, figure a way out of this castle."

"Again with the orders, Arctic," Krispin said. "And I don't think that escaping from here would be the best thing."

"Why not?"

"They aren't going to kill us," Krispin said. "They need to hold us here to ransom us out. We just need to wait. I will protect you here, I promise."

"Then we wait," Arctic said.

Both Krispin and Arctic sat down on benches attached to the wall. They both breathed a heavy sigh as they could only wait for something to happen.

Chapter 17

The Cerrado castle was a beehive of activity. People were moving everywhere with an exuberance of energy that suggested important work needed to be done. The courtyard was full of people who were engaging in their daily commerce who were all unaware of the events that were going on in the throne room of the castle.

Within the throne room, Queen Mala was sitting on the Honor Throne, her black dress flowing around her body as she laughed at the dealings of the room. Two of her guards were holding Duke Asmout in the middle of the room while another was cracking his bare back with a whip. The queen motioned for them to stop and move to the back of the room while Duke Asmout fell to the floor. The duke tried to stand but couldn't get up further than his hands and knees.

"Duke Asmout," Queen Mala boomed from the throne. "Are you enjoying the new management of your castle? I hope you are, I worked very hard to get this set up the way I wanted it."

"You will never succeed," Duke Asmout shouted. "My children will destroy you."

"I don't think so," Mala said. "My spies tell me that Prince Alos, the strongest and bravest of your children, has been destroyed by a powerful necromancer…something I need to look into, it sounds like this Princess Ashlynn is more powerful than I'd thought possible. Your elegant daughter Princess Ambriss decided to cast her lot with Prince Atin. They couldn't find what they were looking for and they have now joined up with the bandits."

"My youngest," Duke Asmout said. "Tell me what's happened to my precious little Arctic."

"The youngest one, Princess Arctic," Queen Mala said, with a sinister grin. "Hasn't been seen in a long time. The guard she was with, Hibit, lost her in the Blue Cerrado Forest. Hibit and the cat, Snowflake, have been wandering around the forest trying to locate her. They met with a warrior princess who believes that she can help them but it will be for not, the princess has disappeared without a trace."

"Not my little Arctic," Duke Asmout wailed. "Not her."

"Silence!" Mala shouted. "Now, former duke, you have to address your subjects. There have been rumors since your children left. People are wondering what is going on and why the children haven't been seen. You will tell the people that everything is going well, Cerrado is prosperous, and its people will be happy. Know one thing Duke Asmout, my people know all of your hand signals, know all of the secret phrases that you use with your top military. You will refrain from using any of them when you are speaking. You will give no indication that anything is wrong by your words or actions."

"You will not succeed," Duke Asmout said. "You will be defeated."

"There is nothing that can stand in my way," Queen Mala said. "You were the last stronghold of the country and you fell without any problem."

"How did you survive?" Duke Asmout said. "The Former King killed you."

"The Former King was weak," Queen Mala sneered. "He couldn't kill me. I was injured and dying and placed in the Blue Cerrado Forest where I was left to die. The magic powers of the forest were to conceal me from any necromancers but Mystic Seven the Red was able to feel my calls. He came to me and saved me. This time though, I am correcting the mistakes that I made before. I spent the last twenty years building my strength, using Mystic Seven to gain control and power within Cerrado, and to build my spy network. I know everything that is going on."

"The bandits will destroy you," Duke Asmout said.

"Ornthal will offer control of the bandits to me as a marriage dowry," Queen Mala said. "He will fall to his knees before me and do anything to prevent me from destroying the bandits. They are a cowardly group that will do anything to survive."

"This will not stand," Duke Asmout said.

"Guards," Queen Mala said. "Take the duke to the balcony and have him give his speech. Then throw him in the dungeon."

The guards picked the duke up off the floor and dragged him out of the room. Queen Mala stood and began pacing around the room. She was nervous, uncertain of what was going on. Mala kept looking at the entrances, waiting for someone to enter. Finally, Mystic Seven the Red rushed into the room and bowed before the queen.

"I've got many reports for you, my Queen," Mystic Seven said.

"Tell me of the women that have been seen in the castle," Mala said.

"They are members of Prince Atin's harem," Mystic Seven said. "We haven't been able to catch any of them but they are everywhere. We have determined that there are two different ones...we think. He had four total, three disguised as men and one openly as a woman. We know that the woman is with him. The other one has yet to be spotted."

"She has to be somewhere," Mala said. "Find her."

"Our best guess is that she's with Atin," Mystic Seven said. "Either in hiding, monitoring what's going on and protecting the prince, or hiding in plain sight posing as someone else. Either way, there's little chance that even with our vast network of spies we will be able to find out. Atin has hidden her far too well."

"That's not acceptable, Mystic," Mala said, with a harsh tone. "I want those women in the castle in the dungeon, and I need to know where the other one is."

"I will tend to it personally," Mystic Seven said.

"Now to bigger things," Queen Mala said. "Princess Ashlynn. I had heard the reports of what she was able to do to Prince Alos. Alos was very powerful. Who is Ashlynn?"

"We are working on it," Mystic Seven said. "We are searching through time and space to find out who she is. We have a number of ideas, but nothing is confirmed."

"We have to know before we move forward," Queen Mala said. "Someone who thought that I was dead could think that they could take power. I will not allow my empire to fall apart because we didn't know who we were dealing with. I don't care what it takes...we must find out who she is."

"You cannot think that it is one of your sisters," Mystic Seven said. "Bala and Tala are dead. You killed them both yourself."

"She is the right age," Mala said. "I fear that she is the daughter of one of them. If either of them had a child and were able to pass knowledge to them about what happened then they would be upset with me. This could damage our plans. We can adjust and compensate, but we have to know who she is first."

"We are working on it," Mystic Seven said. "We will find the information that you require, my Queen."

As Mala was about to speak, a guard rushed into the room. He bowed before them, trying to catch his breath. He appeared to have been running through the castle and had an extremely happy look on his face.

"What news do you bring?" Mystic Seven asked.

"We have one of them," the guard said, between his heavy breaths. "One of the women that we've been trying to catch."

"Where is she?" Mala asked. "Has she said anything yet?"

"She is in the dungeon," the guard said. "In the deepest levels. We have many guards on her so there's no chance of escape or rescue."

"Good," Queen Mala said. "Take me there now."

The guard led Mala and Mystic Seven out of the throne room and into the castle. The group descended into the dungeon, going down many flights of stone stairs. They were in the bowels of the castle, so deep in the earth that the torches they carried barely lit up the area around them. The guard took them through twists and turns in the dungeon before coming to a hallway that was full of other guards.

There was only one way out from the cell, having to go through all the guards to get there. Mala and Mystic Seven walked to the gate of the cell and looked inside to see the woman standing in the cell. She was in the center of the cell, with her arms chained to the ceiling and her feet shackled to the floor. It was the same woman who'd disappeared in front of Mystic Seven before. She had the black, short, choppy hair, and the gray tights he'd seen in the courtyard. The woman still wore a smile on her face as she looked over the people at the gate of her cell.

"You will tell us what you are doing here," Queen Mala shouted.

"Just hanging around," the woman replied.

"No, what are you doing in the castle?"

"Just hanging here."

"What were you doing in the courtyard," Mystic Seven yelled. "What were you doing when you disappeared before my eyes?"

"What were you doing in the courtyard?" the woman said, with a giggle.

"Guard!" Mala commanded, "Whip her."

"Wait," the woman said, as one of the bigger guards stood with a whip in hand. "I'll be good. I'll talk. What do you want to know?"

"What are you doing in the castle?" Mala said. "And one more smart remark, you will be whipped."

"I was given instructions by Prince Atin to remain here and figure out what was going on," the woman said. "He was certain that something didn't feel right about Mystic Seven the Red's premonition. Prince Atin wanted to know what was going on in the Cerrado Castle."

"And what of the other women that we've been tracking?" Mystic Seven asked. "There was another woman in the courtyard...the one with the white hair. Where is she?"

"She is somewhere within the castle," the woman said. "I do not know where at the moment. We had times that we scheduled to meet to exchange information."

"There were four total people with Atin when he left the castle," Mala said. "We've accounted for all but one. Who is the other one and where are they?"

"I cannot answer that because I do not know," the woman said. "Atin kept things hidden from me as well."

"Can you help us capture the other woman in the castle?" Mala asked.

"If I refuse?" the woman asked.

"Then we have no use for you," Mala said. "And you will die down here."

"Not giving me many options to work with," the woman said.

"Wait a moment," Mystic Seven said. "You seem to know much, do you know who Princess Ashlynn from the Windswept Plains is?"

"She is someone very powerful," the woman said. "I know that much. I also know that she should not be trusted and has questionable motives. Beyond that, I have no information about her."

"I don't like this," Queen Mala said. "There's too much that we don't know. I want to have a better picture of what's going on here. We must have all the kids destroyed before we fully reveal that I have returned. If someone knows before the time is right, it could hinder the plans. Cerrado will cower before my feet. I will rule this land the way a ruler should...with fear and terror. The peasants will cower."

"The Former King will stop you," the woman said. "You will never be able to stop him."

"He's a coward," Mala said. "Where is he? Answer that. He disappeared and left Cerrado to fend for itself. We've seen what that causes. Now it's my time, the time that I should have had over twenty years ago."

"There is no way for you to win this, Mala," the woman said. "You have no idea who you are going up against."

"What are you talking about?" Mala asked.

"There are many things that you don't know," the woman said. "Many things that you think you know, but you don't. Duke Asmout and his children will kill you. There's nothing you can do to prevent that."

"Strong words coming from someone who's chained up," Mala said. "Perhaps if my guards whipped you a few times it would make you see what is really going on here. Guard, take some of the arrogance out of this one."

As a guard started to walk toward the cell, a powerful gust of wind blew through the cell, extinguishing all the torches, casting the dungeon into pitch blackness. The guards barked orders, confusedly getting the fires going again. When the torches were relit, standing in the middle of the cell was the woman with white hair and the green dress. She had a smile on her face and was staring right at Mala. All of the guards froze, not knowing what to do. Mala was stunned speechless. Before anyone could say anything, a cloud of smoke filled the cell and when it had cleared, both of the women who'd been in the cell had vanished without a trace.

Mala stood with her jaw hanging open, not knowing what to do or say. Mystic Seven the Red was trying to get into the cell to see what kinds of tricks were being played. Neither of them had ever seen something of this nature before, but both knew that they were up against a powerful opponent.

Chapter 18

The sky was a perfect blue that gave way to a deep red and pink as it kissed the horizon. The air was filled with the unique aroma of the flowering trees mixed with the wide and winding river that separated the trees from the grassland plains that extended to the west. There wasn't a cloud in the sky as the bright sun illuminated everything in the forests and fields.

The lazy day was almost unremarkable until three bolts of lightning caused the bright day to get even brighter. The lightning was accompanied by three cracks of thunder so powerful they caused ripples in the river. From a separated outcropping of flowering trees—trees that had formed an arch together—Lacey, Hibit, and Snowflake emerged from the glowing arch before the trees moved apart and the arch disappeared.

Both Hibit and Lacey were looking for something as Snowflake was sniffing the air. The cat sneezed from the pollen coming from the trees. Snowflake looked over the trees then to the river, realizing that something was wrong, even if the other two didn't understand yet.

"We have to find Arctic," Hibit said. "We cannot return to the castle unless we have her. I will spend the rest of my life searching for her."

"We will find her," Lacey said. "Even if we have to search through every arch that is in Cerrado. We will not stop until she is safe."

"I keep telling you that the arches are a kids' story," Hibit said. "There's no truth to them. There's no such thing as a magical arch between trees that will take you somewhere else Lacey. We need to form a plan to be more effective in our search."

"Where are we?" Lacey asked, looking around.

"We are in the Blue Cerrado Forest," Hibit said.

"The Blue Cerrado Forest is full of northern hardwood trees," Lacey said. "Mixed with some conifers. These trees are softwood flowering trees."

"What?" Hibit asked, looking over the trees. "This is impossible. These trees cannot grow in the Blue Cerrado Forest. The season isn't long enough and there's too much moisture for them."

"It looks like they are growing well," Lacey said. "And look at that, look at the river."

Lacey was pointing at the river that was running near them. The trio rushed over to it and looked at the greenish water flowing between the banks. The river was over one-hundred-feet wide and looked very deep. There were some fish jumping in the middle of the water. Hibit looked up and down the banks, seeing that the river came from the trees—with a bend that hid the river from their view.

"How is this possible?" Hibit stuttered as Snowflake drank from the river.

"That was one of the legends about the arches," Lacey said. "There was a period of amnesia when you went through them."

"What do you mean?" Hibit asked.

"We were in the Blue Cerrado Forest," Lacey said. "And now we're here and we don't know how that happened. We went through the arch! The full memory of what happened won't return to us for hours, according to the legends of the arches. I've heard many people talk about what an arch will do to a person, and this is exactly what they said would happen."

"Then where are we?" Hibit asked. "I don't recognize any of this."

"The water has a green tint to it," Lacey said. "And those are flowering trees. My guess is we are in the west. This has to be the Emerald River, and this is the Dawn Forest."

"That's impossible," Hibit said. "It would take weeks to travel the distance between the Dawn Forest and the Blue Cerrado Forest by foot. Even by river would take days. How could we have gotten here?"

"The arches," Lacey said. "I'm telling you that they are real. That's why you can't remember how we got here. It's the only way we could have traveled that fast."

"If that's true," Hibit said. "Is Arctic around here?"

"She could be," Lacey said. "If we went through the same arch she did. It could depend on how long ago she went through. Arctic may have not stayed around. She may have even gone back through the arch."

"And if we go through the arch, it's not guaranteed we'd get back to the Blue Cerrado Forest?" Hibit asked.

"That's correct," Lacey said. "There'll be an arch there, but there's no way to know where it leads until you go through it."

"What's the plan then?" Hibit asked. "We may or may not be in the same place that Arctic arrived. And she may or may not have stayed in this area. If she jumped through a number of arches then she could be anywhere in Cerrado."

"The arches lead to more places than just Cerrado," Lacey said.

"That's comforting to know," Hibit said. "I don't know what to do. The Duke is going to have my head on a pike for this."

"Oh, my God!" Lacey exclaimed.

Hibit looked at Lacey and saw that she was staring up the river where it broke from around the bend. Lacey looked stunned stiff. Hibit turned and was blown away by what he saw. On the river, coming around the bend, were three pirate ships. The first was small, with a single green mast capped by a gray flag marked with a white embossed figure of a griffin.

The second ship was the largest, with three gray masts. A gray flag was flying at the top, on the bow, and on the stern. The second ship was massive—multi-leveled, with three rows of cannon ports visible above the waterline. Hibit could see many pirates rushing about the deck and on the back quarter of the ship. On a deck raised ten feet above the main deck, stood a big man in gray and white clothing standing at the wheel of the ship. The man wore a large gray hat with a feather sticking out the back.

The third ship was a cross between the first two—two masts with the gray and white flag flying high at the top of the first mast. The ships were moving quickly through the river, cutting through the water as the pirates on the decks sang a pirate tune. The harmonics of the pirates seemed out of place for the pirate's fierce reputation, but Hibit felt the pirates were something more than they seemed. As the ships got closer to where Hibit, Lacey, and Snowflake were standing, Lacey grabbed Hibit and Snowflake and rushed them behind a grouping of trees.

As the ships passed, Hibit could see the man who stood in the captain's position on the second ship. As he got closer, his true size was seen—a massive man, with a large gray hat. His tights and tunic were gray with white accents, tight, and fit his muscular body type well. The man had long black hair that fell around his hat with a neatly trimmed beard. His arms were crossed in front of him with a stern look on his face as he watched his mates work. Hibit knew who this man was and felt intimidated by him, even though he was so far away.

The ships passed where the group was hiding—around another bend and out of sight. The group waited a moment before they exited the trees and walked back to the river. Lacey walked out first, followed by Hibit and Snowflake. Following Snowflake was Jade, the Nature Watcher. She watched the others as they tried to figure out who the pirates were.

"That has to be Captain Creature," Hibit said.

"Who?" Lacey asked.

"Captain Creature," Hibit said. "His ships are The Puma, The Leopard, and his biggest flagship, The Lynx. They sail the seas, oceans, and rivers of Cerrado. The rumors of their exploits are legendary. Wine, rum, women, and swag. They are fierce pirates that leave no survivors and take whatever they want. Duke Asmout had people keeping a close eye on these pirates."

"He kept an eye on them?" Lacey asked. "Why didn't he ever stop them?"

"Because they had such a reputation," Hibit said. "But in our investigations we found they did very little, if any, piracy. We have no idea where the legends came from but we cannot find one city that's been sacked, or one person that's been kidnapped by them. It seems like they sail around Cerrado…and that's all we really know about them."

"That sounds so strange," Lacey said. "How can you not know what they do?"

"They sail the waters of Cerrado," Jade said. "Waiting for the time that they are needed to help the land and save it from evil."

"I doubt they would do that," Hibit said.

Hibit and Lacey both did a double take on Jade. Neither heard her sneak up on them nor did they know where she'd come from. Lacey drew her sword and held it on Jade, looking her over. Jade was in her green billowy pants that were dancing in the breeze and her matching green bandeau top. Jade didn't have her jacket on, nor did she have any weapons to defend herself, so she raised her arms shoulder height and held them palms open toward Lacey.

"I mean you no harm," Jade said.

"Where did you come from?" Lacey barked. "What is your purpose?"

"My purpose?" Jade asked. "I suppose it is to guide lost souls like yours, Lacey DuLake."

The shock of Jade speaking Lacey's full name almost caused her to drop her sword. Lacey staggered two paces back before regaining her composure. She pointed the sword directly in Jade's face.

"How do you know who I am?" Lacey asked. "Who are you?"

"I have watched you, Lacey," Jade said. "I have watched you preparing for you moment. I know that you are strong and true, even if you don't have the most experience. You wish to become a knight, proper and formal, and your king needs you now."

"There's only one person you could be," Lacey said, sheathing her sword and dropping to her knees. "You are Jade, the Nature Watcher. You are responsible for the waters of Cerrado, correct?"

"That is right," Jade said.

"Then I fall before you and offer my services to you if you help us on our quest," Lacey said. "We must find Princess Arctic. She is the only one who matters right now."

"She might be," Jade said. "Or she might not be. Time will tell. Princess Arctic is in the Raven Head's dungeon right now. She is with a man who is helping her on her quest."

"Man?" Lacey asked. "What man?"

"I do not know him," Jade said. "I have not seen him before, nor do I believe that he is from Cerrado. He is protecting her though. He's helping her on the quest."

"Raven's Head?" Hibit asked. "How long will it take us to get there? We must get to the princess and rescue her."

"There are more pressing issues right now," Jade said. "I have been trying to convince my siblings to help in this fight, to fend off the evil that is covering Cerrado now. They do not wish to be bothered with such things. I've tried to explain to them that they cannot avoid the evil that's coming to the land. I have sent them into the kingdom to help but I do not know if they will follow through with my plans. Our parents want them to help, too."

"Your parents?" Lacey asked.

"Father Time and Mother Nature," Jade said.

"To the point though," Hibit said. "What is more important than saving Princess Arctic right now? We must get to Raven's Head and save her. The bandits will be asking for massive tributes to spare her life and who knows where the heart of this man lies. He may help her or kill her. We do not know and won't find out sitting here talking."

"Queen Mala has taken the Cerrado Castle," Jade said, flatly. "Duke Asmout didn't stand a chance. Mystic Seven the Red had everything in place for her return."

"Are you suggesting that we return to the castle and help the Duke out?" Hibit asked.

"No," Jade said. "The one who needs the most help is Prince Alos."

"But Prince Alos is the strongest and wisest of all the children," Hibit said. "How could he need more help than the others?"

"He rode to Princess Ashlynn at the Windswept Castle," Jade said. "Princess Ashlynn is far more powerful and sinister than he could have ever imaged. She is even more powerful than Queen Mala."

"Who is she?" Lacey said. "How could she be more powerful than Mala?"

"That, I cannot say," Jade said. "I cannot see across the time and space that she has come from. There is an abundance of magic that is flooding Cerrado right now. I have never in my years felt this much power in the air."

"If Princess Ashlynn is so powerful," Hibit said. "Why is she content to rule a small area within Cerrado that's in dispute where she has to share her power?"

"Princess Ashlynn is biding her time," Jade said. "The Necromancer, Oliver, placed many different curses on the 'Knowledge of Cerrado' and one of them prevents Mala from opening and using the book. The Necromancer Oliver created the book as a balance of power to Mala. He saw her abilities with magic and knew that no one would be able to stand alone against her, so he created the book so others could stop her. One of the curses that was placed on the book prevents Mala from opening the book. Mala was planning to take control of Alos and have him open the book for her. She didn't count on him encountering someone as powerful as Ashlynn."

"And Ashlynn is holding Alos in the Windswept Castle dungeon?" Hibit asked.

"That is correct," Jade said.

"Then what are we to do?" Lacey asked. "Windswept Castle is a long distance from here."

"Not if you travel with me," Jade said. "Prepare yourselves and follow me. We will not allow Cerrado to fall into the hands of evil."

Jade walked to the waters of the Emerald River. Hibit, Lacey, and Snowflake followed her to the banks of the river. Jade tested the waters with her bare foot before walking knee deep into the water. She motioned for the others to follow her into the water. Slowly, cautiously, Hibit and Lacey walked into the water. Snowflake watched them and paused for a moment before following. Once they were all in the same spot, the water started to agitate. Hibit, Lacey, and Snowflake were nervous, but Jade's smile seemed to put them at ease. The churning of the water got stronger and stronger until Jade reached out, grabbing Hibit and Lacey while having her arm touch Snowflake. When she touched all three of them at the same time, they all disappeared, and the water returned to a still calm.

Chapter 19

The Raven's Head castle was flushed with activity. There were bandits dropping off swag, accountants recording all the booty that was coming in, and bandits enjoying the fine pleasures that come with being a bandit. In the main courtyard there were four horse-drawn carts. Three of them were delivering treasure, one was a hearse that was being prepared to transport troops.

Ornthal, the undertaker, Prince Atin, and Princess Ambriss were standing near the hearse. Atin and Ambriss were wearing the black outfits of the bandits, looking for all to see like they belonged with this treacherous group of murdering thieves. Atin seemed to fit in much better than Ambriss.

"That will be your first mission with us," Ornthal said. "Transport the two persons of ransom to our secret hideout at Yorehill Manor and guard them there. You complete this mission successfully and you will be full members of the bandits."

"I still don't trust them," the undertaker said. "We should have professionals doing a job like this. If they lose the prisoners then we will be out massive amounts of money."

"They will be just fine," Ornthal said. "Don't make the mistake of thinking that we won't have someone watching you at all times. If you think that you're going to double cross the bandits then you have another thing coming to you."

"There's no need to worry about that Ornthal," Atin said. "We will deliver for you without question. We can handle anything you give us."

"What are their qualifications?" the undertaker asked. "How do we know that they can handle this mission?"

"They can do it," Ornthal said.

"We've never let anyone down before," Ambriss said. "We can handle anything."

"He lets his wench speak for him," the undertaker said. "I don't know if I want to let these two go."

"Everything will be fine," Ornthal said. "Now, go to the dungeon and get the two that are to be taken."

"It shall be done," Atin said, bowing to Ornthal before taking off with Ambriss in tow.

"Nice work," Ornthal said, once Atin and Ambriss were in the castle. "You played off of me to instill doubt in them. They will work all the harder now to prove that they can handle the load."

"I still have some reservations about them," the undertaker said. "Something didn't seem right. I feel like I know them from somewhere."

"You worry too much," Ornthal said. "They will be dead once the pair is delivered and we can ransom the Princess from Yorehill. I have already crafted a letter that will be sent to Duke Asmout."

"Rumors abound that trouble is brewing in Cerrado," the undertaker said. "We have the youngest princess...the eldest prince is said to be trapped in the Windswept Castle...and the middle children haven't been seen. All four children were sent into Cerrado on quests. There has to be a reason. I've heard that evil is gathering and that is why the children are away from the safety of the castle."

"What do the prophets say?" Ornthal asked.

"Necromancers say that Queen Mala is returning," the undertaker said.

"If that were true then we would be in danger as well," Ornthal said. "But I doubt that she would go after the bandits. The seats of power within Cerrado will rise against her. They would never allow her to hold power again."

"Let's hope that's true," the undertaker said.

Ornthal nodded as he watched his bandits rushing about their day. Ornthal knew that changes were coming to Cerrado but he'd survived changes before and he knew that he could survive changes again. For the bandits, a new body in the Honor Throne was just another day. Replace one monarch with another. Surely as the sun would rise the next day, Ornthal and the Bandits would survive a new ruler at the Cerrado Castle.

Krispin and Arctic sat in the dungeon waiting for something to happen. They had only been in the dungeon for one night so far and didn't have any idea how long it would be before word reached the duke that Arctic was being held. Krispin kept thinking about Holly—about her eyes, her hair, her giggle, and how he couldn't wait to tell her about the adventure that he was on.

Arctic was apprehensive. Even though she knew that Krispin was an honorable man, she'd heard many stories of people being held in dungeons and girls being forced to do things they didn't want to. Arctic wanted so badly to be back in her warm room, playing a game with Snowflake, the only concern being in the great hall in time for supper while it was still warm. As Arctic thought about how things had gone wrong on her quest, she caught herself many times looking—longing at Krispin.

"Why do you need an adventure to win Holly's heart?" Arctic blurted out. "I just don't understand it."

"Holly is the most desirable woman in my entire village," Krispin said. "Every man wants to marry her. Holly longs for an adventure of her own. She doesn't want to stay in the little village, so by showing her that I can have an adventure, I will prove that we could have an adventure together. The adventure is to prove my love for her."

"What's she doing to prove her love to you?" Arctic asked.

"Well...it's just that...what you have to understand is...you're just too young to understand," Krispin said.

"What's to understand?" Arctic asked. "I think love shouldn't cost anything. When you find that person that you click with, you just love each other. There'll be rocky times and some work, but there's no need to prove love, you just know it. All it requires is that you give your heart completely to the person that gives you their heart."

"If it only were that easy, Arctic," Krispin said.

"So, if Holly needs an adventure to pick you over the other guy," Arctic began. "What is she doing for you to pick Holly over other girls?"

"You just don't understand, Arctic," Krispin said. "Who else would I pick?"

"There has to be someone," Arctic said.

"Who?" Krispin pressed again. "You?"

"No!" Arctic exclaimed. "That's not what I meant."

"Sure you didn't," Krispin said. "You want me, don't you?"

"No," Arctic said. "Don't be silly."

"You're the one with the silly school girl crush," Krispin teased. "I don't know, maybe you need to have an adventure for me."

"No, I don't," Arctic said. "Knock it off, Krispin. Stop being mean."

"Stop being mean?" Krispin said. "You're the one ordering me around all the time. You've been mean to me most of the trip."

"Whatever," Arctic said. "Jerk."

"Wow," Krispin said. "So...how did your father become Duke of Cerrado?"

"You really want to know?" Arctic asked.

"We are going to be here for some time," Krispin said. "I don't want to fight with you and we need to pass the time. How did your father become the Duke?"

"It was a different time," Arctic said. "Cerrado was in dark times. There were evil things that were lurking about. The king and queen died and their daughters weren't of age to rule yet. That's when the Former King took the reins of the country."

"Who was the Former King?" Krispin asked.

"He was a knight in the royal family," Arctic said. "He would have been Mala's uncle, I believe."

"No," Krispin said. "I meant what was his name?"

"No one ever knew," Arctic said. "They called him The King when he was on the Honor Throne. When Tala, the eldest of the sisters was about to come of age, The King was going to turn control over to her but she died. Then, Bala, the next sister died. Everyone thought that The King was killing them, wanting to keep control for himself. He denied it. I wished that everyone would have believed him. A mob formed and demanded that he leave the castle. The King agreed, to the surprise of everyone. He knew what was going on and he also knew that if he said it out loud he would be accused of many things. The King left and Mala took the Honor Throne. It didn't take long to figure out what happened. Mala had not only killed her parents but her sisters as well."

"She killed them all?" Krispin asked. "No one figured it out?"

"The Former King did," Arctic said. "I don't know how he knew, but he did. The King had troops ready. Mala was a horrible leader. She made the people suffer and cower before her. The King had done much to eradicate the evil that was in Cerrado. He had made Cerrado a peaceful and prosperous place. Things were so much better when he sat on the throne. The King had an army ready to go when the people realized the truth about Mala. Before she was able to secure power he led his armies on her and destroyed much of what she had done. Mala had mistakenly thought that The King had been defeated, so she didn't have any defenses ready to go against him. There was a final battle in the Blue Cerrado Forest. Everyone thought that The King had killed Mala."

"Why did he leave?" Krispin asked.

"This is where the story gets strange," Arctic said. "He came to my father who had been sitting in a minor castle in the northlands. He asked if my father would sit in the seat of power, the Honor Throne, at the Cerrado Castle until his return. My father accepted, as would anyone if The King had asked them. The King had a very special sword that he showed my father. The King said the sword would remain in Cerrado, hidden, and my father would know him by the sword. The King said my father and the people wouldn't recognize his face."

"So, no one knows where The King went or why he had to leave?" Krispin asked.

"He never told anyone," Arctic said. "He came to my father right after the battle. The King and my father made one appearance together where they told Cerrado what was going on. There was much sorrow that day. The King had driven most of the evil out of Cerrado. My father drove what evil was left, out. There have never been such prosperous times in the kingdom. Now we have this disaster. I wish that the Former King would return and save my family."

"It must be hard to have all the weight of Cerrado on your shoulders," Krispin said. "Well, on your family's shoulders."

"I have had a very happy life," Arctic said. "I've never had to want...well..."

"Well what?"

"I've wanted real friends," Arctic said. "I've wanted people to play with. Snowflake is great but she's not a person. For the last few years I've wanted a boyfriend. I've wanted to see the world. I've had everything I want except the freedom to explore Cerrado on my own. There's so much I haven't experienced. Enough about my family, tell me about yours."

"I'm a shepherd," Krispin said, proudly. "Like every male in my family. This is the first time that I've left my little village. I tend sheep all day, just like my father did and his father did and their father's before that. I've dreamed of leaving that little village and striking out on my own, doing something important, seeing the world, then returning and continuing the family legacy."

"That sounds amazing," Arctic said. "Did your father ever leave the farm?"

"He did," Krispin said. "He went to university in London. That's where he met mother. They were married and had me before he returned to the paddocks. I was always so jealous of him. He got to experience so much when he was away. I wanted something like that."

"So, has your adventure been everything you wanted it to be?" Arctic asked.

"It has been," Krispin said. "I couldn't have imagined this much before, so how could I have ever wanted it. I thought my adventure in the Moon Forest would last a few days and I would be back within the week.

It's been so long now, I hope that Holly hasn't forgotten that I'm returning before the wedding."

Arctic winced at the mention of Holly's name. She didn't know why but Arctic hated hearing that name. She didn't have the experience to realize that as they were being taken across Cerrado, that Arctic was starting to have feelings for Krispin. She was still mad that he wouldn't follow her orders like her servants would, and that he was challenging her at times, but those things were also creating an intense attraction in her. Arctic was confused as to what she was feeling and didn't know how to express it, but she was certain she wanted to get Krispin to notice her.

"I'm sure Holly's forgotten about you," Arctic said, with a grin. "You've been gone too long now."

"I doubt that," Krispin said. "Holly will always remember me. She'll never forget our walks home from school. She will never be happy with Chester and she knows that. I'm the only one that can save her."

"I wish someone would save me," Arctic said.

"Save you from what?" Krispin asked.

"Look at what life has in store for me," Arctic said. "My father, in trying to protect me, never let me leave the castle. I have no real friends and no real experiences. Once I get back from this adventure I will be placed back inside the safety and boring routine of the castle walls. When I turn twenty-one, I will be shopped around for some boring prince to marry, beginning a life of a marriage that I didn't want, to someone I never knew. I want to look for love, I want to have fun. Once I'm married I'll be hidden behind castle walls again, watching the world pass me by. It's so unfair."

"Life is unfair," Krispin said. "But you have the opportunity to make something different. Once we complete your quest you can show you father that you are ready for more. He might even let you find your own husband."

"I wonder what will happen next in our adventure," Arctic asked. "This has been a wonderful trip already."

As Arctic finished speaking, the cell doors opened and Atin and Ambriss walked in with two other bandit guards. They looked stunned for

155

a moment as they looked at Arctic and Krispin. No one was really sure what to say, these were the last people Arctic expected to come into the cell and Arctic was the last person Atin and Ambriss expected to find in the cell.

"What..." Arctic started to speak.

"Silence, prisoner," Atin barked. "You are not allowed to speak. Can't have you trying to spread your lies as you beg for your life."

Atin winked at Arctic as Ambriss gave her a sympathetic smile. Ambriss grabbed her sister by the arm as Atin grabbed Krispin. They led them out of the cell, through the dungeon, and to the hearse waiting outside. Outside the door of the hearse was a large black casket. One of the guards opened the casket as Atin and Ambriss put Krispin in the casket on his back before putting Arctic in on top of him, facing each other. They closed the lid as Arctic was more confused than she'd ever been in her life.

Chapter 20

The Windswept Castle was in the middle of a violent thunderstorm. The sky was so dark it was almost black, with only the light from the bolts of lightning streaking across the sky like a crack spiraling out on a pane of glass. Rain was pouring down, heavy drops hurling to the ground so fast they almost hurt when they landed.

Inside the castle, Princess Ashlynn was having a blast torturing Prince Alos. She had his footmen arrested and thrown in the dungeon while she took time to kill them slowly—one at a time, in various ways. The first she killed was Sir Wayne, taking all of his life essence for herself. At each death, she forced Prince Alos to watch. Princess Ashlynn had Prince Alos in the throne room, bound to a small cage, while she taunted him. The prince had been so weakened by Ashlynn's magic that he could barely keep his head up.

"Beg for your life," Princess Ashlynn said. "I love it when they beg."

"I will never beg before a witch such as yourself," Prince Alos said. "You will die. My siblings will make certain of that."

"Of all the people dying," Ashlynn said. "I would think you would be more worried about yourself...not me. I have no intentions of dying."

As Ashlynn mocked Alos, Rishi walked into the throne room with two guards dragging one of Alos's footmen behind them. The soldier looked to have been beaten and from the blood and position of his leg, it appeared that his left leg had been broken. The guards threw the footman in the middle of the floor before the cage Alos was trapped in.

"This one is ready for processing," Rishi said. "He has been properly handled."

"There are so many of these troops for processing," Ashlynn said. "Rishi, you handle this one yourself. You could use a magical boost. Take his life for yourself."

"With pleasure," Rishi said, kneeling by the side of the man.

Rishi placed her hands on the man's head and chest. She closed her eyes and began to concentrate. A reddish glow began to form between her hands and the man's skin. The red appeared to be coming out of the man's body and into Rishi's hands. The man began to scream as the pain hit him. Alos could only look on, not having the ability to defend himself, let alone his men. The footman screamed for a moment longer before he drew his last breath and died.

Rishi stood, looking stronger—more powerful than before. She almost seemed to be glowing red for a moment, the same red glow that Alos had seen going between his man and Rishi's hands. Ashlynn clapped as she walked toward Alos.

"As you can see," Ashlynn said. "There's nothing you can do to stop us. Now we are going to discuss terms. I have to have the powers of the Ryder family. You will send a message that Tybin Ryder is to come here for marriage. You will marry us and the union will be consummated. Once the act has taken place I will kill Tybin in his sleep. Tobin will hear and march troops here but we will be ready for them...killing them all, along with the rest of the Ryder family. By the time all this has taken place, Queen Mala will have taken Cerrado and the final battle between your family and her army will have been decided. We will then kill the winner and take Cerrado for our own."

"And your rule will last for eternity," Rishi said. "You will be the most powerful ruler that Cerrado has ever seen."

"You will never have victory," Alos managed to say.

"You know nothing," Ashlynn said. "I am more powerful than you could ever imagine. If you only knew the truth about it...the truth about who I am. There isn't much time left. We need to move quickly. Once we finish with your troops the Ryder family must be here. You must tell them to come here."

"I will do no such thing," Alos said. "I will never aide you in any form. You will just have to kill me."

"If that's what it takes," Ashlynn said. "I will kill you and all your siblings. It will be harder to take Cerrado that way, but it can still be done. Oh, Prince Alos, you should reconsider. You and I could make such a powerful team together. With our combined powers we could rule Cerrado unchallenged for eternity."

"Eternity is such a long time," Alos said. "You shouldn't be so certain of things that you cannot see."

"You are in no position to make such proclamations," Ashlynn said. "You will see…"

Ashlynn was going to continue but something distant caught her attention. At first she didn't know what the issue was, why her intuition was telling her that something had happened. Ashlynn looked around the throne room before looking to Rishi.

"Did you feel that?" Ashlynn asked.

"My senses are not as attuned as yours," Rishi said. "But yes, I felt something strange, my Queen. I cannot explain what it was."

"Someone used magic to sneak into my castle," Ashlynn said. "That is the only thing it could be."

"There is no one powerful enough that would risk that," Rishi said. "No one with that level of power knows about you yet. There would be no reason to do that."

"There is one group of people," Ashlynn said. "The Nature Watchers."

"They are nothing to fear," Rishi said. "They are supposed to watch nature but they are all immersed in personal pleasures. The only one that hasn't destroyed themselves is Jade, the river watcher, but even she has experimented with those things that consume a person. There is no reason for them to get involved in this."

"Their parents got involved before, so I wouldn't put it past them again," Ashlynn said. "I trust them not. Search the castle. Someone entered. I want them placed in the dungeon and I will confront them there."

"It will be done," Rishi said.

Rishi started barking orders to the guards in the room and everyone started to rush through the castle. Ashlynn sat in her throne, stewing at the fact that someone would challenge her. Ashlynn glanced to Alos before standing and summoning the 'Knowledge of Cerrado.' Ashlynn started reading the book as she plotted her next moves.

In an empty corner of the courtyard, a single pool and fountain slowly leaked water out of its side. There hadn't been maintenance done to the fountain in years. No one even bothered to look it over to see if it needed repairs. As water slowly trickled out of the cracks, the water in the fountain started to churn. It only took a few moments before Jade, Hibit, Lacey, and Snowflake appeared in the fountain. The group looked around to see where they were at.

"This is the Windswept Castle," Hibit said. "How did you do that?"

"I have powers," Jade said. "I can travel through the waters of Cerrado. I learned that from my mother. She was so good that she could appear from a single drop of water, anywhere in the land."

"What are we to do here?" Hibit asked.

"We have to save Prince Alos," Jade said. "He is held here and is in danger of being killed."

"Princess Ashlynn wouldn't risk killing him," Hibit said. "The repercussions that would come about from killing one of the children would be far too great."

"Don't count on it," Jade said. "You do not know how powerful Ashlynn has become. She is a powerful necromancer, much older than she looks. We need to move quickly to save him. Follow me."

Jade raced toward a door to enter the castle. Hibit and Lacey paused before they took off after her. Snowflake let out a giant sigh and yawn before she chased after the group. They caught up to Jade and stalked down a corridor. They were looking in the open rooms, trying to

160

find a passage that would lead them to the dungeon. As they walked, the corridor filled with guards holding swords. Rishi was leading them.

"Halt!" Rishi ordered. "Who are you and what are you doing here?"

"We are trying to find the dungeon," Jade said.

"Then you're in luck," Rishi said. "Take them to the dungeon and lock them away to rot."

The guards grabbed the group and roughly took them through twists and turns throughout the castle, leading downwards toward the dungeon. The dungeon was empty when they arrived, no one else in sight. The guards threw the entire group into one cell and locked the gate. The group looked around, trying to see if there was a way out.

"Now what do we do?" Hibit asked. "How can we save anyone when we are in here?"

"Can I trust that you will do the right thing when the time is right?" Jade asked, taking a step back so she was standing in a pool of water on the floor. "Can you believe that I'm on your side and will do everything I can to help you win this?"

"We are in a dungeon thanks to you," Lacey said. "You're track record isn't the greatest right now. We have our job of saving Arctic but we are a long ways away from her and we are trapped in a dungeon. I find it hard to find the faith to trust you right now."

"You must find the faith to trust me, Lacey DuLake," Jade said. "You are going to be very important before the final game is played. Everyone has their role to play, myself included. Ashlynn will be here soon to question you, and ask why you are here. She will be confused and upset that I brought you here. The Nature Watchers have never gotten involved in the affairs of Cerrado or any other world before. This will throw a curve into all of her plans. You must save Alos and kill Ashlynn before you continue the search for Arctic. That much I know for sure."

"You ask for much and give nothing," Lacey said. "Is that all you can say?"

"Yes," Jade said.

161

The water in the pool that Jade was standing in got choppy before Jade disappeared and the water returned to calm. Both Hibit and Lacey were stunned. They were alone in the dungeon now, not knowing what to do. They looked at each other for any idea of what should happen.

"I really don't like her," Lacey said.

"I don't know," Hibit said. "I believe that there's more going on that she told us. I've studied the Nature Watchers and their parents. They wouldn't side with evil. There's too much at stake."

"Who are their parents?" Lacey asked. "Is it true?"

"They are the children of Father Time and Mother Nature," Hibit said. "They watch nature and are supposed to prevent evil from walking the lands. The others haven't been doing their jobs. Jade didn't start doing her job until recently. The rumors are that she's been on Captain Creature's ships. They say that he saved her from the path she was going down and now they are romantically linked."

"Why would she bring us here?" Lacey asked.

"It might be the case that it's safer for us to be in a dungeon than it is to be out in the open of Cerrado," Hibit said. "What do you think, Snowflake?"

Snowflake perked up her head and looked at Hibit with a quizzical look on her face. She yawned before walking in a circle and finding a spot to curl up on the floor. Hibit smiled as the large cat purred loudly while drifting off to sleep.

"What a cat," Hibit said. "Sleeps more than any creature that I've ever seen."

"We need to find a way out of here," Lacey said. "We cannot be hindered in our actions. We must save Alos."

"Saving Alos is the last thing you will be doing," Princess Ashlynn said, stepping in front of the cell gate. "Am I to assume that Jade, the lady of the rivers, was the one who brought you to my castle?"

"She did," Hibit said. "Before she left us here. We have no idea why she brought us here...or why she left us here."

"You lie," Ashlynn said. "You should know that Alos is on the verge of death. I have defeated him and have been draining his life. I will do that to so many other people before I destroy Mala and take Cerrado for my own. There is nothing...no force, no family, and no army that can stop me. Even Queen Mala and her evil forces do not have the power to prevent me from taking this land as my own."

"You talk too much," Lacey said, drawing her sword. "Open this gate and let's settle this in the open. I challenge you to open fencing."

"To the death?" Ashlynn asked.

"Is there any other way?" Lacey asked.

"Very well," Ashlynn said.

Princess Ashlynn stepped away from the gate as the gate swung open. Lacey walked out as the gate snapped shut, keeping Hibit and Snowflake in the cell. A sword manifested in Ashlynn's hands and she pointed it right at Lacey. The pair circled around each other in the open area of the dungeon. They tapped swords as an indication to start the fight.

Lacey rushed forward but Ashlynn simply smiled while dropping her sword. Ashlynn used magic to drop Lacey to her knees. Lacey tried to fight but the overwhelming power of the magic prevented it. Lacey dropped her sword as she crumbled under the power of the magic. Ashlynn used her powers to push Lacey back into the cell. The gate opened and closed just wide enough to allow Lacey through. Ashlynn took Lacey's sword and looked it over.

"This is a very nice sword," Ashlynn said. "I've only seen a few that could equal this blade. Where did you get it?"

"From the people I escaped from," Lacey said.

"This was one of Mala's swords," Ashlynn said. "I would recognize this sword anywhere. Mala loved this sword. She must be very sore that you have it. If you escaped from her cells, you must be very powerful and crafty. I will have to have a guard on you at all times to make sure you don't escape here."

"What are you going to do with us?" Hibit asked.

"I'm going to kill you slowly," Ashlynn said. "I'm going to use you to enhance my powers. There will be no one who will stand before me. I must ask you though, Lacey DuLake...being in Mala's dungeons you must have had the chance to learn the dark arts...learn the power of magic, but you don't have any powers. Why didn't you choose to defend yourself with real power?"

"I do defend myself with real power," Lacey said. "I use my heart, my inner strength...not cowardice and hatred like you do."

"You fear the awesome powers that I have?" Ashlynn asked.

"I don't fear you," Lacey said. "I pity you. You have powers that can destroy anything but you cannot be protected from yourself. All your power and you cannot control yourself."

"Fool," Ashlynn said. "I cannot wait to destroy you. Get comfortable, you're going to be in this dungeon for a long time. But don't get too comfortable, I will kill you."

With that ominous warning, Ashlynn walked away from the cell gate. The last thing that either Lacey or Hibit heard was Ashlynn telling the guards to extinguish all the torches in the dungeon. The group was cast into utter and pitch darkness as they had nothing to do but sit—waiting to see what Princess Ashlynn's next move would be.

Chapter 21

The river water moved lazily on the midsummer's day. The current wasn't fast as animals drank from the banks without care or concern for the day. As uneventful as the day had been, in an instant it changed as three pirate ships came around the bend. The animals scattered in all directions as to hide from the massive ships that were floating down the river.

The pirates aboard the ships were singing a shanty—their deep, gruff voices raising up in harmonics as they worked the rigging and the decking—expertly sailing the ships through the river channels. On the biggest ship, The Lynx, in middle of the pack, Captain Creature stood next to the wheel, watching his men work. The captain was a big man—strong and fit, wearing garments cut especially for him, to fit his muscular body style—brown pants, a white button shirt, brown vest, and brown captain's hat.

Captain Creature navigated the ship along the banks of the river, maneuvering the biggest ship between the narrow banks with ease—a task that he had done many times before. The captain knew his ship and the rivers like the back of his hand. There was nothing in those waters that could have surprised him. As Captain Creature looked over the banks of his river, a small puddle of water next to him started to get agitated. The captain smiled as Jade appeared on the deck of the ship from the water.

Captain Creature instructed one of his men to take his position at the helm as he walked to Jade and kissed her. The pair walked over the decking of the ship. Each pirate stopped what he was doing to salute the captain as he walked by. Creature and Jade made their way to the bow, kissing and looking over the scenery before Jade began speaking.

"Everything is going to hell," Jade said. "I did as you commanded but I understand not. Captain Creature, all of the children are in trouble."

"Everything is darkest before dawn, my love," Captain Creature said. "Trust."

"I do trust you," Jade said. "I've given you my heart completely. You saved me and I fell in love with you that day, Creature. I couldn't love another after you, but I have to know what we are doing. Everything has turned against the children."

"I dabbled in all possible futures Jade," Captain Creature said. "I predicted what each course of action would bring about. There is much that I don't know or couldn't account for, but there is much that I can do. This is the only way."

"But Ashlynn has Alos," Jade protested. "The guards were on us as soon as we entered the castle. They knew. Ashlynn is far more powerful than you could have thought."

"Not more powerful than I could have thought," Captain Creature said. "It just means that she's someone we didn't expect. I know who she is, and so do you."

"Impossible," Jade said.

"Nothing is impossible, Jade," Captain Creature said. "Are your siblings on board with the plans?"

"I believe so," Jade said. "When Mother and Father called us, I feared the worst. They want us to help. The others weren't as excited for this chance to prove our worth as I was."

"The time has come for Cherry to play a role in this," Captain Creature said. "She must be the next person the boy from the other world sees."

"I think we should kill him," Jade said.

"Death is not a light decision to make," Captain Creature said. "Nor is it ours to deal with."

"But Arctic is on the verge of losing the ability of having a unicorn appear to her," Jade said. "If they act on the feelings that they are having for each other, all will be lost. Only a blade that is laced with the magic of a unicorn's horn could kill Mala. It would have to pierce her black, evil heart. I think that Ashlynn needs to die in the same way. With her powers a normal death wouldn't be enough, correct?"

"You are right," Captain Creature said. "But we cannot kill the boy. He has a very important role to play and his love for the girl from the other world will prevent him from acting on his feelings for Arctic. He will stay true to this Holly that he loves."

"We can only hope so, my love," Jade said, kissing Captain Creature's cheek.

"Princess Arctic is not mature enough to handle her quest on her own," Captain Creature said. "This boy will protect and guide her as she discovers herself and her role that she must play in all of this. The day will come when everything is made clear."

Jade was about to speak when a pirate rushed up to them. The pirate was tall and lank, with sunburnt leathery skin and stringy blonde hair. He saluted Captain Creature before speaking.

"Captain," the pirate said. "We are approaching the nexus point. We can continue to sail down the river and make haste for the Cerrado Castle or we can use an arch...although, none are appearing right now."

"Slow the ships to a crawl," Captain Creature said. "We must get to the Bloodgrass Plains. That is where we will be needed next."

"The Bloodgrass Plains?" Jade asked as Creature nodded yes. "That will take at least three jumps. Who knows how long it will take for the arches to appear to us. We could be waiting for days."

"Then we wait for days," Captain Creature said. "Do it at once."

The pirate saluted and rushed away. In an instant the pirates were working quickly to bring the ships to a slower pace. Pirates were using flag signals on the bow and stern to signal the front and rear ships of the convoy. Within moments, the ships were stopped—floating openly in the slow currents of the river.

"Now you must summon your sister," Captain Creature said. "Bring Cherry here and we will instruct her on what to do."

"I will try," Jade said. "But I do not know if she will be willing. We must get below deck. I don't want the other pirates to see her."

The Captain nodded as they walked to the stairs to go below deck. They made their way through the dimly lit ship to a grand room in the stern. The room was big, with a large table with wine and food set upon it and chairs surrounding it in the middle—a desk to one side, maps and globes on the other. In the one corner of the room were two large, comfortable looking chairs that faced large windows. The room was decorated with gold and silver trinkets and paintings and statues from many different worlds.

Jade walked to an open area of the room and pulled a small bag from her jacket pocket before taking her jacket off and tossing it on a chair. She pulled the contents out of the bag—a handful of plain grass. Jade breathed a heavy breath before tossing the grass in the air and twirling her fingers. There was a rush of wind in the room before Cherry appeared.

Cherry was very confused as she looked around her new surroundings. She was in her cherry-colored dress that matched her cherry boots and her long cherry hair. She looked at her sister and smiled before glaring at Captain Creature. Cherry saw a bottle of wine on the table and poured herself a goblet, taking a sip before she sat down in a large, comfortable chair.

"And to what do I owe this pleasure, dear sister?" Cherry said, in a mocking tone. "I was having such a fun time out in my grasslands. I have the most wonderful friends there. You should come and join us sometime. You would find it much more fun that sailing around on a dumb ship."

"Cherry," Jade said, approaching her sister. "Do you remember the conversations that we had with Mother and Father?"

"Of course I remember them," Cherry said. "Help Cerrado...blah, blah, blah...be a good person...blah, blah, blah...you're perfect and we are disappointments..."

"They didn't say that," Jade interrupted. "They were making the point that I have done the task I was appointed with. Cherry, you have so much potential. You could make your name legendary."

"That's your dream, Sister," Cherry said. "I just want to spend time with my friends. We were getting ready for the most wonderful of parties. There's going to be hundreds of people there, with a band and all the booze and food that you could imagine." Cherry looked over to Captain Creature. "Dear captain, I've heard much about you. He must be fun,

Sister. Bring him to the party and he can entertain us with his pirate stories."

"I am not a performer," Captain Creature said. "I am a man of action. I don't watch while others work. We have a task to do and you have your role to play."

"You're not going to let this go?" Cherry asked with a heavy sigh. "What do you need me to do?"

"There's a hearse that's traveling through your Bloodgrass Plains as we speak," Captain Creature said. "Inside the casket are two people."

"Dead bodies?" Cherry recoiled in horror. "No way. I'm not touching a dead body. I'm not getting near a dead body."

"They aren't dead," Jade said.

"Then why are they in a casket?" Cherry asked.

"An evil is using the casket to transport them," Captain Creature said. "You need to intercept them before they reach their destination."

"And what will that do?" Cherry asked.

"Much," Captain Creature said.

Cherry waited for the captain to continue, but he didn't. Cherry was beginning to weigh her options. She knew that the party would be starting soon and if she was tied up with this she would miss the beginning, if not the entire party. He friends would be upset that she wasn't there, but Cherry also knew that her parents and Jade wouldn't let her slip out of the responsibilities of what she was supposed to do.

"I intercept them," Cherry said. "What do I do with them?"

"The people who are transporting them need to be taken to the Windswept Castle," Captain Creature said. "There Princess Ashlynn will deal with them. Why they are taken there isn't your concern. They need to end up in that castle."

"And the pair in the casket?"

"Tell them to unhitch the horses from the hearse," Jade said. "And tell them to ride. They are to go to the banks of the river. We will pick them up from there."

"Why can't you do this?" Cherry asked, trying one more time to get out of working. "It seems like this is a task that you could handle."

"I have other responsibilities," Jade said. "Some that include getting my brothers to help with these plans as well."

"Cinnamon and Cobalt aren't going to help you," Cherry said. "Cinnamon's a drunk. Cobalt smokes too much grass and spends all his time with his women. Cinnamon may have been one of the best swordsmen in all the land when he was younger, but once he set out on his own, he lost his abilities. I would wager that you could best him now, Sister."

"I wouldn't challenge him," Jade said. "He was an expert with the blade and we are going to need his expertise again. He will be very important to what's coming. He will have to train someone in the combat."

"Good luck with that," Cherry said. "What will Cobalt do?"

"When the time is right," Jade said. "He will guide a pair of people through his forest. They will need to find something, and he will have to help them."

"He's so lost in his own mind and you expect him to guide others?" Cherry laughed. "Once again, good luck with that. You have such grand plans, Sister. Are these your plans, or did the captain here come up with them?"

"We worked them out together," Jade said.

"You two are not yet married, are you?" Cherry asked.

"We have not married yet," Jade said. "We won't marry until Cerrado is at peace."

"Then if you aren't married," Cherry said, with a grin. "Maybe I could borrow your captain for the night. He looks like such a handsome, strong man."

"I didn't know you liked men," Jade said.

"I like to sample everything," Cherry replied.

"The answer is no," Jade said. "We are not married but we are committed to each other."

"You speak for him?" Cherry asked.

"No," Captain Creature said. "Although, she knows me well. Cherry, we are wasting time. Do you agree to help with our quest or not?"

"I agree," Cherry sighed. "I fear I won't get a moment's peace if I refuse. I can intercept and send them on their way. You two better be right though, we better be working for the right side."

"We are, Sister," Jade said. "I will send you on your way. Thank you."

Jade twirled her fingers and the grass on the floor started to swirl in the air. Cherry waved and smiled at Captain Creature as she disappeared from the room. The room went calm as Jade kissed Captain Creature. The captain was about to speak when they heard multiple cracks of thunder rumbling in the sky. There were flashes of lightning going on all around the sky.

"We've entered the arch," Jade said. "We should be at the plains soon."

"Then all has begun," Captain Creature said. "Come with me."

Captain Creature took Jade by the hand and led her through the ship and back to the deck. When they emerged they came out on a bright sunny day with reddish-tinted grass as far as the eye could see. There wasn't a single tree in their field of vision. Some of the pirates on the deck were confused as to what had happened, but Captain Creature and Jade had been through the arches so many times they knew what to expect and didn't experience any levels of amnesia. Captain Creature and Jade walked to the helm of the ship as Creature took the wheel. Jade kissed him as they looked out over the plains—wondering if they had the ability to defeat the evil that had befallen their land.

Chapter 22

The large, black, horse-drawn hearse was speeding down a narrow trail that snaked alongside the six-foot-tall reddish-tinted grass. Atin whipped the horses to get them to travel as fast as they could. Ambriss, sitting on the bench next to Atin, kept looking behind them, watching for the two horse riders that she thought she saw following them. Ambriss scanned the rear horizon but didn't see any trace of them.

"Don't fret, Sister," Atin said. "Whatever will happen, will happen. If there is someone following us, I'm sure it's for a good reason."

"I'm worried about our little sister," Ambriss said. "Why is she in this casket? Who is the boy with her? What happened to Hibit and Snowflake?"

"She's having an adventure," Atin said. "She's doing okay. Better than we are."

"What do you mean?" Ambriss asked.

"Ornthal didn't realize who we were," Atin said. "Those who are following us are going to make sure that we are killed once we reach Yorehill Manor."

"They wouldn't dare kill us," Ambriss exclaimed.

"Why not?" Atin said. "The bandits feel that something evil is taking over Cerrado. They don't trust anyone to begin with. And two strangers show up wanting to join?—they can't take the risk that we are here to gather information from them."

"You seem to know a lot about the bandits," Ambriss said. "Why is that?"

"I may have an insider or two," Atin said.

"Do you know Ornthal?" Ambriss asked.

"I know enough about him to know that I don't want to know him," Atin said. "He is a cold-blooded killer. Ornthal takes what he wants and gives nothing back."

"Don't you do the same, Brother?" Ambriss asked.

"I don't," Atin said. "I have a moral code that I live by—some lines that I would never cross, no matter what the cost. There is no need to kill or take to live the life you want. Ornthal has no code that he lives by. He does what he wants and listens to no one. In the end it will catch up with him, possibly destroy him. His men are not loyal to him. His women fear him."

"And I suppose that your women love you?" Ambriss asked. "They don't pleasure you out of fear and privilege?"

"They do love me," Atin said. "I treat them wonderfully. I make them feel like women. We all know what our deal is, and we honor it."

"What do they get?" Ambriss asked.

"A life," Atin said. "They are not merely toys for me to play with. They get to go out into Cerrado and have adventures, live wonderful lives, and never have to want for anything. If they don't get the job done, they know that there's consequences, so they do everything in their power to get the job done."

"The one that you were with," Ambriss said. "What is her name?"

"Why do you wish to know her name?" Atin asked.

"Because you are in love with her," Ambriss said. "I could see it in your eyes and hers when you were standing near each other. It is obvious to anyone who can see. You two are a couple."

"I admit," Atin said. "There have been less women in my bed since she came around, but that does not mean that we are in love."

"You're in love," Ambriss said, with a big smile. "Admit it."

"I admit nothing," Atin said. "I wonder if Arctic is in love with that bozo in the casket with her."

"They looked like they had concern for each other," Ambriss said. "If they were to fall in love and act upon it, then Arctic won't get to see a unicorn."

173

"I think we have bigger problems than her seeing a unicorn," Atin said. "We have to deliver them, but we risk getting killed once we drop them off."

"Will the bandits kill Arctic?" Ambriss asked.

"No," Atin said. "I'm sure they know that she's very valuable. They will ransom her out from Yorehill Manor, asking for massive amounts of gold, silver, and treasure to give her back."

"Arctic must be so scared," Ambriss said. "Can we please stop for a little while? I want to talk to her and make sure she's safe."

"We cannot," Atin said. "If there are people following us, and they saw us opening the casket, then the situation could change. We have a good idea of what their plan is now."

"How do we make sure that we don't get killed when we arrive?" Ambriss asked.

"We will have to slip out of the Manor upon our arrival," Atin said. "Then search out information. This is going to require stealth and courage. We will slip through the Manor and find what we need."

"You make it sound so easy," Ambriss said.

"Be ready for action in a moment's notice," Atin said. "There could be a lot of trouble ahead. They said we were to go down this path for at least two days. How are our passengers supposed to eat or relieve themselves? We will need to let them out after a bit. You can speak with Arctic then."

"She looked so dirty," Ambriss said. "They must have seen some serious action. I wonder how they ended up this far away from the Blue Cerrado Forest. She must have a wonderful story to tell."

As the hearse was going around a bend in the path, Atin pulled the horses to a stop. Standing in the middle of the road was Cherry. She was waiting for them as Atin tried to calm the horses. Atin and Ambriss stayed on the bench of the hearse, looking at Cherry standing in the middle of the road. Atin had a hand on his dagger, ready to throw it at a moment's notice.

"Who are you?" Ambriss called out.

"I am here to protect my grasslands," Cherry said.

"Then you must be Cherry," Atin said. "Lady of the grasslands. I have heard much about you."

"What you have heard may or may not be true," Cherry replied. "I am not here to explain my actions to you."

"Then why are you blocking our way?" Ambriss asked.

"Like you, I have a quest to complete," Cherry said. "I am supposed to make sure that evil doesn't take control of these lands...take control of Cerrado."

"Then it would be best if you allowed us to make our way," Atin said. "We have the same goals in mind. We need to complete our mission."

"You will not make it to Yorehill Manor, Prince Atin," Cherry said.

"You know us," Atin said, with a wolf grin. "Many know the wolf prince. We are wasting time. What is your play then?"

"Both of you, come here," Cherry said.

Atin and Ambriss looked at each other before dismounting the hearse and walking toward Cherry. Atin had his daggers drawn and was ready to strike, indicating to Cherry that she needed to move with caution. Cherry smiled at the pair before motioning them to take her hands. Slowly, Atin put one of the daggers back in its sheath and took her hand. Ambriss took the other hand. Cherry smiled and in an instant the trio was gone.

The horses were agitated but they stayed in place. All was calm and quiet around the hearse until two bandits on large black horses rode up. The men looked around the hearse and at the horses. They both wore looks of disbelief on their faces. Neither could understand what they'd seen. They searched the area until they met back at the horses.

"I know what I thought I saw," the first bandit said. "But nothing can disappear like that. Something must have happened to them. Who was the girl in red with them?"

"I've never seen one like that," the second bandit said. "There must be some powerful magic going on here."

"Our orders were to kill them upon their arrival at Yorehill Manor," the first bandit said. "What should we do, bring the hearse there and unload the cargo, or kill the passengers now?"

"We weren't supposed to kill the passengers," the second said. "Just the ones bringing them. Ornthal would have our heads if we did that."

"Something went wrong here," the first said. "We must act now."

"You will do no such thing," a female voice said, from behind them.

The two bandits turned and saw a tough-looking woman in brown leather, holding a large sword, standing behind them. It was Atin's woman. They had no idea where she'd come from or how she was able to sneak up on them. They had been following the hearse since it left Raven's Head and had never once seen her.

"Who are you, woman?" the first bandit asked. "Who are you that sneaks upon us in silence?"

"Who I am is no concern of yours," the woman said. "I am going to kill both of you."

The woman started moving forward as the bandits drew their swords. The group was in a standoff when Cherry appeared behind the bandits. The woman was stunned that Cherry was there, out of the blue, standing behind the men. Before the men knew what was going on, Cherry placed her hands on their shoulders and the three of them disappeared. The woman stood in shocked silence. She didn't know what to do. She was about to take a step toward the hearse, but Cherry reappeared.

"Sheath your sword," Cherry said. "You do not want to stand against me. You saw what I did to them and you know what I can do."

"What happened to Atin?" the woman shouted.

"He's safe," Cherry said. "I promise you that. Now sheath your sword. I don't want to have to kill you, but if you threaten me I will have no other choice."

The woman slowly put her sword away but didn't take her hand off the hilt.

"Now, where is Atin?" the woman asked.

"He's safer than you are about to be," Cherry said. "Sorry."

With lightning speed, Cherry rushed to the woman and the instant the two touched they disappeared, leaving just the hearse and the horses on the empty plains. It was only a moment before Cherry reappeared. Cherry opened the rear door to the hearse and pulled the casket out, letting it drop to the ground with a resounding thud. Cherry undid the latch and opened the lid before helping Arctic and Krispin out of the box.

"Thank you so much," Arctic said, as she looked around.

"Yes," Krispin said. "Thank you. I didn't know how much longer I could have stayed in there."

"Just be glad that I'm little," Arctic said. "If I was heavy you would have been smothered in there."

"Where are we?" Krispin asked.

"You are on the Bloodgrass Plains," Cherry said. "From here you are to take this hearse and drive it to the river. Once you are there you will wait."

"Wait for what?" Krispin asked.

"You will know it when you see it," Cherry said.

"Who are you?" Krispin said.

"I am Cherry," Cherry said. "The watcher of the grasslands of Cerrado."

"You are a Nature Watcher," Arctic said. "I didn't know you were helping in the affairs of man."

"We just started," Cherry said. "I'm not overly thrilled about it. Just do what I said. Take this to the river and all will be made clear there."

With that, Cherry disappeared. Both Krispin and Arctic were stunned. They looked around the area they were at, then to each other. Something deep inside both of them caused them to rush to each other and hug. They almost kissed, but pulled away at the last moment.

"It's good to be out of there and safe," Krispin said. "I'm glad you are safe."

"I'm glad you're safe, too," Arctic said. "But I wish I knew what happened to my brother and sister. Where did they go and why were they with the bandits."

"What roles were they playing again?" Krispin asked.

"Atin was going to find the lost sword," Arctic said. "While Princess Ambriss was going to search out the immortal river. I don't know why they would be with the bandits."

"What do you think we should do?" Krispin asked.

"You're my knight," Arctic said. "You are the one who's supposed to be leading and protecting me."

"Who was that girl?" Krispin asked.

"She is Cherry," Arctic said. "The daughter of Father Time and Mother Nature. She is one of the quintuplets...the four that were born together and watch the nature."

"Father Time and Mother Nature?" Krispin asked. "This is a strange place."

"There are many strange things here," Arctic said. "But I can think of one that is stranger than everything else."

"What is that?"

"You," Arctic said.

"Me?" Krispin said. "You are far stranger than I. You're eighteen and on a unicorn hunt."

"You think a woman's heart can be bought," Arctic said. "You have to go to the ends of the earth for this Holly, but she is doing nothing for you."

"You still don't understand," Krispin said. "I doubt you'll ever be able to understand."

"That's because it doesn't make sense," Arctic said, with a smile.

"We need to keep moving," Krispin said. "We have been going for a long time now. We are running out of time before Holly and Chester's wedding. I have to return before then. I'm sure that this adventure will make Holly fall into my arms."

"Won't that be great," Arctic said, sarcastically, as she climbed onto the hearse. "Come on, if she said to go to the river, we should go to the river."

"Okay," Krispin said.

Krispin climbed onto the bench on the hearse. He took the reins of the horses and cracked them, causing the horses to take off running at high speed. Although Arctic was still worried about her siblings disappearing, she had a feeling that things were starting to go their way.

Chapter 23

The sun shone high above the vibrant, lush sheep paddock. The fluffy sheep were lazily grazing in the gentle breeze while Kale Risdell walked along the bank of a still river. Kale took great pride in his flock, knowing that his wool commanded top dollar at the village market. Kale liked to think it was because his sheep were the happiest, calmest sheep in the land. The stone wall that his ancestors built made it so the sheep couldn't see what was outside their paddock and no predators could see in.

Kale knew that the day was going to come that his son Krispin would seek his fortunes elsewhere, and that he may or may not return to the farm when his adventures were over. Kale had hoped that Krispin would have been older when the adventure began, allowing Kale more time to instruct Krispin on the ways of the world, and that not every place is as peaceful or nice as their little village.

As Kale walked along the river he noticed that he was being shadowed on the outside of the wall. Someone was following him. When Kale would stop, the person behind the wall would stop. Kale could just barely make out the top of the person's head. It only took Kale a moment to realize what was going on as a massive smile came across his face. Kale began to jog along the riverbank, quickly shifting directions multiple times to confuse the stalker behind the wall.

Every shift of direction, Kale moved closer to the wall. When he was just about to the wall, Kale jumped on top of the wall and then dropped right in front of the person who was chasing him. Kale scared the daylights out of his wife, Mary, who was trying to play a joke on him. Mary rushed right into his arms for a kiss. The pair was laughing.

"One of these days, Kale Risdell," Mary said, with a big smile. "I will catch you off guard."

"You'd need to get up pretty early in the morning to do that, my love," Kale said. "But I do love the fact that you keep trying. Don't ever stop."

"I won't."

The pair kissed again before Mary picked up a picnic basket she had been carrying. Kale took Mary by the hand and they walked to the gate in the wall and entered the paddock properly. The pair walked to a small outcropping of trees and sat down in the shade. The sheep watched as Mary took out fruit and sandwiches from the basket.

"MLT?" Kale asked, biting into the sandwich.

"Mutton, lettuce, and tomatoes," Mary said. "But don't tell them." Mary pointed to the sheep. "They wouldn't understand."

"I doubt they would," Kale said, with a smile.

The pair ate their lunch in relative silence. They commented on the clouds, the grass, and news from the village up the road. Kale was happy with the sheep this season—they were gaining weight and had full coats of wool. He knew they would have a fine crop this year. As they were finishing their lunch, Kale looked to Mary and could tell she was very upset.

"What's troubling you, my dear?" Kale asked.

"Krispin," Mary said. "I wish we could have had more time with him to prepare him for the outside world. There's so much he doesn't know."

"I'm sure he's doing wonderfully," Kale said. "He'll have stories to last a lifetime."

"But will he be safe?" Mary asked.

"I'm sure of it," Kale said.

Mary was about to ask another question when the gate to the paddock opened. Kale turned to see Chester and Holly walking into the pasture. They walked hand in hand right up to Kale and Mary.

"Chester and Holly," Kale said, standing. "How may we help you on this fine day?"

"Krispin and I have some unfinished business," Chester said. "I want to make sure he knows his place around here."

"What Chester meant to say was, the wedding date is fast approaching," Holly said. "We were wondering if you've heard any word from Krispin yet."

"I'm sorry," Mary said. "Krispin walked into the Moon Forest almost two months ago and that's the last anyone has heard from him."

"Really?" Holly asked with concern.

"Really?" Chester asked at the same time with glee.

"I'm afraid so," Kale said. "He's out there somewhere. I pray every day for his safe return."

"He will have a wonderful adventure to tell us about, I'm sure," Holly said.

"It will make fine entertainment for our wedding," Chester said. "There's no way that he could do something grand. No offense, but Krispin was always so plain."

"Don't be so quick to judge, Chester Van Brunt," Mary said. "Krispin has a destiny just as you do. And you never know where that path is going to lead. Just walking through the forest, going between the trees, there could be pathways to places you can't possibly imagine."

"You had an adventure, right, Mr. Risdell?" Holly asked.

"I did," Kale said. "I went to university in London. I studied the stars. I met many wonderful people. I met Mary there."

"Hang on a second," Chester said. "I've heard rumors that Mary wasn't from London. You met her elsewhere. People don't know where she's from."

"I've never put much stock into rumors Chester," Kale said. "Repeating them can get you into trouble...especially when they're not true."

"How do you know if they're true or not," Chester asked. "If you don't ask around for confirmation?"

"You go directly to the source," Kale said. "And ask them. But before you do that, you must ask yourself if you think the rumor could be true or not. Let's say you think it's true, the next thing you need to ask yourself is if the person the rumor is about will even confirm or deny it to you. You could embarrass yourself by asking something stupid to someone you don't want to upset."

"Is it true?" Chester asked. "You don't look like you're from London. You don't talk like it either. And I've never heard of a girl from the city coming out to a little village such as ours and being happy."

"You speak with many London women?" Holly asked in an accusing tone.

"I've spoken with a few," Chester said. "You're not from London."

"You have much to learn, Chester," Mary said. "But you are right about one thing, I'm not from London. I've been there a time or two, but it's not where Kale and I met."

"Where did you meet?" Holly asked.

"We met in a grand castle," Mary said. "Kale was confused and alone, not knowing which way to turn. He was like you, Holly...at a major turning point in his life. He wasn't thinking about who to marry, but if he was going to continue with his astronomical research or if he was going to come back to the family farm and be a shepherd."

"I can't believe that you returned," Chester said. "You were in London and could have gone anywhere in the world and you returned here."

"Sometimes home is the best place, Chester," Kale said.

"When I first saw him," Mary said. "I was very surprised. I didn't know how he'd gotten into the castle. It didn't take long to figure out the story. We met with another friend and talked the night away. It was a grand time. I'll never forget that first night. There was magic in the air."

"Like the first time Chester told me he loved me," Holly said, with starry eyes.

"Much more than that," Mary said. "We fell in love that first night and were married right away. We didn't stay in my land very long before we came back here."

"Where do you come from?" Holly asked. "How would we get there? Is it far?"

"You can't get to it from here," Mary said. "It's a faraway land."

"Do you ever wish to go back and visit?" Holly asked. "Do you miss your family?"

"My family died," Mary said. "The day before Kale came, my family died. I didn't have anywhere else to turn. They were murdered, and I was afraid that someone would come for me too. I didn't know what to do and when I looked into Kale's eyes, I knew that I wanted to look into those eyes forever. They were perfect beyond words. I've thought often about my home and the castle where I grew up, but I'm happy here."

"You grew up in a castle, yet you're happy in a cottage that's almost a shack?" Chester asked.

"Yes, I am," Mary said. "There's so much more to life than castles, parties, and power. I wouldn't trade anything I have now to go back."

"Even if things were different?" Holly said. "You wouldn't go back to that life?"

"Not without Kale," Mary said. "He would have to be with me. I would go anywhere with him."

Mary leaned over and kissed Kale. He smiled and kissed her back.

"As long as I'm with him I have everything I could possibly want," Mary said. "There may be a day when duty calls me back to my homeland, but Kale will be with me and everything will be well."

"I can only hope that my life is as happy as yours," Holly said. "You sound like you have everything a person could ever want."

"Almost," Mary said. "I just wished I knew that my Krispin was safe and sound. I so desperately hope that everything has gone well for him and that he will return to us soon…happy, and ready to take his place on the farm."

"I hope that like you, Kale," Chester said. "Krispin has found his love off in another world."

"That's very possible," Kale said. "When you expand your vision outside of the world you know you can meet so many people that you never even knew were possible."

"What kind of strange people did you meet on your travels?" Holly asked.

"I met all different kinds," Kale said. "I met a wizard who saw backwards, I met a woman that had lived for hundreds of years yet only looked to be in her teens, I met a man that claimed to have read every book ever written, I met a group that had sailed every ocean on the planet, I met a woman who could tell you what your future held, I met many diverse and interesting people. You must always keep your mind open, you never know who might want to pop in."

"It sounds like you had a grand time," Chester said. "But once we're married, I've booked us passage on a steamer. We're going to sail around Africa to the land of the pyramids. I bet Krispin's adventure won't be able to top that. We'll be gone almost a year."

"That sounds like it will be a very fun time," Kale said. "Must have cost a fortune to plan."

"It did," Chester said. "I will have to work a long time to pay it off but it will be worth every moment. I cannot wait to see the world."

"I wish you well on your trip," Mary said. Then added with a sly smile, "As long as Krispin doesn't have a better adventure before then."

"We're going," Chester said, in a huff. "Good day."

"Sorry about him," Holly said. "I do pray for Krispin's safe return. I really do."

Holly rushed to catch up to Chester, closing the gate behind them. Both Kale and Mary were laughing as the pair left.

"Oh, they will make a great pair," Kale said. "They were made for each other."

"Do you think Krispin will find someone when he's on his adventure?" Mary asked.

"I do hope so," Kale said, kissing his wife before returning to his sheep.

"Kale," Mary said, as she walked to her husband. "I better help you watch the sheep today."

"I would love nothing more," Kale said, as he kissed his wife. The pair held hands as they started walking around the paddock.

Chapter 24

The Windswept Castle appeared almost a ghost town, save for the massive amounts of guards that were hidden strategically throughout the grounds. There was only one guard who was out in the open, slowly walking along the top of the castle walls, holding a large bow with a quiver full of arrows on his back. There was an arrow loaded into his bow, ready to fire at a moment's notice.

The day was bright and sunny—a slight breeze preventing it from becoming too hot. The air was heavy, with a humidity that indicated that very soon the sky could be dark with rain, although no clouds could be seen in the sky. As the archer paced along the top of the wall, Sir Bromas, in his full knight's armor with a massive shiny sword at his side, approached the archer.

"How goes the day, Archer Augustus?" Sir Bromas asked.

"Quiet," Augustus replied.

"Has there been any movement today?"

"None," Augustus said. "Something's not right today. The animals aren't out. The air is heavy and I feel something…I don't know."

"There are many things we need to be concerned with," Sir Bromas said. "We need to be certain of our actions before we act. Things in Cerrado are speeding up. Princess Ashlynn is on edge right now. Something strange happened here."

"What?" Augustus asked. "I heard the rumors that people were brought here by a strange magic. Something that the princess was unable to prevent. Is it true?"

"It's not that she can't prevent it," Sir Bromas said. "She was simply caught off guard. I wouldn't worry too much. The princess has everything under control."

Just as Sir Bromas finished speaking, almost to thumb his words in his nose, a gust of wind turned into a whirlwind in the middle of the courtyard. In an instant, Sir Bromas saw Prince Atin and Princess Ambriss appear. Sir Bromas motioned quickly to the guards that were in the alcoves of the castle courtyard. They were on the pair in an instant.

Sir Bromas rushed toward the pair in the middle of the courtyard. When he reached the ground, off the wall, he drew his sword and began running toward where the pair was being held. As he was almost to the pair, another woman appeared next to them. Both of the first people looked shocked that the other woman arrived. Sir Bromas rushed to the center of the guards, pointing his sword right in Prince Atin's face. Sir Bromas instantly recognized who he was holding at sword point.

"Prince Atin, Princess Ambriss, and a strange woman," Sir Bromas said. "Strange magic that you seem to be using. We have some other people who arrived here like that."

"This is the Windswept Castle," Prince Atin said, looking around. "How in the name of Cerrado did we get here from where we were at?"

"Don't try to lie your way out of this," Sir Bromas said. "You and your people have been trying to take the Windswept Castle for years. Take these swine before Princess Ashlynn. She will want to know what is going on here."

The guards grabbed Atin, Ambriss, and the other woman, and roughly forced them toward the entrance to the castle. Sir Bromas looked back toward Augustus who was still on the wall. Bromas flashed a hand signal to the archer, indicating to keep his eyes open for anything that might happen and to bring all prisoners to Ashlynn.

Princess Ashlynn sat on her throne, staring at the people who'd been brought in front of her. She smiled a crooked smile as she looked the trio over like they were meat, to be devoured by a hungry tiger. The guards held all the prisoners back four paces and Sir Bromas stood between her and the captives. Princess Ashlynn motioned for Bromas to approach her.

"Are they who I think they are?" Ashlynn asked softly so only Bromas could hear.

"They are," Sir Bromas said.

"Welcome," Ashlynn boomed so everyone in the room could easily hear her. "Prince Atin and Princess Ambriss. I do welcome you very much to my Windswept Castle. You have come here to pay me a visit. What news do you wish to discuss?"

Atin and Ambriss exchanged a confused glance.

"We were brought here," Atin said. "We are on a quest and have questions to ask you. We wish to determine if you know anything about the on goings of Cerrado."

"They lie," Sir Bromas said. "They arrived in a very strange way. There was nothing in the courtyard and then they were standing there…the royalty first, then the strange woman. They appeared out of thin air."

"Interesting," Ashlynn said. "We've had other people arrive here like that…people that I think might be related to you."

"Who would that be?" Princess Ambriss asked.

"An old family friend and trainer…Hibit, I believe his name is," Princess Ashlynn said. "He was accompanied by his cat and a strange girl."

"Who was the girl?" Ambriss asked.

"I believe that it was Jade," Princess Ashlynn said. "One of those damn Nature Watchers. She disappeared after we provided them with lodging and food. She was very rude. Jade brought them here in the same way you arrived. Why did Jade bring you here?"

"Jade didn't bring us here," Atin said.

"Who did?"

"Cherry."

"The lady of the plains?" Ashlynn asked. "I can understand why Jade would be involving herself in our affairs, but Cherry? That makes no

189

sense at all. Cherry has other things that she's concerned about. Helping the duke and his family aren't one of them."

"Maybe her parents or sister forced her to help," Sir Bromas said. "There are other forces we don't know about."

"I know about them all," Ashlynn snapped. "There isn't a force in Cerrado that I don't know about. Why haven't my spy networks informed us about this?"

"Princess Ashlynn," Ambriss began to ask. "Our brother…the honorable Prince Alos, the fox prince…came here to make a request of you. Where is our brother?"

"Your brother practices necromancy," Ashlynn said. "But he doesn't practice it that well. Alos and I had a sparring session. He was powerful…for a normal person. I could have destroyed him with the snap of my fingers. He was weak compared to what I can do. He is in my dungeon now."

"Interesting," Atin said.

"What?"

"Where did you become so powerful?" Atin asked.

"I've trained," Ashlynn said.

"So has Prince Alos," Prince Atin said. "I've watched my brother. I know what he can do. Alos has become a very powerful necromancer. He did so to protect Cerrado from that very necromancy. What I find so interesting is how did you learn the powers, Princess Ashlynn? How did you become so powerful?"

"There was a trainer that I went to," Ashlynn said, with a smile.

"Really?" Atin asked. "I've gone through many records of Cerrado. I know all the trainers of the dark arts that have ever existed."

"You didn't know about this one," Ashlynn said.

"They are all bound by an oath," Atin said. "One that you appear to have broken."

"If you knew anything about the oath, you would know that it cannot be broken," Ashlynn said. "You don't know anything about magic. Tell me, who is your woman?"

"I am no one's woman," Atin's friend said, stepping forward. "I am myself, witch."

"You dare call me witch?" Ashlynn asked, standing. "I could kill all of you and your siblings in an instant. You have no idea the forces that you are dealing with. I should kill you all where you stand for what you say."

"You couldn't kill me," Atin's friend said. "You think you have powers? Try me, witch."

Ashlynn rushed forward and tried to cast magic at the woman. The woman stood stone-statue still until Ashlynn was almost on top of her. In the blink of an eye, the woman was standing behind Ashlynn. Ashlynn spun around, confused at what had happened. She rushed the woman again...in the blink of an eye, the woman was sitting on the throne. Princess Ashlynn stopped and glared at the woman.

"You have an interesting trick," Ashlynn said. "You can move in the ether, yet you don't attack. Where did you learn your powers?"

"I have my secrets as you have yours," the woman said.

"I still have yet to receive your name," Ashlynn said.

"That's because I haven't said it," the woman said. "And I don't believe that I'm going to. I think that would shorten the way between us. I believe that I've seen all that I care to see here. I have other tasks that I need to attend to."

With that, the woman disappeared from the room. Ashlynn looked around confused—upset. She walked right up to Atin and put her finger in his face.

"You will tell me right now who that woman is and where she was trained," Ashlynn commanded. "And you will also tell me what she is doing with you."

"I have never know her real name," Atin said. "Names weren't needed, nor wise when we first met. Since then we have grown together but have not had reason to exchange that information."

"You lie," Ashlynn yelled. "Why do people always lie to me? I want the answers right now. Who is that woman?"

"Get used to disappointment," Atin said. "Now tell us what we need. Give us the information that our quests require."

"I will do no such thing," Ashlynn said. "I need to figure out what's going on in Cerrado. What brings you out on these quests?"

"Surely my brother told you that," Ambriss said.

"I want to hear what your story is," Ashlynn said. "I want to hear you tell it."

"We've been sent to find items to save our father," Ambriss said. "Someone threatens his life and we are determined to save him."

"Who threatens him?" Ashlynn asked.

"That we don't know," Ambriss said. "Our Mystic Seven the Red has seen someone killing father. We will not allow that to happen. Cerrado will not fall nor will it suffer like it had in the past. Our family will hold this land until the Former King returns."

"Guards," Princess Ashlynn shouted as she returned to her throne and sat down. "Put these two in the dungeon. I want all guards to be on the lookout for the woman that was with them. If she's seen in the castle then she is to be killed."

The guards took Prince Atin and Princess Ambriss out of the throne room. Only Ashlynn and Bromas remained. Ashlynn got herself comfortable on her throne as Sir Bromas approached the throne. He stood at her side silent until she was in a position she found comfortable.

"I want those two put in a cell with the others," Ashlynn said.

"My Princess?" Sir Bromas asked, confused. "All together?"

"I want the three children," Ashlynn said. "Along with the teacher, cat, and the strange woman with them. Put them in the same cell and have a pair of guards standing nearby...listening. I want scrolls of everything that is said. They will give away their true intentions."

"You suspect that more is going on than they let on?"

"Much more," Ashlynn said. "I know who Mystic Seven the Red is. He was in Queen Mala's court. He was her most trusted necromancer."

"You think the Queen has already returned?" Sir Bromas asked. "You think that Mala is trying to take Cerrado?"

"If she is, we cannot permit her to succeed," Princess Ashlynn said. "I must kill her and destroy all of her forces before she can gain any reasonable power in Cerrado. If Mala is able to take the Cerrado Castle before anyone knows that she is back then it would be very hard to remove her from power."

"What is our play then?" Sir Bromas asked.

"First we must know everything that is going on," Princess Ashlynn said. "We must know what they know. We must also find out where the little sibling is...the sister, Arctic. We cannot have a child of Duke Asmout running around Cerrado. They must all be dead when I take the throne."

"No one will be able to stop you, Princess Ashlynn," Sir Bromas said. "No one knows that you are coming."

"They'd better not," Princess Ashlynn said. "I will be like a spring storm, appearing out of nowhere on a clear, calm day, with a power that most didn't know was possible. They will bow before me and fear me. Once they know the truth of the matter, then all will fall before me. I have laid in waiting for years. My vengeance will be swift and true. No one will ever know what happened. I will destroy them all. Cerrado will become a dark place, the way the land should look."

Princess Ashlynn stood and walked out of the throne room. Sir Bromas stood for a moment, replaying everything that had just happened, trying to remember if there was any hidden meanings or double talk in the conversations that they had. Sir Bromas knew that he had chosen the right side so many years ago, and now that all his patience and waiting was about to pay off. He knew that Princess Ashlynn was going to take Cerrado and he would be the head of the military—a military that would control Cerrado with an iron fist.

Chapter 25

Krispin and Arctic rode on the hearse as they passed through the tall grass of the Bloodgrass Plains. The narrow trail was winding, and even though they were sitting high on the bench of the hearse the pair couldn't see the horizon due to the tall grass gently swaying in the light breeze. Krispin kept the large black horses moving as fast as they would go, trying to get to the river as quickly as they could. Krispin didn't know why they needed to go to the river, but with the warnings they were given he didn't want to waste any time.

Krispin looked over to Arctic who was sitting next to him. She hadn't said a word since they had taken off on the hearse. She was looking at the grass on the plains with longing, concerned eyes. There were large plains animals—buffalos, mammoths, antelopes, and the rare Cerrado Plains Green Bears, all grazing and playing on the plains. Arctic let out a heavy sigh as she turned toward Krispin.

"Do you think that we'll ever find a unicorn horn?" Arctic asked.

"I'm sure we will," Krispin said. "Someday we will find one. Do unicorns live on these plains? Is there somewhere nearby that we could find one?"

"They keep to the Blue Cerrado Forest," Arctic said. "That's the only location we can find them. They keep to themselves and will only appear to certain people. Pure people."

"We will get there, Arctic," Krispin said. "Then we will return to the Moon Forest and tell Holly about this amazing adventure. The wedding is fast approaching though. I do hope that my parents aren't too worried about me. I wish I could get word to them that I am okay."

"How did your parents meet?" Arctic asked.

"Dad had been to university," Krispin said. "In London. They met there. I've never really heard much about it. They never talked about it. Why do you ask?"

"I love hearing about how people fell in love," Arctic said. "I've always wanted to myself. I've always hoped that some amazing prince would come and sweep me off my feet. Unfortunately, since I'm the youngest, I will be arranged to be married to someone."

"Is that how your parents were married?"

"It was," Arctic said. "They were both from prominent families, and they thought that binding them together would benefit both families. I don't know if they ever loved each other, but they were each able to tolerate the other. I want to know what falling in love feels like."

"Have you ever felt love with someone?" Krispin asked.

"There's a man that I've been having strange feelings for," Arctic said. "Sometimes I think it is love...other times I think loathing. It's a very strange feeling."

"Who's the man?" Krispin asked. "What's he like?"

"I don't want to talk about it," Arctic said.

"You were the one who brought it up," Krispin said. "What's wrong, is he ugly?"

"No," Arctic snapped. "He's handsome."

"What else?"

"I'm not talking about it," Arctic said. "You wouldn't care anyway, you're so hung up on your stupid Holly...who needs to be bought."

"I'm not buying her," Krispin protested.

"You have to prove yourself to her," Arctic laughed. "Yet, she doesn't do anything to prove her love to you. It will be a match made in heaven."

Krispin was about to respond to Arctic, trying again to make her understand how amazing Holly truly is, but they went around a bend and saw the river. The water was moving fast, and the river was very wide— over one-hundred feet between the shores. The water had a strange greenish tint to it even though it was clear.

In the water was a pack of buffalo that were wading near the shore. They were to their bellies in the water as they drank and wallowed in the cool water on the hot day. There were other smaller animals near the buffalo that were drinking and playing in the water. Krispin stopped the hearse near the water and the pair dismounted and walked along the river.

"What are we supposed to do here?" Krispin asked. "She never gave up any instructions."

"I guess we just wait," Arctic said. "There must be some reason for us to be here."

"It's already been a long day," Krispin said, with a yawn. "I think it would be best for us to get a nap in before the next part of this adventure starts. Who knows where we're going to end up next."

"I agree," Arctic said. "I guess a little sleep would do us good."

Krispin and Arctic both spread themselves out on the ground, using the soft grass as a bed. Krispin didn't know what to expect, but with what they'd already been through he knew that anything was possible. Krispin was beginning to realize that all the limits he thought he had about the world, no longer applied. Krispin's mind was racing with all the things he'd experienced and all the things that were about to come.

Krispin noticed that Arctic had fallen asleep the instant she was on the ground. Krispin was starting to take more notice of Arctic, and was thinking about how much fun they could have together once the adventure was over. Krispin couldn't figure out why he was thinking so much of her when he knew that he had to get back to Holly. Krispin figured that once the adventure was over and he was married to Holly the memory of Arctic would begin to fade away. With that though, Krispin closed his eyes and drifted into a deep sleep.

"WAKE UP!" a gruff voice boomed over Krispin.

Krispin's mind had been reeling in a dream. The shouting jarred him awake, yet his eyes hadn't opened yet. Krispin could hear many

196

people around him and could hear that the horses were agitated. Krispin slowly opened his eyes—just a slit, enough to see out of. When he looked out, his eyes opened wide and Krispin sat up, stunned at what he saw.

On the river, three large ships dropped anchor in the channel of the river. Smaller rowboats were on the shore. Krispin couldn't imagine who would be sailing ships that big on the river. He looked up at the people around him and could see pirates. There was a man the others were deferring to as he was closest to Krispin and Arctic.

"Who be ye who's sleeping by my seas?" the man said.

"I am Sir Krispin the Brave," Krispin said, as he and Arctic stood. Krispin got Arctic behind him, to protect her from the pirates. "Who are you that sneaks up on a pair of sleeping people?"

"I am Captain Creature. You take a great risk sleeping on the shores like that," Captain Creature said. "What are you doing here?"

"We are on a quest," Krispin said. "We were told to come to the waters and wait."

"Told by whom?" the captain asked.

"Cherry," Arctic said. "The Lady of the Plains."

"That's the last line," Captain Creature almost shouted. "To the ship with them."

The pirates cheered as they grabbed Krispin and Arctic. Krispin could only imagine what was about to happen to them, but he was surprised that the pirates were being relatively gentle with them as they loaded them into a rowboat and rowed them to the main—and largest— ship that was on the river. Krispin and Arctic climbed up the side of the ship, followed by the rest of the pirates.

On deck there were many more pirates cleaning the decks and working the riggings. As they were being moved toward a door that led beneath deck, Krispin noticed that Captain Creature was giving orders that the anchors be lifted and they start sailing again. Krispin and Arctic were taken to a small room that had no windows and was lit by candles. The room was dank and the air was stale. There were chairs in the room, basic and wooden—but nothing else. Captain Creature entered, whispered something to a guard that was with him, the guard left the room, and the captain closed and locked the door.

"We could have killed you out there," Captain Creature said. "You wouldn't have even known what happened."

"We are very important," Krispin said. "You kill us and you will have every knight in all of Cerrado searching for your blood."

"I've been up against worse odds," Captain Creature said. "Believe me, you are safe here and will not be hurt...I promise you that. I know who you are."

"Then you know, Captain, that I must be released," Arctic said. "There is much work to do and I cannot fail on my quest."

"That much is true," Captain Creature said. "I'm afraid, young Princess Arctic that things are much worse than you'd thought. Your siblings, Alos, Atin, Ambriss...along with Hibit, Snowflake, and a warrior named Lacey DuLake...are all prisoners of Princess Ashlynn in the Windswept Castle."

"Then we must go there and free them," Arctic said. "They have their quests and we must help them. How soon can we get there?"

"There are other plans for you, Princess Arctic," Captain Creature said. "You see, I have been watching the waters of Cerrado for many years. I know what is coming and what will be needed. There is much evil that has befallen Cerrado. Only the return of the Former King can destroy the evils that walk our lands."

"Why didn't the Former King kill Mala?" Krispin asked. "How was she allowed to stay alive? For that matter, why did the Former King leave?"

"There are rumors," Captain Creature said. "I believe that he couldn't kill Mala. She had too much magic. A normal sword will not kill a witch with her powers. The same goes for Princess Ashlynn. To destroy them, a degree of magic will be needed. I think the Former King was hurt in the battle. He was dying as well and needed to go somewhere to regain his strengths for the final battle. The war that tore Cerrado apart, never stopped."

"You know much, Captain Creature," Krispin said. "You are the Former King, correct? Hiding in plain sight?"

"No," Captain Creature said, with a hearty laugh. "I am not the Former King. I knew him well though. He was a good man that was thrown into a bad situation. He made the most of it and held Cerrado together when many would have let the darkness cover the land. The Former King will return one day...and on that day, I hope that I will be the first to bow before him."

"You've sailed these waters for many years, correct?" Arctic asked.

"Many times many," Creature said.

"How many?"

"Hundreds."

"Then you've tasted the waters of the Immortal River," Arctic said.

"I have," Captain Creature said.

"And you have a unicorn horn to keep you looking young," Arctic said.

"I do not," Captain Creature said. "When you drink the waters of the Immortal River you remain that age as long as you keep drinking a little of the magical waters every so often. A unicorn horn would make a person look younger."

Krispin looked to the captain then to Arctic. He couldn't understand everything that had gone on, but on some level, things of Cerrado seemed to be making more sense to him. Krispin was accepting what the Captain was saying—somehow knowing the captain was speaking the truth. Krispin didn't know what to make of everything, but he knew that his time in Cerrado was getting more limited by the day.

"What is our play then?" Krispin asked. "Where do we go from here?"

"You need to complete your quest, Princess Arctic," Captain Creature said. "Krispin Risdell, you need to become a proper knight. You need to learn how to fight. Both of you will have a need to protect yourselves and others very soon."

"I've never been in a fight before," Krispin said. "I've gotten beaten up…but I've never fought back."

"You will fight back now," Captain Creature said. "Come with me."

Captain Creature opened the door and exited the little room. Krispin and Arctic exchanged a glance before following the captain. They rushed through the ship and to a room near the stern on the first level below the deck. The room was large with many yellow-colored windows allowing light into the room. The room was heavily decorated with different kinds of treasure. The walls were covered with intricately woven fabric tapestries, and the floor was covered with soft rugs. Both were made of rare fabrics from the farthest corners of Cerrado.

In the middle of the room was a large crate made of hardwood. Captain Creature approached the case and opened the top. Inside was a shelf that contained over twenty different swords. Both Krispin and Arctic peeked inside the crate and looked at the swords. Krispin could see that many of the swords were made from gold or silver, encrusted with diamonds and jewels. He thought that the contents of the crate were worth more than his parent's farm.

"You will both need a sword," Captain Creature said. "These are some of the finest swords that I have. You will each pick one now and use it for training and fighting."

"Ladies first," Krispin said, motioning for Arctic to pick.

Princess Arctic looked in the crate and picked up a couple different swords—feeling their weight, looking at their features. Arctic finally decided on a shorter sword—European styled, with a blade that bore a pinkish tint, with pink jewels in the golden handle. Arctic swung the sword in the air, mocking a battle, showing that she knew a little about handling a sword.

"This is the sword that I choose," Arctic said, proudly holding the sword up.

"Interesting choice," Captain Creature said. "Why do you pick that sword?"

"It's shorter and lighter," Arctic said, looking at the sword. "I can handle it better. I don't have the strength to handle the bigger swords. This one will suit me better. Plus, it's pink and it looks like a girl's sword."

"Interesting reasoning for an interesting choice," Captain Creature said. "That sword will be very good for you. Krispin, you're next."

Krispin looked over the swords. He'd never handled a sword before in his life. Not knowing at all what made up a good sword or a poor one—Krispin lifted some of the swords, held them in his hands, and made striking motions in the air—trying to see which one felt the best. To Krispin, all the swords felt cumbersome and heavy. There was one sword that stood out to Krispin. Where most of the swords looked new and never used, there were some that had nicks and scratches. One of the older swords, a European styled sword that had a large blade and plain bronzed handle, and was decorated with an ornate blade carving of a shepherd guiding his flock. When Krispin saw that mosaic, he knew he'd found his sword.

"I choose this one," Krispin said.

"That sword is old and used," Captain Creature said. "Why do you choose that one?"

"It's basic," Krispin said. "You don't need a lot of fancy jewels or gold when you are fighting. This weapon has everything a person needs. The other reason I chose it was because of the shepherd on it."

"What does that have to do with anything?" Captain Creature asked.

"I was a shepherd when I was in my land," Krispin said. "Oh, I'm sure Holly will love this adventure...getting a sword from a pirate. There's been so much going on, and the wedding is fast approaching."

"Wedding?" Captain Creature asked. "What wedding?"

"I came on this adventure to win the heart of the woman of my dreams," Krispin said. "She said she would marry me if I had an amazing adventure."

"That doesn't sound like love at all," Captain Creature said. "That sounds like a very stupid reason to get married...an adventure."

"Thank you!" Arctic screeched. "That's what I've been telling him since I met him."

"So, what is this little strumpet doing to prove her love to you?" Captain Creature asked.

"She doesn't need to do anything," Krispin said. "I know that once I explain this adventure, she'll love me for sure. Holly doesn't need to do anything."

"I wish you the best, but you are in for a huge surprise," Captain Creature said, as he took a large silver sword from the crate. "Now, Krispin...let's see what you can do."

Captain Creature and Krispin moved to the middle of the room, both pointing their swords at the other. Krispin was almost shaking because he was so scared. Captain Creature was so big and intimidating— a fierce pirate, hundreds of years old—and Krispin was supposed to stand against him in a sword fight. Creature motioned for Krispin to attack. Krispin took a deep breath and moved forward, swinging. It only took Creature two motions to have the sword out of Krispin's hand and have Krispin on his back.

"I told you I have no fighting experience," Krispin said, as Arctic helped him up. Krispin picked up his sword. "It would take forever to get me proficient enough with this sword to be ready for a fight. We don't have that kind of time."

"We will have plenty of time, Krispin," Captain Creature said, as he picked up a water goblet and poured the water on the ground. "Now, Princess Arctic...let's get someone here to test your swordplay abilities."

There was a breeze in the room, and from the puddle of water, Jade appeared. Jade smiled as she silently took her green leather jacket off and drew her sword. Arctic looked at Jade with massive eyes. Arctic thought that she knew who the strange, green-haired woman was, but she couldn't be sure. Jade pointed her sword at Arctic as Arctic raised hers. The women engaged quickly—Jade dictating the pace. Arctic was able to keep up with Jade but Jade was not engaging with full power. After a minute of fencing around the room, Jade pushed Arctic to the corner and disarmed her.

"You must be Jade," Arctic said, with her hands in the air and her back against the wall. "The Lady of the Waters. It was an honor to cross blades with you."

"You know your history well," Jade said, sheathing her sword and bowing to Princess Arctic. "I participated in the wars of the past, fighting alongside Captain Creature. You have talent. You've practiced with a sword before."

"Growing up in the castle," Arctic said, picking her sword up. "I was instructed on defense, along with my normal education."

"Instructed by people who knew that if they so much as scratched you they would be beheaded," Captain Creature said. "They went very easy on you."

"No, they didn't," Arctic protested. "They drew blood on more than one occasion. Father told them that my ability to defend myself was more important than avoiding a few training room cuts."

"Your father is a smarter man than I gave him credit for," Captain Creature said.

"I can work with her," Jade said. "What about the boy?"

"He needs more work," Creature said. "He needs much more work than Princess Arctic does. I think that there's only one man that can train him fast enough."

"I know who you are thinking about," Jade said. "I don't know if he's willing to do it...or if he's even that good anymore."

"In the day, he was the best swordsmen in all the lands," Captain Creature said. "There wasn't another person that could stand with him in swordplay."

"But his mind has been lost to wine," Jade said. "I can train the boy."

"You could train him," Captain Creature said. "But then who will train the girl?"

"I can train them both," Jade said.

"If we had more time then I would agree with you," Captain Creature said. "But we don't have that kind of time. You will train the girl and I will call on him for the boy."

"He won't help," Jade said, as Captain Creature took a jar of sand and dumped it on the floor.

"Your parents made it clear that he had to," Captain Creature said.

"I don't know if he's going to listen to them," Jade said.

Krispin looked at the sand that was dumped on the floor. He couldn't understand why the captain would dirty the floor. Krispin still didn't understand why they were going to be trained to fight. As he wondered, a man appeared in the room, right above the spilled sand. The man was tall and fit, with long cinnamon-colored hair that matched his extravagant three-piece suit. The man held a goblet full of wine and looked disappointed with where he was.

"So, this is where you spend your days, Sister," the man said, looking at Jade. "So drab."

"Cinnamon," Jade said. "Brother. We need your help. You were the greatest sword fighter in all of Cerrado at one time."

"I still am," Cinnamon said. "Not even you, Jade, could stand against me. You and your fancy sword fighting and the muscular body you've developed these past decades. I still could defeat you."

"I've no doubt of that," Jade said. "But we need that skill today. I am going to train the girl. I will teach her to be a master with the sword. You need to teach the boy. He needs to be an expert. He needs to know everything there is to know about sword fighting, and you have less than a week to teach him."

"Not interested," Cinnamon said, looking over Krispin. "I will spend some time with the girl though. She looks like she would be very fun to play with."

"You will do no such thing," Jade said. "You will train the boy. Remember what Mother and Father said."

"I'll challenge you for it," Cinnamon said. "Sword fight. You win, I'll train the boy...I win, you train the boy and I get the girl."

"I told you he couldn't do it," Captain Creature said, with a smile. "I told you your brother wasn't the sword master that he used to be."

"I am twice the sword master that I was," Cinnamon shot back. "You don't know what you're talking about, old man. I could destroy you and Jade together."

"Prove it," Jade said. "Prove you are the best. Train this boy so that he's as good as you. If you are the best in the world then you can train him to be the second best."

"I'll make a deal with you," Cinnamon said. "I'll train him and you train the girl. Once they are trained, they will fight. If he wins, then the girl is mine..."

"And if the girl wins," Jade interrupted. "You never touch wine again. You clean up and remain sober."

"You think I would wager my wine on that?" Cinnamon asked.

"If you're scared I would understand," Jade said.

Cinnamon stared at his sister. He knew that she was plotting something. Cinnamon remembered back to all the sword fights that he'd had in his life. There were so many that he couldn't even remember most of them. Cinnamon knew that he hadn't practiced his swordplay in such a long time and he knew his sister was a tricky one that making that bet would surely lead to defeat. Cinnamon realized that his sister had already trapped him—she'd already won the first battle of wits. Cinnamon knew that he had to concede this round and plan for the next. He'd promised his parents that he would help, but he would do it on his own terms.

"Let's try something else," Cinnamon said. "I'll train the boy, you train the girl. In exchange for this training you tell our parents that I have fulfilled my bargain with them...I helped protect Cerrado. This will be the last thing that I do for them. After this I live my life on my terms and I'm not bothered with matters like this again."

"If he wins, then those terms will be honored," Jade said. "Take the boy and train him."

"Come along, lad," Cinnamon said. "We will go to the main deck. I will make you a master of swordplay in less than a week."

Cinnamon and Krispin walked out of the room. Jade smiled as she looked over Arctic. Jade knew that Arctic was about to face a great trial and she wanted the little princess to be ready.

"I promise you this, Arctic," Jade said. "I will help you as much as I can…but there will come a point where you and Krispin are on your own."

Jade raised her sword toward Arctic as Arctic did the same. The women bowed to each other before they started to fence. Captain Creature watched as Jade started giving Arctic pointers on how to handle the sword, how to parry, how to defend, and how to move her feet and position her body. Arctic was enjoying the work and was picking up Jade's advice quickly. Captain Creature breathed a sigh of relief. He knew that after so many years of planning, things were starting to come together.

Chapter 26

Prince Atin and Princess Ambriss were thrown into a dank cell in the dungeon. Both looked over their situation, but before either had a chance to speak, Hibit, Snowflake, and Lacey DuLake were shoved into the cell with them. Ambriss quickly hugged Snowflake who seemed indifferent to the current situation—nudging Ambriss in the way she did when she wanted food. Ambriss petted the cat quickly then stood. She was about to speak when the cell door opened again and Prince Alos was thrown into the cell, landing with a resounding thud on the stone floor.

Alos remained on the ground—topless, in his blue and white pants. He'd been stripped of his sword and daggers, looking almost completely destroyed. He tried to lift himself up to his hands and knees but didn't have the strength. Prince Atin and Hibit rushed to him and lifted him to a sitting position. Prince Alos looked over the cell with despair.

"Then we've all failed our father," Alos said. "Cerrado will be lost to the evil that has befallen our family."

"Don't be so sure of that," Ambriss said. "Arctic is still out there. Still able to fight."

"You've seen the youngest daughter?" Hibit asked, hopeful. "She's still alive and doing well in Cerrado?"

"We saw her right before we were brought here," Ambriss said. "Prince Atin and I had infiltrated the bandits. We were given the task to transport two prisoners from Raven's Head to Yorehill Manor. We put Arctic and a boy into a casket and loaded it into a hearse. We met with Cherry, the lady of the plains and she brought us here. That was the last we saw of Arctic."

"We were brought here by Jade," Hibit said. "The lady of the waters. Isn't that right, Snowflake?"

Snowflake nodded before yawning and laying down—nestling her body at Prince Alos's feet.

"What happened?" Ambriss asked. "How did you lose Arctic, and who is this lady with you?"

"We believe that Arctic stepped through an arch," Hibit said. "I lost her. All the evidence points to an arch. I didn't know what happened but this warrior offered to help me."

"I am Lacey DuLake," Lacey said, interrupting. "I am a knight in waiting. I was taken prisoner by Queen Mala and her servant, Mystic Seven the Red. I'm sorry, but Mystic Seven is working for the Queen. You never stood a chance. He played your father, but I am here to help you. I will lay down my life to help defeat Mala and her evil plans." Lacey bowed on one knee. "I am yours to command my Princes and Princess. Please, tell me how I can serve you."

"Rise up, Lacey DuLake," Princess Ambriss said. "You will have your opportunity to fight for us and become a knight in our service. The first thing we must do is determine how to defeat Mala."

"We should be more concerned with defeating her older sister," Prince Atin said. "Her older sister is much more powerful than Mala is."

"Older sister?" Alos asked.

"What do you mean, Brother?" Princess Ambriss asked. "Tala and Bala were both killed by Mala. We know that. There wasn't another sister. Mala killed her parents and sisters to take the throne."

"Just as the Former King didn't finish the job with Mala," Atin said. "Mala didn't finish the job with Bala."

"Princess Ashlynn," Prince Alos said, still holding his side in pain. "She's...Bala?"

"Yes."

"How do you know this brother?" Ambriss asked.

"Remember when I commented on the oath that Ashlynn had broken?" Prince Atin asked.

"Yes."

"Ashlynn said if I knew anything about magic, I knew that the oath couldn't be broken," Prince Atin said. "She gave herself away. All trainers keep records of who they train and what methods are used. They are all required to give this information to the necromancer elders. This system keeps any one necromancer from getting too powerful. They can keep tabs on each other. There is an oath among them. When Ashlynn said she'd not broken the oath, it confirmed that her name had to be on those scrolls. There is no Princess Ashlynn on those scrolls."

"You do not practice necromancy, Brother," Prince Alos said. "How do you know so much about these things?"

"Some of the women that I associate with, do practice," Atin said. "They keep me informed. This is an interesting play. Mala kills her parents, and the Former King must take the throne until Tala is of age. Tala and Bala are killed, and Mala takes the throne. The Former King fights Mala and defeats her to prevent her cruelty to rule the whole of Cerrado. Now we find out that both Mala and Bala have survived. I knew that these two were powerful, but I never knew they were this powerful."

"What is our play then?" Ambriss asked. "How do we handle the situation, knowing what we know now? If Ashlynn is Bala, then we can be certain that war is on the horizon. The sisters will never be able to find a peace between them."

"I fear that we will be used as the bait in a trap, to draw Mala out into the open," Alos said. "That is the only reason that Bala would keep us alive. My question is, how come she looks so young? Bala should be over forty but she looks half that age."

"There could be any number of powers at work," Atin said. "We don't know what magic she's been playing with."

"What are we to do then?" Lacey asked.

"We need to formulate a plan," Alos said. "But before we figure out that…we need to know whose side the Nature Watchers are on. I can't figure out why they would be getting involved. Why would they bring all of us here?"

"I could see that Jade, the Lady of the Waters, helping us," Ambriss said. "I've heard very good things about her. It's rumored that she's romantically linked to Captain Creature. That she sails the waters of many worlds with him. The big question is the Lady of the Plains. Cherry. I've heard how she spends her time and where her interests lie. I don't understand why she would be involved at all. It's so out of character for her."

"I'm sure their parents had something to do with it," Atin said. "I've spoken with their father a number of times and he's been upset with the way his children have been acting. There have been...complaints."

"You've been in contact with Father Time?" Ambriss asked. "Who aren't you in contact with?"

"I have many contacts throughout Cerrado," Atin said. "From what they've told me, there is much upset within Cerrado. Many people can't figure out why the Former King left. And they don't fully understand why Father was made the duke. Our father is a good man...wise and just. But wise and just doesn't make you a good leader. You need to be able to rule, and command those in your stead, and fend off those that don't agree with you. Father makes the mistake of believing that he can please everyone. That's simply not possible. Alos would be good as a leader."

"And I'm sure you think you'd be better?" Ambriss asked.

"No," Atin said. "There are reasons why I wouldn't want the top spot. I do much better in different capacity. We've seen the girls get involved, I wonder where their brothers are?"

"Cinnamon, the Man of the Sands," Ambriss said. "Cobalt, the Man of the Woods. I have seen neither in my travels."

"Neither have I," Alos said. "Princess Ambriss, what happened to your riders?"

"They are searching for the river on their own," Ambriss said. "When we decided to go with the bandits, I parted ways with them. January and Rose were leading them. I haven't heard from them in a long time. I instructed them to not sent word unless they had found something. I didn't want to risk an interception of messages."

"So they are out in the kingdom," Alos said. "That's good. We may have to get word to them to get us out of here. Atin, Brother, what about your women?"

"Women?" Atin asked. "I have only one woman that travels with me. The others were men."

"Really?" Alos asked with a smile.

"I've never seen a woman grow a beard as thick and healthy as my men have," Atin said. "The others in my group are men, Brother."

"I've seen the others in your group, Brother," Alos said. "Instead of your group, maybe we should call them your harem. I'm sure they could do some amazing things. I can tell by the way they walk…the look in their eyes. You can pad them out to look like barrel-chested muscular men, and paste beards onto their faces, but that does not make them men. Brother, I know they are women."

"Very well," Atin conceded. "Have you ever spent time with them?"

"No, I haven't."

"Good," Atin said. "They are in the castle, monitoring everything that is going on there. We will know everything when my closest companion returns."

"What is her name?" Alos asked. "I know that you are in love with her. I would like very much to know her name."

"Why does everyone keep saying that?" Atin asked. "We are not in love. I do not fall in love like some playful puppy. We have a relationship, yes. Love has nothing to do with it."

"As you say," Alos said. "The biggest question is how do we get out of here? We must get away from Bala and save our land."

"I have information coming to us, Brother," Atin said. "Very soon we shall know what is going on."

As Atin finished speaking, almost as if on cue, his friend walked in front of the cell door. She was carrying a sword that was dripping red with blood. The woman was breathing heavily, with beads of sweat coming down her body. She had a twisted smile on her face as she used a strip of brown animal hide to wipe her sword down before sheathing it. The woman walked to the bars of the cell where Atin walked to her, kissing the woman between the bars of the cell.

"Tell me," Atin said, to his companion. What news have you discovered?"

"There is treachery at the castle," the woman said. "Queen Mala has your father prisoner. She has been forcing him to address the population, telling them that everything is fine, quelling the rumors that you fled the castle in fear...rumors that Mala has had her agents spreading."

"Are the people remaining loyal?" Atin asked. "Is there any agitation within the populace?"

"The people remain calm for now," the woman said. "Our other friends that remain in the castle, have made themselves known to Mala, but only to distract her. Mystic Seven has been led on a merry wild goose chase. They know who they work for but have yet to figure out what they are doing."

"Have you seen any sign of my riders?" Ambriss asked. "What has become of my women?"

"They are still riding," the woman said. "They are searching and are in danger. The trouble they run into isn't as critical as what you are in now."

"What about Arctic?" Atin asked. "Where is our little sister?"

"From the information that I could gather," the woman said, "Arctic and the man with her are headed for a river and are on an intercept course with Captain Creature and his ships. This makes sense since Jade has been linked to the Captain. She could have had Cherry send them there. I know Captain Creature. He is a good man."

"He's a pirate," Ambriss protested. "The rumors of his murder and pillaging spread throughout the land. I wouldn't want little Arctic to end up on one of his ships."

"There is a lot of talk about the captain," Atin said. "But yet we could never find one village that had been sacked, never found one person that had been ransomed, never found anything to confirm those stories. Captain Creature has a fierce reputation and he seems to protect it, but I don't believe that he's the monster that those stories make him out to be."

"But if he has Arctic, what will he do with her?" Ambriss asked.

"It seems the Nature Watcher wants him to have her," Alos said. "At this point there's very little that we can do about it. Friend, do you think that you can distract the guards long enough for us to make an escape from this pit?"

"The guards are all dead," the woman said. "I made sure of that. They are not the problem. The problem is that all the hallways of this castle are guarded with magic. Bala would know if this group was trying to escape. Even if we took separate ways she would be able to sense it. I know how to throw her feelings off so I can move around but there's too many of you that don't know."

"I can handle myself with a sword as well as anyone here," Lacey said. "I can defend myself. I can take Hibit and the cat with me."

"I don't think that's the best idea," Hibit said. "We should wait."

"Wait for what?" Lacey asked.

"What do we have here?" a male voice boomed from behind the woman.

The woman turned to see four massive men—fully armored knights—standing with their swords drawn and pointed right at her. The woman didn't draw her sword immediately. She looked them over, sizing them up, but decided to not press her luck. The woman dropped her sheath as the knights opened the cell and threw her in. The woman hit the stone floor as the knights locked the door. Atin helped his woman up and checked her over.

"Are you hurt?" Atin asked.

"I've been thrown to the ground harder than that," the woman replied. "I'm going to slit their throats in the night before this is over. Mark my words, all four of them will die by my hands."

"When the time is right," Atin said. "For now, we need to wait. There's nothing we can do here. It doesn't look like we'll be able to get away anytime soon."

The group all breathed heavy sighs, fearful of what was happening to their kingdom. Atin knew that Arctic was inexperienced and scared— out in Cerrado, with no one she knew to guide her. Atin and the others could only hope that Arctic would have better luck than they had, and that Arctic would be able to save Cerrado. Everyone sat down in the cell and waited for something to happen.

Chapter 27

The Cerrado Castle was shimmering in the midday's sun. The day was warm and there was a hustle and bustle by the people who were going about their day in the courtyard. No one could have imaged the destruction that was coming to Cerrado. Destruction that was being brought about by the people who were in the throne room of their very castle. No one had yet to even imagine that Queen Mala was once again sitting on the Honor Throne.

In the Cerrado Castle throne room, Mala had taken her place on the Honor Throne. She had complete control of the Cerrado Castle, and Duke Asmout. The duke was in bindings, standing in front of her, while Mystic Seven the Red was looking into his divination ball. Mala was drinking from a golden goblet—the goblet that was reserved for the queen of Cerrado.

As Mala waited for Mystic Seven the Red to finish his divinations, the Nature Watcher—Cherry, the Lady of the Plains—appeared in the room. She was smiling as she ran her hands through her cherry-colored hair. Cherry approached Queen Mala, but she did not bow or make any formal greetings. Queen Mala had expected a greeting but got none as Cherry spoke.

"The deeds you have requested that I do have been done," Cherry said, casually, almost disregardful of the powerful queen sitting before her. "I have trapped almost all the children in the dungeons at the Windswept Castle. I convinced my sister Jade...the Lady of the Water...that we needed to get the others there to save Prince Alos, so she brought some of the helpers. They are all there. The youngest and her knight are with Jade on her beau's ship. They are teaching them how to handle a sword."

"Do they pose any threat to us?" Queen Mala asked.

"They are learning fencing from Jade and Cinnamon," Cherry said. "I doubt that they will learn anything useful. It will be a fool's errand. There are bigger concerns that we need to address though."

"Princess Ashlynn," Queen Mala said. "Why haven't I been able to see her? Why don't I know who trained her or where this little brat came from?"

"She's older than you are," Cherry said. "She's older by four years."

"Older than I am?"

"She is your older sister, Bala," Cherry said.

"Impossible," Mala said. "I killed my sister. There's no way that she could have returned to us. I want everyone in that castle dead."

"She is your sister," Mystic Seven the Red said. "There's no way to deny it. Bala would be the only person who could have developed the powers that Princess Ashlynn is rumored to have. We knew that this was a possibility that we would have to deal with."

"My sisters are dead," Mala said. "I killed them both myself."

"You can deny it all you want, but that doesn't change the fact that you failed in the past," Cherry said, uncouthly. "Bala was able to survive and she is in a position to challenge you at every turn. There's nothing that you can do to prevent her. She's become so powerful that you are now the only person who could kill her. A normal sword piercing her heart wouldn't be enough. Remember, she's had as much time as you had to rebuild herself. There's no telling how powerful she's become. We must deal with her before we take Cerrado, or there could be a civil war that would destroy everything."

"First thing, Nature Watcher," Mala said, standing and stepping up to Cherry's face. "There is no we. You betrayed your parents and family to serve me. You serve me. You are not partners or equals with me. I don't want you assuming that you are on my level. Do you understand?"

"I do," Cherry said.

"No, you don't," Mala said. "You will address me as 'my Queen'. Now, let's try this again...do you understand me?"

"I do, my Queen," Cherry said, mockingly bowing toward Mala. "Is there anything else you would like me to do? Any jobs that you can't handle that you want to place on my shoulders? Is there any way that I can serve you better? Or perhaps…"

Cherry took a couple small steps forward and moved her lips toward Mala's. Mala let Cherry get very close before Mala slapped Cherry so hard that Cherry fell to the ground, looking up with a quivering bottom lip and tears in her eyes. Mala took a step back and let Cherry get to her feet.

"That was a warning," Mala said. "If you persist in mocking me I will consider you a traitor like the rest of your slob family. I will kill you like I am going to kill them. Make no mistake little Nature Watcher. You have no power here."

"Your empire is off to a wonderful start," Duke Asmout said. "No one respects you, and you have more enemies than you ever thought possible."

"Silence," Queen Mala shouted. "I will not be subverted like this. No one can stand in front of me. Cherry, you will kill your siblings. Duke Asmout, you will watch your children die before I kill you. There will be nothing that can stand in our way. Mystic Seven has seen all. Cherry, explain to me again why you sided with me…betraying your family and everything that they stand for."

"They tried to take my life from me," Cherry said. "First, they made me guard the plains. I could think of nothing more boring. I was spending my time attending the most wonderful parties and playing with the most interesting people before I have to go out to these grasslands and wander to help people. Yuck. I hated it. Then, if that wasn't bad enough, I got called to help with this situation. Jade wants to get involved in the affairs of man and help them out. Let her do it, but our parents say that I have to work. Well, I don't want to. I came to you to spite them. I will make their plans fail for trying to make me work. This is my revenge to them."

"How profound," Mala said. "Cherry, take Duke Asmout to the dungeon and wait there for my orders."

"Of course, my Queen," Cherry said, with a curt bow.

Cherry grabbed the chains of the bindings that were holding Duke Asmout and started to guide him out of the room. Mala and Mystic Seven watched as they exited the room. Mala looked over the throne room, looking for more of the women that had been tormenting them throughout the castle. Mala motioned for her mystic to get closer to her so they could speak with hushed voices.

"Have there been any more sightings of the women in my castle?" Mala asked.

"They have been seen everywhere," Mystic Seven the Red said. "We haven't been able to catch them. We still don't know exactly who they are, but we are quite certain that they were the ones who were dressed as men with Prince Atin. We do not know how much information they have obtained."

"This is not acceptable Mystic Seven," Mala said. "Use every art available to you and tell me what they know. We must be able to stand against them."

"I have been trying everything that I have," Mystic Seven said. "They are...protected."

"Protected?"

"I cannot explain it," Mystic Seven said. "I've never come up against something like this. They are powerful and have a very peculiar defense. I believe that they are sending information about what's going on here to Prince Atin, although I haven't been able to figure out how they are getting the information out. We've seen nothing to indicate spies moving information on the roads or rivers. We are blind to them."

"If we are blind to them, there is only one possibility as to who these women are," Mala said. "Just as I was blind to my sister, Bala...they must be Bala's daughters. Is it possible that they survived as well?"

"Anything is possible," Mystic Seven said. "I was taken aback when I heard about Bala, so it is possible that her daughters are out there...somewhere. What do we know about them?"

"She had at least three daughters," Mala said. "I've often suspected that Atin's main woman was Bala's oldest daughter, April. When I killed Bala, two of her daughters were with her. I know they died. I was certain they died. They were the younger two. April was in the lands of Cerrado somewhere. I sent huntsmen out to find her and they brought back the hearts of four women, all of whom thought that they had the heart of April."

"Then we don't know for certain if she ever died?" Mystic Seven said.

"Not for certain," Mala sighed. "There was a time when we were growing up that I remember. Bala was around fourteen and I was about ten. It was during that summer she was spending a lot of time with a boy. They were together all the time. She was sent away to a private school for about a year. The boy was to become her husband, but I took care of him when I took care of her. It was about a year after they returned that she had April. There could be a daughter that's even older that we don't know about."

"That would be horrible," Mystic Seven said. "We don't even know how many there are or if any of them survived. If they are the women with Prince Atin, do you think they are working with their mother or are they on their own?"

"All actions indicate that they are aligned with Prince Atin and his family," Queen Mala said. "We need to capture one of them and find out for sure who they are. If they are the daughters of my sister then we have to kill them at once. I want those women found and questioned. They may even know if there is an older sister. We have to know for sure what we are looking at."

"We will, my Queen," Mystic Seven said. "These women will not have an advantage over us...as for Princess Ashlynn, Bala, what is our move?"

"We have to destroy her before she has her plans in place," Mala said. "Gather our troops. We will march on the Windswept Castle and draw her forces out. They will be confused that the attack is coming this early. They won't be prepared. Our troops will defeat hers while I kill her. Properly this time. Our best weapon will be the element of surprise. She will not be ready for the attack."

"Our troops will be readied at once," Mystic Seven said. "And the Duke? What are we going to do with him?"

"He will stay in the dungeon until we kill him," Bala said.

"There's one other contingency, my Queen," Mystic Seven the Red said. "You survived your killing, Bala survived her killing, there's a possibility that Bala's daughters survived…"

"State your mind plainly," Mala barked.

"I was looking into the divination ball," Mystic Seven said. "I couldn't confirm or deny either possibility. What if Tala, your eldest sister, survived as well?"

"I thought that's what you were getting at," Mala said. "If she has survived then we will find her and kill her as well. I don't care how much of this land we have to search, we will find and kill them if they have been left alive. Take the Nature Watcher and find out for sure."

Mystic Seven the Red and Cherry stood in the middle of a massive graveyard set in the middle of a forest. The pair had used Cherry's ability to quickly travel to get to the location, hundreds of miles from the Cerrado Castle. The sky was dark at the cemetery. The trees surrounding it were dark, gnarled, and twisted. There were animals that stalked the pair on the outside of the rusted old fence that separated the burial ground from the darkened forest.

The pair was accompanied by multiple guards who were in the process of digging up four different graves. He knew that three were the daughters of Bala, and one was Bala herself. He still didn't rule out that there was a fourth daughter somewhere out there. But here in this graveyard, were the graves for April, May, and June. The guards started to hit the wooden caskets—one by one, slowly pulling each pine box out of the ground.

When all four boxes were out, Mystic Seven the Red opened each casket, one at a time. It didn't surprise him at all that each one of the boxes were empty. The turn of events was expected. This only served to confirm what he'd suspected.

"They have a leg up on us," Mystic Seven said. "They must have many powers if we weren't able to see this coming."

"They were planning this from a very early time," Cherry said.

"What do you mean?" Mystic Seven asked.

"I remember my parents talking about this," Cherry said. "They said that Captain Creature was getting involved. This is when he met Jade. The Captain found a strange boy and he used that boy to protect the Former King. Jade took a liking to Creature and they have been together ever since."

"What do these girls have to do with the Former King?" Mystic Seven asked.

"I don't know," Cherry said. "I know that my parents promised protection to certain people. And it was my parents...well, mother, specifically, who set some of these things in motion. I never received more information than that. They didn't really trust me at the time. They still don't, and it's a good thing. If I knew more of the information I would share it with you."

"Who is Captain Creature?" Mystic Seven asked.

"I don't know," Cherry said. "I know that he's very old though. He has very strange maps. Maps that show him things that other people don't know."

"He has the maps of all the arches in Cerrado," Mystic Seven said. "I've heard that before. I would say that he's the Former King, but he's been around too long. I would bet that he knows who the king is. We need to kill Captain Creature."

"Can I do it?" Cherry asked.

"You freely offer?"

"I've seen him and wanted him," Cherry said. "But he ignored me and chose my dopy, do-everything sister. I want to hurt both of them. I will kill them both."

"Very well," Mystic Seven said. "Take me back to the Cerrado Castle and I will inform Queen Mala on the situation as you go and take care of Captain Creature and your sister."

Cherry smiled and took Mystic Seven by the arm as the pair disappeared from the cemetery, leaving the guards to rebury the graves and to find their own way home.

Chapter 28

The three ships towered over everything along the river banks, sailing swiftly in the currents of the crystal clear waters. All the animals that were along the river took notice of the ships coming. When they were close, the animals would rush and hide, fearing the strange floating monsters were invading their space. Captain Creature rarely took his ships down the narrower rivers of Cerrado, preferring to stay out on the seas and greater lakes.

On the deck of The Lynx there was a massive swordfight going on. Cinnamon, still looking suave in his cinnamon-colored three-piece suit was in fast action with Krispin. Krispin had gotten himself clean up from all the dank dungeons he'd been in, and was wearing green trousers. He was battling it out with the Nature Watcher. Krispin's exposed upper body was drenched in sweat, and was starting to show the muscle he'd been developing since his adventure started. When Krispin had cleaned up the first time on Captain Creature's ships, he'd hardly recognized his body— having developed so much. Krispin was certain that Holly would love it.

The pair continued to lunge and parry, quarte and riposte, pouring every ounce of strength they had into the fight. They were moving all over the deck as Captain Creature and some of his pirates watched from an upper deck. The pirates were making comments, amazed at how good Krispin had become in such a short time. Krispin loved practicing with Cinnamon and felt that he was becoming very adept with the blade. As Creature watched, Jade walked up behind him, placing her hand on his shoulder.

"He's very impressive," Jade said, watching intently.

"I've never seen someone take to fencing this fast," Captain Creature said. "He has an intuitive sense of how to handle that sword. He has the nuances of fighting that take years of practice to develop. I'm very impressed."

"Does this mean that he's ready to fight for the girl?" Jade asked. "Do you think he's ready to defend her in Cerrado?"

"He's been defending her all along," Captain Creature said. "Most wouldn't have lasted as long as they did with all the troubles they went through. I must say, his devotion to get back to this friend of his is quite impressive."

"Cerrado will need him though," Jade said. "We can't let him go back."

"He has a family there, Jade," Captain Creature said. "He has a life there. One day he will have to make a choice. I can only hope that he makes the choice that we all want him to make."

"But we can't tell him that, can we?"

"No," Captain Creature said. "How's the girl? Can she handle a sword now?"

"HOLD," Jade shouted to Krispin and Cinnamon. "Men, take a break. I need to demonstrate Princess Arctic's skill with a blade. Pirate, get the princess and tell her to be on deck for an exhibition."

One of the pirates rushed into the ship while Krispin and Cinnamon sheathed their swords and walked up the stairs to stand beside Captain Creature. Krispin used a towel to wipe the sweat off his face and chest before drinking from a bucket of water. Cinnamon only took a small drink of water—barely a gulp, before pouring wine in his goblet and sipping.

Jade took to the deck of the ship, removing her leather jacket and hanging it on a post. Using a strip of green cloth, she bound her hair into a ponytail before she looked over her knives and the fighting floor. Jade stretched for a moment before a door opened and Princess Arctic walked onto the deck.

The princess's body was wrapped in a fine cloth robe, white with blue markings that extended from her neck to her feet. Arctic had her blonde locks up, bound and decorated with gold rings befitting a princess, not someone who was about to enter a swordfight. Princess Arctic slowly untied the belt around the robe and let the robe gently slide open before she quickly took the robe off and hung it on the same post as Jade's jacket.

When Arctic turned around so Krispin could see her face, Krispin felt a flutter in his heart. Like him, Arctic had cleaned up from the dungeons and Jade had given her fine lotions so that her skin glowed and radiated beauty. Arctic had on white fine fur boots that went to her knees with a gray wrapped dress that clung tight to her body from the top of her chest to the tops of her thighs. Both the boots and the dress were decorated with black and blue markings.

Krispin could only stare. For the first time since he'd gotten to Cerrado, he was only thinking of Princess Arctic. Holly was nowhere in his mind. For the first time since his adventure with her had started, Krispin wasn't looking at Arctic like she was an annoying little sister, but a woman. A woman who was independent, strong, and intelligent. Krispin realized that Arctic was looking at him. She was smiling, knowing exactly what he was thinking.

Arctic pulled her sword from its sheath and began circling around Jade, who held a dagger in each hand. The women bowed to each other in the customary fashion of a friendly dual. Once the formalities were out of the way, both women began to circle—crouched down to lessen the exposed body area, and moved quickly, but with a set pattern.

Jade let Arctic come in for the first attack. Jade quickly and easily defended it. Arctic backed up and twirled her sword in her hand, realizing that Jade wasn't going to be going easy on her today. Jade rushed in, feigning to the left, but striking toward the right. Arctic didn't realize the sneak attack, but was quick enough to defend. The pair started circling again.

Captain Creature watched Princess Arctic intently. He knew that she'd had some training with weapons in that castle but only as much as was necessary to defend herself for a short time. The duke had believed that she would always have guards and escorts around her. As the clanging of the daggers on the sword filled the air, Captain Creature could tell that Arctic was ready.

As the women fought all over the deck, their blades shimmering in the daylight, their bodies becoming cover in sweat, the ships sailed on down the river. The women fought and fought, Princess Arctic having an answer for everything Jade was trying with her. Jade wasn't fighting at full power, but the fight was very intense nonetheless.

After a full ten minutes of fighting, Jade made the motion for them to stop. She bowed to Princess Arctic to signify that the match was over. Arctic bowed back and sheathed her sword. Both of the women walked toward the deck where Captain Creature and Krispin were standing. They stopped just below the men.

"Captain Creature," Jade called out. "Do you approve of my training?"

"Princess Arctic looks to be very adept with her sword," Captain Creature replied. "I am very impressed with you, Princess Arctic."

"I'm impressed as well," Krispin said. "Good job, Arctic."

Princess Arctic beamed with pride. "Thank you. I was nervous that I wasn't going to meet your standards, Captain Creature."

"You did a wonderful job," Captain Creature said. "Now, everyone gather in my chambers. We have to discuss what is coming next."

The captain turned and made his way into the ship. Jade did the same, not bothering to grab her leather jacket. Krispin looked over Arctic, who was looking back at him. Their eyes met and were locked for a moment before they both followed into the ship.

Captain Creature was looking over a map of Cerrado that was focusing on the area around the Cerrado Castle and the Blue Cerrado Forest. He was looking at the rivers that ran between them. The waterways had strange marks on them that Krispin couldn't identify. The marks looked like two trees leaning over the rivers.

Jade had poured goblets of water for herself and Arctic. The women tapped their glasses together before drinking. Krispin couldn't help but notice how much more mature Arctic seemed now. How she seemed to be glowing and had a power about herself. She didn't look like that helpless lost person he'd first encountered in the forest.

Krispin had yet to put a top on. Although the water she was drinking felt so refreshing going down her throat, Arctic couldn't help but look at Krispin's muscular chest. He'd been working extensively with

226

Cinnamon—and the training was paying off. Arctic thought the pair of them together could handle anything that came their way.

"Now we are going to head to the Blue Cerrado Forest," Captain Creature said.

"That will take a long time to get to," Princess Arctic said.

"Don't be so certain of that," Captain Creature said, as three mast bolts of lightning illuminated the bright day and three cracks of thunder rocked the ships. "Once we get to the forest you two will disembark the ship and go into the woods. There you will find your unicorn horn, Princess Arctic."

"I am ready for my quest," Princess Arctic said. "I know that with Sir Krispin the Brave by my side, I can achieve anything."

"I believe, Princess Arctic, that you could achieve anything on your own," Jade said. "With Krispin by your side you could rule any world that you choose."

"I am ready," Princess Arctic said.

"I am ready as well," Krispin said. "I do not fear anything. I know now that we have within ourselves the ability to handle anything that comes our way."

"That's good, Krispin," Captain Creature said. "Because there is a war coming. The whole of Cerrado could be torn in two. The evil Queen Mala will stop at nothing to rule here again, bringing about a horrible winter of destruction that will forever scar Cerrado in ways you can't possibly imagine."

"There is another force," Jade said. "Something that wants to control Cerrado. If these two forces collide, then there's a hope that they will eliminate each other. If one of them survives, then there will be nothing to stop them."

"The Former King will return," Krispin said. "He will help us. I have a feeling that once we obtain the unicorn horn, Princess Arctic and I are going on a quest to retrieve him, correct? Is that the real mission that you've been training us for?"

"You are perceptive," Captain Creature said.

"And once the Former King returns," Princess Arctic said. "He will lead his armies to defeat all the evils that walk in Cerrado."

"That would be the hope," Jade said. "We have waited a long time for his return. There has been much speculation as to why he left, where he went, what happened to him."

"You don't know?" Krispin asked.

"Unfortunately, no," Jade said. "We have an idea, but he didn't tell us everything that was going on. We failed that day. We assumed that he had killed Mala. We thought that it was going to be the end of it. We were wrong."

"If only we had a genie," Princess Arctic said. "Genie's exist in all lands and their powers could come in handy now. A genie…"

"No genies," Captain Creature almost yelled, interrupting. "They are horrible creatures that only take pleasure in destruction. I would never use one of those demons."

"Genies can be helpful," Arctic said.

"I would rather lose than be indebted to a genie, but this time we will not fail," Captain Creature said. "We have waited and planned. You will play an important role. Both of you. Fate dealt you a hand and you have played it well. You have walked a path that led you here. You have a destiny. You both could have chosen to walk away, to stop before you got this far, but you both persisted and now the final battle is near. Follow me."

The group followed Creature to the upper deck. Both Krispin and Arctic were amazed that they were looking out over the Blue Cerrado Forest. The blue tint to the trees gave a perfect indication to all who looked that they were in the magical forest.

"How is this possible?" Arctic asked. "This journey should have taken a long time."

"I have a map of every arch in Cerrado," Captain Creature said. "A map of every arch in every world. I know exactly where they lead and at what times of the day they will appear."

"What created the arches?" Krispin asked.

"Cerrado was created when the first realm, a land of magic was destroyed," Captain Creature said. "The arches were the last remnants of the magic to manifest itself. They are connectors. Some of them spilled into other worlds, like the world that has the Immortal River. The magic of the arches are just as powerful today as they were when they first formed."

"How was the land of magic destroyed?" Krispin asked.

"That's a story for another day," Captain Creature said. "That story would take many days to tell. Some of the evil that destroyed that land infected Princess Ashlynn, Bala, and her sister Queen Mala."

"There's no magic in the land that I'm from," Krispin said. "My land would be so much more interesting if there was magic there."

"There's magic in every world, Krispin," Jade sad. "There's magic in every land. You just have to be in tune with it. Most people ignore it, push it aside. They don't want to deal with the consequences of magic."

"Consequences?" Krispin asked.

"Just like there is good and evil," Jade said. "And just like good and evil is separated only by the intent that we use it for, magic can be used for good or evil. The magic is very seductive and if the intent slips to using, to taking, to destroying, then the magic, and the person, will slip to evil, be consumed by it. The consequences of using magic can destroy a person just as fast as the magic itself."

"I understand," Krispin said.

"As do I," Arctic said. "But Jade, why doesn't Captain Creature want to use a genie? They can be found, and would be helpful. I've thought about trying to find one since we started our quests."

"He had a bad experience with one," Jade said. "Not him…his parents. It's a long story and he doesn't like to talk about it, but Captain Creature will not use genies for anything."

"All genies do, is destroy," Captain Creature said. "Nothing more."

"Come on, Arctic. We don't have much time," Krispin said.

The pirates helped Krispin and Arctic into a small boat and then lowered it to the water. Krispin used the oars to paddle to the shore. Krispin and Arctic exited the boat and began to walk toward the forest—both ready to take on anything that could come their way.

Chapter 29

The air outside the Windswept Castle seemed electrical on this overcast day. There was something that had the animals on edge—like they knew of a grand battle that was about to begin. The people who were moving about did so with caution—looking toward the sky, almost as if they were expecting it to fall.

In the heavy breeze most of the birds had bunkered down and were avoiding flight, but on this day, a single raven was flying toward the castle. The blackbird was large and flew direct, with a purpose. He landed on the sill of a window high in the castle. The bird paused only a moment before flying away but a close observer would have noticed a hand taking something from around the bird's ankle.

In the throne room of the castle, Princess Ashlynn paced. Word had come to her that Mala had started moving troops, but they were close to the Cerrado Castle so no confirmation could be given on where the troops were headed. Ashlynn couldn't figure out how Mala could have discovered that she was alive, but all of her advisors had tried to calm her—warning her against jumping to conclusions before they knew for sure which way the army was heading.

Sir Bromas swallowed in a dry throat as he read a scroll. The scroll confirmed what Ashlynn had believed and what everyone else tried to talk her out of. Bromas knew that now he was the one who would have to deliver this message to Ashlynn. Sir Bromas knew that he could be killed for what he was about to read.

"This message confirms it, my Princess," Sir Bromas said, reading a small scroll. "Queen Mala's armies are heading in this direction. They march directly for the Windswept Castle."

"I told you!" Ashlynn yelled, pacing. "I told everyone that we needed to be ready. It's those damn Nature Watchers. They brought all of those people here so that we would kill them and they could spy on us. I bet that's why they did it. As they play tricks on us, we shall play tricks on them."

"Our best bet would be to fortify," Sir Bromas said. "Dig in and be ready to defend the castle. We must make sure that they cannot penetrate our defenses."

"FOOL!" Ashlynn said, as she rushed over and slapped Sir Bromas. "I should have your head for such cowardice."

"It's not cowardice, Princess Ashlynn," Sir Bromas said. "This message indicates that thousands of troops are marching in this direction. We do not have enough forces to stand against that. If we use the defenses of the castle, then we would stand the best chance. You know that the only way you can die is by your sister's hand. We must make sure that we don't lose."

"I'm not going to defend this dump," Princess Ashlynn said. "Then flee, only to wait another twenty years to claim what should rightfully be mine...Cerrado."

"There are not a lot of other options," Sir Bromas said.

"I remember when my witless little sister tried to kill me," Princess Ashlynn said. "It was shortly after Tala had died. The word was spread through the kingdom that it had been a riding accident. I knew that wasn't true. Tala was incredibly adept at riding horses. I instantly went on my guard and started learning things that I could do to extend my life. I wanted to find a unicorn horn but a unicorn would have never presented itself to me so I went on a quest to find the Immortal River."

"But that is only a legend," Sir Bromas said.

"It could be," Princess Ashlynn replied. "I was here, staying at the Windswept Castle when the blow came. Mala had been tracking me. The only reason that I was able to survive was that the queen was giving birth to a daughter when I was killed. I used what necromancer powers I'd learned to put my memories, my spirit, and my soul into the body of that little baby princess. I figured that if I was going to have to grow up again, I might as well do it as a princess."

"It's a good thing that you'd started practicing necromancy," Sir Bromas said. "You would have died otherwise."

"It's a very good thing," Princess Ashlynn said. "I always wondered what happened to the soul of that little girl who was supposed to have this body. I guess it's wandering Cerrado as a ghost. Or maybe it found a body to take. Either way, I had to survive. It was nice because I already knew how to do everything. It was simply a matter of waiting for this body to be developed enough to handle it. I had many different plans as to how I was going to take Cerrado back, and the first thing I had to do was get this body's parents out of the way. That was easy enough. Now all that planning is thrown out the window because of my sister. I had it planned perfectly. I was going to offer myself as queen to the former king when he returned, saying that he needed a queen...and that would end the feud between my family and the Ryder Family. Once we were married and I had full rank and title, I would have killed him."

"How?"

"That's not important," Princess Ashlynn said. "Poison, accident, or murder blamed on someone else...as long as he died. Then I would have been sole ruler of Cerrado. Now that Mala's returned it has messed everything up."

"If we don't dig down in the castle, what is our move then?" Sir Bromas asked.

"They will rest a half day's march from the castle," Princess Ashlynn said. "Her troops will be tired from the long march carrying heavy battle gear. They will make camp...most likely at the opposite edge of the Windswept Forest. If we wait until they have almost finished making camp to attack, that's when they will be at their weakest. We can strike heavy there and wound many of her troops. If we can then set traps throughout the forest, there will be nothing left of her force when they arrive at the castle walls."

"Remember that Mala is the only one who can kill you," Sir Bromas said. "We cannot discount that the troops are a diversion to draw you out. We can get all the troops that we ever need, but you have to be protected. I have a delicious plan. We send for the Ryder Family...Tobin and Tybin. We petition them to help us. They will not know why troops are headed this way, but you offer your hand to the one that leads the group that kills the attackers."

"And then both the Ryder boys end up in strange attacks," Princess Ashlynn said. "The remaining troops that were loyal to the attackers somehow get in and destroy them. I like this plan. Have our troops ready in case the Ryder Boys don't get here in time. I want to be certain that we have everything covered."

"It will be done," Sir Bromas said, as he rushed out of the room.

Princess Ashlynn paced in the room before she looked out the window and over her castle and subjects. She had been waiting patiently for so long for this day to come. Ever since her sister had tried to kill her, Bala had taken a new name, a new look, and made it work for her. Ashlynn knew that many people were conspiring in Cerrado, but she knew that she would win.

As she was looking over the castle, a guard walked in with two bound women. The women both wore the blue leather pants, sleeveless tunics, and hats of the famed Cerrado women riders—the women that would ride with Princess Ambriss into battle. The guard was a large man and was easy able to handle both women by himself. The guard forced both women to their knees before Princess Ashlynn.

"Princess Ashlynn," the guard said, bowing. "We have captured these two sneaking around the castle grounds. They were looking about and they are the riders who support Princess Ambriss."

"I know who they are," Ashlynn said. "Their clothing gives them away. Guard, leave us."

The guard bowed and quickly left the room. Ashlynn studied the women. One of them—the bigger, prettier one—looked familiar somehow. Ashlynn was certain that she knew this woman.

"You there," Ashlynn barked. "What is your name?"

"I am January and this is Rose," January said.

"Oh, my God," Ashlynn said. "Daughter."

"I beg your pardon?" January asked. "You are the evil Princess Ashlynn who has done much to destroy the Windswept Plains and harbors a war with the Ryder Family."

"But you are," Ashlynn said. "I am Princess Bala. I took the body of Ashlynn when she was a baby because my sister, Mala, tried to kill me."

"You would have been not fifteen years old when I was born," January said.

"It was a scandal in the royal family, yes," Princess Ashlynn said. "That's why you were taken from me.But you are my daughter. You know of your sisters?"

"I have no sisters," January said.

"You have three younger sisters," Ashlynn said. "April, May, and June."

"Those are the names of the women that associate with Prince Atin," Rose said. "I know them, and know they were Princess Bala's daughters."

"Think," Princess Ashlynn said. "You resemble them, don't you? When you look at them, it's almost as if you are looking into a mirror."

"You're right," January said. "I've often wondered about that...how the four of us could look so alike, albeit with different skin colors."

"You are all my daughters," Ashlynn said. "You don't share the same father as those three though, yours was a man from the deserts who entertained me one night."

"Then why do you have my leader locked in your dungeon?" January demanded. "I am here to free her and her companions down there. They are the rightful rulers of Cerrado until the Former King returns."

"He won't return," Ashlynn said. "He's dead. I'm sure of it."

"Impossible," Rose said.

"Not at all," Ashlynn said. "He would have returned by now. My family is the true bloodline. Mala acted out of jealousy. She couldn't handle never holding the throne. She never will. I will. I ask you now, daughter...join me."

"Never," January said. "I am loyal to my lady, the great and honorable Princess Ambriss."

"I will ask you again," Ashlynn said. "Join me."

"My heart, body, and soul belong to Princess Ambriss," January said. "I took an oath of honor to serve and protect her always. Where she commands, there will I go. If my blood is spilled, as long as it protects my Princess. That is a vow that cannot be broken, even if you are my mother."

"I will ask you one last time," Princess Ashlynn said, through gritted teeth. "Join me."

"You will have to kill me first," January said. "That is the bond that I have with my princess. I believed you dead, so I forged on with a new family. They treated me proper and respectful, and I will lay down my life for them. That is the bond that we have. I would never join with someone who practices necromancy in an effort to gain unlimited power."

"Then you will die," Ashlynn said.

"If that is the fate that is destined for me," January said. "Then so be it. I will not betray my princess."

Ashlynn twirled her fingers and in an instant she was in her battle gear with a copy of the 'Knowledge of Cerrado' on a flaming pedestal beside her. Ashlynn began to conjure a spell but something inside of her wouldn't let her do it. She couldn't kill her own daughter. January looked up to her mother, still uncertain if it was true, but she had no fear. She was dying to protect the one that she loved and served.

Ashlynn let a sympathetic smile come across her face. She instantly changed back and the book and pedestal disappeared. Ashlynn motioned for both January and Rose to stand.

"I only hope that one day you will be this loyal to me," Ashlynn said. "I can't kill you. I can't kill my own daughter. I will have you two placed in a cell until I figure out what to do with you."

Ashlynn snapped her fingers and a guard rushed in. Princess Ashlynn flashed him a hand sign and he took January and Rose out of the room. Ashlynn smiled, knowing that both women had bought what she had said. That kind of loyalty could come in handy. Ashlynn didn't know exactly how she would use it, but she knew that at some point, January's love and devotion to Princess Ambriss would allow Princess Ashlynn to kill them both—and if she was lucky, maybe even more of the royal family along with them.

As Princess Ashlynn returned to her throne, Sir Bromas rushed into the room. He looked excited. The knight bowed before the princess before standing.

"Word has been sent," Sir Bromas said. "The Ryder Family should be here soon so we can ask for their help."

"And lead them to their deaths in the process," Ashlynn said. "Good work, Sir Bromas. This is turning into a wonderful day."

Princess Ashlynn stood up and walked to the window. She looked out over her castle and kingdom—a kingdom she knew was soon going to get much bigger.

Chapter 30

The sky over the Blue Cerrado Forest was overcast with the remains of a rainstorm recently past. Water droplets fell from the leaves— a reminder of the storm that had doused the area with water. The ground was muddy, but the blue-tinted trees and plants all looked clean and refreshed, like the rain was long overdue.

Sir Krispin and Princess Arctic trudged their way through the mud as they made their way deeper into the forest. They lost sight of the river almost immediately. It had been almost an hour since they were able to hear the running waters. Krispin, with his sword at his side, and Arctic, with her daggers at her waist, were walking close together. Krispin offered the princess his hand every time there was something to climb over.

"Tell me, Krispin," Arctic asked. "Tell me about your parents' farm."

"It is a simple farm," Krispin said. "We have a number of different paddocks that we rotate the sheep between. We always have a couple hundred sheep. We sheer them and sell the wool. Dad commands some of the highest prices in the market for his wool. It is known as the finest in the market. I would watch dad with the buyers. They would be haggling on the price for his wool, and he would remain firm on his price. He always got the price he wanted. He would always say that if they wanted to pay less, then they should buy a lesser quality of wool. He always stands his ground...always keeps his convictions."

"It's rare to find men like that," Princess Arctic said. "So many people go on whatever whim seems convenient at the time."

"Dad and mom truly love each other," Krispin said. "Dad said that he was always looking for other worlds and that he wouldn't be happy until he found one, but yet he said that every day that he's been with mom, he's been happy. I know that Holly and I will be happy together once I finish this adventure."

"Holly again," Arctic said. "I thought that with everything that you've seen here in Cerrado that you would have realized that she's not the only woman in the world...your world or this one."

"If I didn't marry Holly, who would I marry?" Krispin asked.

"I don't know," Arctic said.

"You?" Krispin asked. "Am I supposed to marry you?"

"No," Arctic said, defensively. "That's not what I meant. I was just pointing out that it doesn't make sense that you need to prove your love to her when she's doing nothing for you. Love doesn't need an adventure to be there…just two people who care about each other. Care about each other enough to put up with them during the bad and hard times."

"Again, you're an expert on love," Krispin said, with a laugh. "You, who hasn't even experienced anything closely related to love."

"I've experienced something like love," Arctic said. "There's a man who I truly care about. I couldn't imagine that it is anything but love. I want to be with this person at all times. I want to share the world with him. I want him to hold me on stormy nights and run with me through the surf on moonlight nights with stars twinkling over our heads. This man makes me laugh and keeps me on my toes. That's the kind of man that I want. What is it about Holly that makes you want her?"

"She's beautiful," Krispin said. "The way her hair bounces when she walks, the way the light catches her blue eyes and they twinkle like diamonds. The way she laughs, the way she always challenges me, pushes me…"

Krispin trailed off. He realized that he was describing Princess Arctic—not his Holly. He didn't know what that meant. Ever since he'd watched Arctic practice with Jade, he'd been noticing her in a different light. There was something about this princess that he couldn't ignore. Krispin wondered if he should ask Arctic if she felt the same way but then he thought about Holly—how he'd promised to return to her with the story of this amazing adventure. Krispin knew that when he dazzled Holly with this story, she'd fall into his arms and they'd live happily ever after. Krispin knew that love would conquer all.

As Krispin was lost in thought of Holly and Arctic, a twig cracked somewhere in the distance behind them. Krispin and Arctic got behind a giant fallen tree and hid. They looked toward where they had been, and waited. It only took a moment for three horrible looking, little green goblins to come through the trees.

The goblins were small, only about four feet tall, and covered with shapeless brown tunics holding short swords. The goblins had stringy hair, grotesque faces, and almost appeared to be covered in some kind of slime. Arctic gasped when she saw them, starting to shake.

"What are they?" Krispin asked.

"Goblins," Princess Arctic said. "They live in the forests. They will kill us and steal anything of value."

"That's good," Krispin said.

"WHAT?" Arctic shouted in a whisper. "How can that be good?"

"We have nothing of value," Krispin said. "They won't get anything from us."

"That won't stop them from killing us," Arctic said.

"They're so little though," Krispin said. "Surely they don't pose a threat to us. I will fight them and defeat them."

"Krispin!" Arctic said, trying to stop him. "Goblins are amazing fighters. You don't stand a chance against three of them."

The words were spoken too late. Krispin had already jumped from their hiding place and pulled his sword out. Arctic could only pray that he would be able to stand against the three goblins, even though she knew how fierce the gold stealers were. Princess Arctic got her daggers out and ready to use as Krispin approached the goblins with his sword drawn.

"Hear me now," Krispin said, bravely. "Pass through here and no harm or trouble will befall you and your people."

"What gives you the bravado to challenge us?" one of the goblins shouted in a guttural voice. "You cannot stand before one goblin, let alone three. Sheath your sword and drop to your knees and I promise that we will kill you swiftly, without pain."

"I will not," Krispin said. "You cannot harm me."

The goblins only laughed as they circled around Krispin. Krispin tried to keep his eyes on all three but they spread out so he couldn't focus on more than one. As Krispin was looking at one, the goblin behind started to rush in. The only reason Krispin was able to defend, was that he heard the goblin's feet splashing in the mud as he tried to rush toward him.

Krispin deflected the goblin's sword and offered an attack the goblin was barely able to escape from. As the goblin was rushing off, another rushed in. Krispin quickly realized that no matter what he did, he couldn't defeat all three at the same time. He needed to separate them. Krispin noticed that a smaller tree was laying on the ground. Krispin rushed to it and jumped up, taking the higher ground, and limiting the options for the goblin's attack.

The goblins didn't give up easily. They tried to rush from the front and back at the same time. Krispin was able to knock the sword out of one of the goblin's hands. Krispin used his sword and was able to pierce the goblin in the heart. One of the goblins fell, leaving only two left. The other two were stunned that Krispin was able to slash their friend down.

"Impossible," one goblin shouted. "Where did you learn to handle a sword? Goblins are some of the best swordfighters in Cerrado."

"Obviously not that good," Krispin said. "He fell quickly and easily."

As both goblins were about to rush Krispin at the same time, Princess Arctic jumped out from behind her hiding spot and rushed toward the goblins. She was impressed that Krispin had defeated the one goblin, but there was a good chance he could fall with two left.

Arctic slashed her daggers toward one of the goblins but he was ready for her. Krispin started to fend off the other goblin but he lost his balance on the log and had to jump down. The sound of clanging metal filled the forest. Krispin was trying to remember everything that Cinnamon had taught him about fighting. There was so much to remember, and the little goblin was moving faster than Cinnamon ever had.

Krispin noticed that every time the goblin slashed forward, he would pause—turning toward the left. As Krispin tried to figure out how to use that to his advantage, he noticed the other goblin had Princess Arctic on the defensive. She was moving backwards, fighting valiantly, but losing to the faster goblin. Krispin caught the goblin as he paused and was able to knock it to the ground.

Krispin looked over and saw the other goblin had Arctic pressed up against a tree. He was laughing as he knew that he had Arctic defeated. Krispin's heart skipped a beat as he froze, not knowing what to do. As Krispin's mind was racing in all directions, a glint of light caught his eye. He noticed that the goblin he'd knocked to the ground was swinging a sword toward him.

Krispin reacted without thinking, dodging the sword and quickly attacking the fallen goblin. Krispin made sure his sword pierced the goblin's heart. The goblin gurgled before slumping dead on the ground. Krispin rushed toward Arctic. The other goblin didn't even see Krispin coming as he was swinging his sword toward Arctic. Arctic didn't see what happened. She had her eyes closed in fear of what was to happen. But in an instant, the goblin was gone. Princess Arctic opened her eyes to see a headless goblin body sprawled on the ground before her, Krispin's sword dripping with green goblin blood.

"Are you hurt?" Krispin asked.

"No," Arctic said. "Thank you."

"I was so worried about you," Krispin said. "When I saw he had you against the tree I feared the worst."

"That's how I felt when I saw you trying to defeat all three," Arctic said. "We could have easily taken them together, if we'd just worked together."

"At least you didn't order me this time," Krispin said, with a smile.

"I know that you wouldn't listen to me anyway," Arctic smiled back.

The pair hugged. As they pulled apart they looked deep into each other's eyes—almost moving in for a kiss, but they held back. The pair was surprised to hear someone clapping behind them. The pair turned, swords ready for action, but they were stunned at who they saw. There was a handsome man standing there with long cobalt-colored hair that matched his cobalt-colored three-piece suit. At first, Krispin thought that it was

Cinnamon, since it looked exactly like his sword trainer. But the color gave the man away.

"You must be Cobalt," Krispin said. "The man of the Forest."

"That I am," Cobalt said, puffing on a long-stemmed golden pipe. Three exotic, beautiful women stepped out from behind trees, wearing the finest clothing that either Krispin or Arctic had ever seen. They stood beside Cobalt. "That was an impressive fight."

"We had to defend against the goblins," Arctic said. "They would have killed us otherwise."

"They would have," Cobalt said, sharing his pipe with his women.

"Did you watch the entire fight?" Krispin asked.

"I did."

"Why didn't you help?"

"I avoid fighting," Cobalt said. "There's no need for it. I have no reason to fight."

"Then why have you shown yourself to us?" Princess Arctic asked.

"There is much to do and my parents have demanded that I do my part," Cobalt said. "I have no desire or care for what is going on here, but I have to do what my parents command. With that being said…Princess Arctic, you are searching for something, correct?"

"I am looking for a unicorn so I can collect his horn to help my father," Arctic said. "I need to get the horn, which was my quest."

"Very well," Cobalt said. "My friends here could not see a unicorn but I believe that you can. Princess Arctic, are you pure of heart, body, and soul?"

"I am," Princess Arctic said, proudly.

"Very well," Cobalt looked to one of his women. "Check her."

One of the women walked over to Arctic and began to inspect her. She placed a hand on Arctic's arm and squeezed. Arctic felt strange as the woman looked her over. The woman looked Arctic in the eyes, looking deep, in her, and through her, before she turned and faced Cobalt.

"This girl is pure," the woman said.

"Very good," Cobalt said. "Princess Arctic, you will receive your unicorn horn."

As Cobalt spoke, the group heard a snap of a twig behind them. Princess Arctic turned and looked, seeing a beautiful snow white unicorn with a large ivory white horn. The unicorn walked right up to Arctic, allowing her to pet the majestic beast. Arctic laughed as the unicorn seemed to sneeze as he shook his head.

"You're a good boy," Arctic said. "Very good boy."

The unicorn shook its head harder and the horn on his muzzle fell off. Arctic picked it up and held it up high. Arctic was beaming with pride as she looked at the horn.

"Thank you so much, unicorn," Arctic said. "Thank you."

The unicorn bowed to Arctic before turning and walking back into the forest. Arctic put the horn in a sash at the waist of her wrapped dress. Her smile was bright and beaming. She'd completed her quest. Now she could hold her head high and rush back to the castle to save her father. Arctic rushed to Krispin and the pair embraced.

"We did it," Arctic said. "Thank you so much for helping me."

The pair looked deep in each other's eyes. Krispin couldn't help but notice how big and bright Arctic's eyes were. They were twinkling like nothing he'd ever seen before. Arctic had an air of power about her— something that was so compelling, so inviting, that Krispin started to lean his head toward her. Arctic started smiling even more. Krispin paused just before their lips touched.

"Don't stop," Princess Arctic said. "Not this time. Kiss me."

Krispin complied. As the pair's lips touched, Cobalt and the women with him saw the sparks flying between the two. There was magic in that kiss. Something that both Krispin and Arctic felt deep within their very being. As quickly as the magic started, an image of Holly came into Krispin's mind. He pulled away and swallowed hard.

"Arctic," Krispin said. "I can't. We shouldn't have."

"What are you saying?" Arctic asked horrified.

"Holly," Krispin said. "I have to return to her. We have to tell her about our adventure."

"Damn Holly!" Arctic yelled, as she let out a scream. "Krispin, I love you. I know you love me. I felt it in that kiss. How can you think of Holly when I'm here with you right now?"

"Arctic," Krispin said, putting his hands up. "It just that..."

"No," Arctic shouted. "All of this meant nothing to you? We've walked through Cerrado together and faced much more than anyone could have ever imaged. I gave you my heart and you reject it?"

"Holly," Krispin said, again.

"Guard that horn well, Arctic," Cobalt said. "There was passion and love in that kiss. A unicorn will not appear to a woman who's had any passion or love with a man. You will not see one again. Your first kiss was a very powerful one. Very few women get a kiss that powerful for their first time."

"Then my first kiss was a complete and total waste," Arctic said, with tears in her eyes. "It is something that I do not wish to remember. Thank you, Krispin Risdell. You destroyed my first kiss. Come on, let's get back to the stupid ship so we can go tell your stupid girlfriend about this stupid adventure."

Arctic walked away in a huff. Krispin walked over to Cobalt.

"I hurt her, didn't I?" Krispin asked.

"In ways you can't possibly imagine," Cobalt said. "Love is a very funny thing, Krispin. It's unpredictable and unpreventable."

"I didn't mean to hurt her," Krispin said.

"So often people don't mean to do things, Krispin," one of the women said. "People get so caught up in what they are doing they don't see the consequences of their actions until it's too late."

"How can I make it up to her?" Krispin asked.

"I cannot tell you that," the woman said. "But it's going to have to be a major gesture."

"What?" Krispin asked.

Before the woman could answer, Cobalt and his women disappeared in front of his eyes. Krispin tried to figure out what the women had said. Krispin decided that he would make it up to Arctic somehow as he rushed to catch up to her.

Chapter 31

The boats were still anchored off the river bank as Arctic got to the little rowboat. She put all her strength into it but she couldn't move the boat into the water by herself. Krispin caught up to her, easily pushed the boat into the water, and offered his hand to her to help Arctic into the boat. Arctic didn't even acknowledge Krispin as she got into the boat on her own.

Krispin got in and began to row, steering the little boat to The Lynx—Captain Creature's flagship. The entire time Krispin was trying to think of something to say to Arctic, something he could say to her that would smooth over what had happened in the forest, but he couldn't think of anything to say. As they got to the ship Krispin tried to help Arctic out of the boat by steadying her arm, but she pulled it away before he could help her.

"Don't you dare touch me," Princess Arctic said, with venom in her voice. "I don't ever want to see you again. I know I agreed to tell Holly about this adventure, and I will, but after that I don't want to see you again."

"Princess Arctic, you have to understand," Krispin pleaded. "Holly is…"

"I don't care," Arctic said, as she started climbing the ladder on the side of the ship.

Krispin and Arctic got to the deck of the ship to see the waiting Captain Creature and Jade. They were in a conversation of their own, looking at a map of Cerrado. It almost looked like they were planning an attack on the Windswept Castle. Arctic slammed the unicorn horn down on a table.

"I got the horn," Arctic said. "Can we please get moving?"

"I sense that something went wrong," Captain Creature said.

"Can we please just get moving?" Arctic pleaded. "Go back to his world, drop him off, and I'll tell his bimbo about what happened here. I don't want to see him again."

"It's not that simple, Princess Arctic," Jade said. "You two are bound together for more of this quest. Your work together isn't finished."

"What?" Krispin said. "The wedding is tomorrow. I have to get back to my village and let Holly know about this before she marries Chester."

"Sometimes much is expected of us, Krispin," Captain Creature said. "Sometimes we have to sacrifice things that we want for the good of the kingdom. There is an evil that has befallen Cerrado and we will only have one chance to succeed...or all will be lost."

"No," Krispin said. "I have to get back now. This is my only shot to show Holly what I did for her. This is my only chance to tell her about my adventure."

"Krispin, I have a map that shows all the arches in Cerrado," Captain Creature said. "The maps show when the arches will appear and where they lead to. Without this map you will never find the right arch. There are four arches in that grouping of trees that you entered and only one of them goes to your world. There are hundreds of arches that exist in Cerrado."

"Golly gee, wow," Princess Arctic said, sarcastically. "Can we please just get moving? I really want to just get moving. There's no point in arguing about this."

Princess Arctic stormed off the deck and went below into the ship. Jade watched Arctic walk away before casting a glance toward Krispin. She could tell that something major happened, so Jade rushed after Arctic. Captain Creature had also noticed the unspoken interaction between the pair. He waited until Jade was out of earshot before speaking.

"What happened?" Captain Creature asked.

"We shared a tender kiss," Krispin said. "Before I pulled away and said that I couldn't because of Holly."

"That was a mistake," Creature said.

"Why?" Krispin asked.

"Go to your chamber and get some sleep," Captain Creature said. "You will have a mission tonight that will require that you are well rested."

"What is it?" Krispin asked.

"You shall see tonight," Captain Creature said.

Jade rushed through the ship to get to the chamber where Arctic had gone. The chamber was bare, save for the bed and wardrobe against the far wall. There was one circular window allowing light in. Arctic had thrown herself on the bed and was sobbing—her arms covering her head that was buried in the mattress. Jade paused for a moment before speaking.

"What's wrong, Princess Arctic?" Jade asked.

"He kissed me," Arctic said. "But then he yammered on about that twit, Holly. How can he choose someone that forces him to prove his love, while giving nothing back, when I'm right here? I wouldn't ask him for anything."

"Men are finicky things," Jade said. "You never know what they are thinking or what their motives are. I'm very sorry about it Arctic, but some things just need to take their course. I'm sure there's someone out there for you."

"You want to know what the worst part about the whole situation is?" Arctic asked as she looked up toward Jade through blurry eyes.

"What's that?"

"I really love him," Arctic said. "And I said that I didn't want to see him again, but that's not true. I want him to speak about me the way he speaks about Holly. I want to see that magical look in his eye when he's thinking about me...not Holly."

"Men are hard to predict," Jade said. "When I first started dating Captain Creature, his actions were very strange indeed. It took me a long time to get him to look at only me and not other women that he wanted. If you want a relationship to blossom you have to take action. You cannot wait for love to just happen. You can't force it either, but you can subtly and gently nudge it along."

"What should I do?" Arctic asked.

"Be there for him," Jade said. "Make yourself attractive to him. You can do it, Arctic. I know you can."

Jade left the room as Arctic sat up on her bed. She let Jade's words fill her mind. Arctic began to think of all the different ways she could make herself more attractive to Krispin so that he would think about her and not Holly. Arctic believed that she could solve this problem on her own. If she only knew what Captain Creature and Jade had planned for Krispin that evening, Princess Arctic may have wanted to be by his side then—to be there for him when they dropped a bombshell on Krispin Risdell that shattered everything he ever knew about his world...

"Wake up now," Jade said, softly shaking Krispin's shoulder.

Krispin slowly opened his eyes and looked around. It was dark out but there were shafts of moonbeams illuminating the room. Krispin had fallen asleep on top of the bed sheets, still in the clothing that he was wearing earlier in the day. Krispin wiped the sleep from his eyes and looked to Jade. She almost looked like an angel to him—a moonbeam bathing her amazing figure in silver moonlight.

"What's going on?" Krispin asked. "Why are you waking me?"

"We need to take a trip," Jade said. "Take my hand."

Krispin looked at Jade with confused eyes, but something about her face told him to trust her. Krispin slowly reached out and touched

Jade's hand. The instant that he touched her, the pair disappeared from the ship, leaving no trace of them in the room they'd been in.

It took Krispin a moment to adjust to his new surroundings. Unlike traveling through the arch, Krispin had a perfect knowledge of what had just happened. He knew that Jade had transported him somewhere but there was still sleep in his eyes, blurring what he was seeing.

The area was dark, with a full blood-red moon hanging in the sky. There were stars—silver and yellow, that seemed to be pulsing in the sky—brighter then dimmer, brighter then dimmer, and in no discernable pattern Krispin could figure out. As his surroundings became clearer, Krispin let out a gasp—he was in a graveyard. Within the confines of the black iron fence were hundreds of old stone monuments, weathered and aged with vines climbing some. Past the fence were gnarled black trees and darkness.

Krispin swallowed in a throat that had suddenly become dry. He looked past the fence, into the darkness, and saw shadows moving in the trees. Krispin strained to see what the shadows were but he couldn't make any of them out. Krispin started to perspire although he realized how cold and heavy the air felt. In the distance, animals called out with frightening loud calls. Krispin look toward Jade, who seemed very peaceful.

"This is a very special place," Jade said.

"Where are we?" Krispin asked.

"This is a shadow realm," Jade said. "Very few exist anymore. The only way to access this one is through a special arch."

"But I remember how we got here," Krispin said. "I remember going through."

"That is something that I expected would happen," Jade said. "You are going through changes. This place will change you more, expand your mind."

"What do you mean?" Krispin asked. "Who's buried here?"

"Do you see those shadows off in the distance?"

"Yes."

"These graves belong to them," Jade said.

"Ghosts."

"Yes and no."

"What do you mean?"

"They cannot be ghosts since they are not dead," Jade said. "However, they cannot be living since they are not alive. That is the curse of being trapped in a shadow realm. Some of these souls choose to be here for one reason or another. Others were trapped and forced to be here."

"What happened to them?

"It's the magic of Cerrado," Jade said. "Mala would have been taken here if Mystic Seven hadn't found her. This is a protected place where spirits can regenerate themselves after a battle."

"The Former King," Krispin said. "He's here?"

"He was badly injured in his battle with Mala," Jade said. "He didn't have the power to defeat her. She had killed her parents and believed that she'd killed her two older sisters. The powers running through her were nearly unstoppable. This was the only thing we could think to do. We had to determine what it would take to stop her and keep the Former King on the throne."

"Who was he?" Krispin asked. "Am I to bring him back from here? That's why I was needed?"

"Come with me," Jade said.

Krispin followed Jade as they walked past rows and rows of crooked and crumbling tombstones. The shadows on the outer edge of the fence watched every move the pair made. Krispin could feel eyes upon him. It was a sensation like he'd never felt before. He didn't know how to explain where he was. His mind was still reeling from the fact that Chester and Holly's wedding would take place the next day and he was no closer to getting home than he was before they'd gotten the unicorn horn. And now, for some reason he couldn't understand, Princess Arctic was furious with him.

Jade stopped walking in front of a stone slab carved from a block of pure quartz. Above the slab was a granite carving of a king with a massive crown on his head. In each hand was a dagger with a sword laying by his side. The king was adorned in jewels and fine clothing, capped off with a flowing robe. The carving was ornately cut and painted to the point it almost looked real. Krispin was amazed by the quality of the handy work.

"The Former King?" Krispin asked.

"It is," Jade said. "He's buried here. The Former King had to come here because Mala had stabbed him with a tainted unicorn horn."

"Tainted?" Krispin asked.

"Mala had tricked the unicorn to appear before her," Jade said. "That caused the horn to be evil instead of good…darkness instead of light. The Former King, after stabbing Mala, fled here. Above all else, he wanted a peaceful and prosperous Cerrado. He came here to recharge and heal. We knew that one day Mala would be back. It was the only way that we could kill her."

"Then all we need to do is wake him up and he will return to us?" Krispin said.

"It's a little more complex than that," Jade said.

"Is his name written on the stone?" Krispin asked.

"There is a question that you must first ask yourself," Jade said.

"What's that?"

"Can you handle this information?" Jade asked.

"I can," Krispin said. "I can handle anything now."

"Then read the name at his feet."

Krispin looked at Jade then to the feet of the carving. There were leaves covering the area of the stone beneath the feet. Krispin brushed them away and his jaw fell as his eyes got huge.

"I never knew," Krispin said. "What does this mean?"

"It means…" Jade began, but stopped with a shudder. "Something has happened. Come. We must get back."

Krispin took one last look at the name, the stones, the carvings, and the graveyard. So much now made sense to him yet he had many more questions. He could tell that something had bothered Jade to her core that something truly was wrong yet he couldn't figure out what that thing would be. Krispin took Jade's hand and the pair disappeared from the graveyard.

Chapter 32

Krispin, mind still reeling from the information that he'd learned in the shadow realm, returned with Jade to the shores of the river. The sun was just beginning to rise, bathing the entire river and forest in a golden light. The plants and grass shimmered with the morning dew. The beauty of nature wasn't the focal point of all the animals this morning. It was the three massive ships on the river, each a raging inferno with flames dancing high into the sky.

Krispin noticed Princess Arctic was on the shores of the river— soaking, dripping wet, and crying. He rushed over to her and when Arctic heard footsteps getting close, she looked up—eyes lighting up. Arctic jumped to her feet and rushed to meet Krispin. She hugged him before pushing him away.

"I'm still mad at you," Arctic said. "But I am glad that you are okay. Where were you?"

"Jade had to show me something," Krispin said. "What happened here?"

"I awoke to hear the pirates shouting," Arctic said. "There was all kinds of confusion going on. No one knew what to do. I rushed to your room but you weren't there. That's when I noticed the smoke and heard the explosion on one of the other ships. I ran to the deck and could see that they were on fire. I dove off into the river and swam to shore."

"What happened to all the pirates?" Jade asked.

"They ran into the forest," Arctic said. "They were saying that whoever did this would kill them all if they stuck around. None of them wanted to stay."

"But you didn't follow them," Jade said.

"I didn't see Krispin running with them," Princess Arctic said. "I had to know that he was safe. I figured that if he was gone he would return here."

"You stayed here for me?" Krispin asked.

"Of course I did," Arctic said. "I...never mind. You still have to get me home. I'm still your responsibility. Then we have to go tell your bimbo about this adventure. Where did you two go anyway?"

"A shadow realm," Krispin said.

"Shadow realm?" Arctic asked. "What were you doing there? Did you meet someone between two worlds?"

"In a sense, yes," Krispin said. "There is more going on than you'd ever know, Arctic. The final battle will be greater than anyone could imagine."

"Arctic, did you see where Captain Creature went?" Jade asked. "Did he run with his troops or did he go somewhere else?"

"The pirates were saying that he was captured," Arctic said.

"Impossible," Krispin said. "No one could capture Captain Creature."

"It's very possible," Jade said. "They may have gotten to him in his sleep or he may have allowed them to capture him to save the others."

"Where did the pirates go?" Krispin asked.

"They went to an arch," Jade said. "That is the course they are to take if they lose a battle or are attacked like this. They will jump arches until they get to a hidden ship. A massive ship that has weapons that no one in Cerrado knows about. Weapons that Captain Creature obtained from a different world. They will take that ship and the first thing they will do is get the Captain back."

"Where would he have been taken?" Krispin asked.

"This has to be Mala's doing," Jade said. "And one thing that I know for sure about Mala is that she cannot travel instantly like my siblings and I do. Cherry was supposed to be watching some of Mala's doings. It is possible that my sister has joined her."

"Why would she do that?" Krispin asked.

"She cares not for Cerrado or anyone in it," Jade said. "She spends her nights at parties. She's drinking and dancing until all hours of the night, then she sleeps until midday and spends the rest of the day at the beach. She was very offended that our parents requested that she do any actual work."

"We need to save Captain Creature before any harm comes to him," Krispin said. "Jade, can you take us to where he is?"

"He has been taken to either the Cerrado Castle or the Windswept Castle," Jade said.

"I would bet Windswept Castle," Krispin said. "All the others are there and that is where the final battle will be fought. Mala will want him there to gloat that she had victory over him after all the time he spent trying to defeat her."

"Before we go to the castle we need to get the troops," Jade said. "Come with me. I'll take us to the secret hiding place of The Lion, Captain Creature's hidden ship. I will captain it to the Windswept Castle."

Krispin only nodded as he took Arctic by the hand. He desperately wanted to tell her what he'd seen in the shadow realm. Krispin knew that he'd hurt her in ways he couldn't imagine but he was going to do something to make it up to her. Krispin knew that by sundown Chester and Holly would be married and if they didn't win this battle it wouldn't make any difference—he'd be dead. Krispin and Arctic took Jade's hand as they stepped into the shallows of the water and the three of them disappeared as the burning ships began to crumble apart into the water.

The Cerrado Castle and surrounding grounds looked quiet on the overcast day. In the far distance, smoke could be seen rising from what appeared to be three large fires, but the people near the castle didn't concern themselves with that. The fires weren't close enough to pose a threat to them. They were concerned with the rumors that had started to filter throughout the kingdom—rumors that evil had befallen their beloved land. No one was certain that the rumors were true, but everyone walked with an air of caution, just in case they were.

Inside the walls of the castle, in the throne room, Queen Mala and Mystic Seven the Red were looking over their handy work. Standing before them was the Nature Watcher, Cherry—the Lady of the Plains. No longer in her cherry dress, Cherry was wearing black tights, a black tunic, and a cherry-colored cape that was secured around her neck, with a brooch the shape of a raven. Cherry stood before Mala at perfect attention, not moving at all. Her voice had become a flat monotone.

"It has been done, my Queen," Cherry said. "I burned all the ships like you asked me to. I took the Captain to the dungeons at the Windswept Castle. He is in the cell with the others. They are locked tight and have many guards watching them. There is no chance of escape."

"You have done very well," Queen Mala said, from her throne.

"I live to serve you, my Queen," Cherry said bowing.

"I told you she was too valuable to destroy," Mystic Seven the Red said, as he got close to Cherry—close enough to run his fingers through her hair. "With the right combination of poison and magic, I knew she would serve you."

"I live to serve you, my Queen," Cherry repeated before turning to Mystic Seven. "And to please you, my master."

"Impressive," Queen Mala said. "Considering her normal tastes. But did you really need to do that?"

"I'm entitled to a little fun after all the work we've done," Mystic Seven said. "I had to serve that bozo of a duke, listening to him yap on and on, looking at all the women who passed through here…but never got to touch. I needed something."

"Once this escapade is over, this one can be yours for whatever purposes you want," Mala said. "Now that we have all of them right where we want them, we can destroy my sister and then all of her guards. We'll leave them in the castle and let them starve."

"What about the women running around this castle?" Mystic Seven said. "We still have the problem of Prince Atin's women. We know now that they are your nieces. Bala's daughters."

"This Nature Watcher can find them and kill them," Mala said. "That will be your task while we are away at the Windswept Castle. You will find the women that associate with Prince Atin and you will kill them. I would like to question them but I doubt there is a dungeon in all of Cerrado that could hold them…with as slippery as they are. Kill them and show me the bodies."

"Cherry won't stay with us at Windswept?" Mystic Seven asked.

"I don't trust her there," Mala said. "Her brothers and sister will likely be there. The three of them could save their sister from our spells. We have the ability to destroy my sister. She will not be needed there. Have there been any reports as to my sister's actions since the troops started to move?"

"Just as you predicted, my Queen," Cherry said. "Bala, who hides as Princess Ashlynn, sent her troops out of the castle to meet yours in the open fields near the forest. She left minimal guards in the castle protecting her."

"Then the little fool fell right into my trap," Mala said. "We will enter the castle using Cherry's ability to transport. My sister will be unprotected. She will fall quickly. Once that happens, we will take out the rest of the guards in the castle then lock it…allowing those in the dungeon to slowly starve to death."

"What of your troops on the plains?" Mystic Seven asked.

"They should be able to survive the battle," Mala replied. "We will let them fight it out and they will destroy what's left of Bala's army. We cannot have her troops rising up in her name. We must make sure that every single one of them has been destroyed, down to the lowliest squire and page. We cannot risk them revolting after we have taken Cerrado."

"Then we will destroy them all," Mystic Seven said. "This will be a good day for Cerrado. A true and just leader will once again be on the throne. There's just one more thing we need to deal with."

"What's that?" Mala asked.

"The little one," Mystic Seven said. "There haven't been any solid reports on Princess Arctic. We thought the bandits had them but they got away from Ornthal and his men. The reports would indicate that they are with Captain Creature, but we cannot confirm anything."

"Captain Creature is Jade's man, correct?" Mala asked.

"My sister and the captain have shared a bed for many years now," Cherry said. "They do not share their bed with anyone else."

"The captain is going to die in the dungeon of the Windswept Castle," Mala said. "And once this mess is over we will have Cherry kill Jade, Cinnamon, and Cobalt. The Nature Watchers will be destroyed. Princess Arctic will be alone and scared in the wastelands of Cerrado without a friend to turn to. We will place a price on her head and have every lowlife in Cerrado after her. She will turn up dead...and that little problem will be taken care of."

Mala stood and paced throughout the throne room. She wanted to be sure that every person who had ever stood against her would end up dead. Mala wanted to make sure that there would be no traces left of the royal family so no one could ever challenge the bloodline. The only person that she could foresee as a problem was the Former King. She didn't know when he would return but she knew that if he did, and he raised an army before she knew about it, that he could challenge her.

"What about Duke Asmout?" Mystic Seven asked.

"His time is over," Queen Mala said. "Cherry, go to the dungeon right now and kill Duke Asmout."

"It will be done," Cherry said, as she bowed and left the room.

"What about making him watch his children die?" Mystic Seven asked. "I thought you were going to take extreme pleasure in watching him suffer."

"I was," Mala said, still pacing. "But something doesn't feel right. We don't have the luxury of time anymore. We need to finish this."

"I understand," Mystic Seven said.

"Send word to every person under our control," Queen Mala said. "I want everyone looking for the Former King. Anything they can find on him. I want to know where he is, and how we can kill him."

"We will find him, my Queen," Mystic Seven said.

The doors to the throne room opened and Cherry returned, carrying the duke's severed head in her right arm. There was a trail of blood from where she had walked. Mala smiled as Cherry set the head before the Honor Throne.

"The duke has been taken care of," Cherry said, bowing. "What is my next task?"

"Take us to the throne room of the Windswept Castle," Mala said, confidently.

Cherry grabbed the arm of both Queen Mala and Mystic Seven the Red. As they disappeared from the room, Mala knew that the foundation of her empire was going to be a strong one. Mala knew that Cerrado was about to enter a new time—a time of her rule. There was no one in this world or another that would be able to stop them.

Chapter 33

The halls of the Windswept Castle were quiet as Princess Ashlynn rushed to the throne room. She had heard reports of the fighting outside the forests and she wanted to get an account of what was going on. Ashlynn didn't trust that Mala would fight fair, and she was prepared for tricks. Bala didn't know what kind of tricks she would have to deal with, but she was certain that something would be there.

As Bala entered the throne room she saw Sir Bromas reading a scroll as a raven flew out of the window. The look on the knight's face told the story. He was smiling from ear to ear. The momentary joy of seeing her knight excited about the news, was washed away before anything was said. As the door to the throne room closed, Queen Mala, Mystic Seven the Red, and Cherry appeared in the room. Ashlynn snapped her fingers and was in her battle gear, sword already in her hand.

"Mala, dear sister," Princess Ashlynn said, foully. "How lovely that you joined me as I'm about to take Cerrado for my own."

"Oh, dear Bala," Mala said. "I should have killed you properly the first time. It was my mistake that this even happened. It's a mistake that you can bet I won't make again."

"You underestimate me," Ashlynn said.

"I have a Nature Watcher," Mala said. "Cherry...kill her."

Cherry took a step forward, a sword appearing in her hand. Before she could engage with Ashlynn—Krispin, Arctic, and Jade appear in the room. In the confusion, Jade opened a door and a mass of people flooded the room—all the people that were in the dungeon and were helping the children. Prince Alos, Princess Ambriss, Prince Atin, January, Rose, April, May, June, Captain Creature, Hibit, Snowflake, Cinnamon, Cobalt, and Lacey entered the room.

Mala and Ashlynn both looked confused as the people spread out throughout the room. The royal children each had a sword or daggers drawn—as did Lacey, January, and all of Atin's women. Captain Creature was standing to the side, not aligning near any group.

"This all ends here and now," Krispin said. "In the name of the Former King, I banish Mala, Bala, and Mystic Seven the Red from this land. Your ideas of terror will never be seen in Cerrado again."

"Who the hell do you think you are?" Ashlynn said.

"You don't stand a chance against us, pup," Mala said.

"As you can see," Krispin said. "Your dungeons are not as secure as you think they are. We are not afraid of either of you. There is nothing that you can do to scare us anymore. I will end your reigns right now."

"I don't believe this," Mala said. "We have a real battle to do. Cherry, kill this fool now."

Cherry rushed toward Krispin with her sword drawn. The pair crossed blades and began fighting all over the room. It was very apparent that Cherry was the aggressor and that she was far more skilled than Krispin. Some of the others started to move toward the fight, like they were going to help, but Mala used her magic to create a force shield around the fighters—preventing anyone from getting involved.

Krispin was trying to defend against Cherry, but for every move he had, she had two more. Sweat was beginning to roll down his brow and the tinging of steel on steel filled the room. No matter how hard Krispin tried, he couldn't get inside Cherry's guard. The Nature Watcher smiled, seeing that Krispin was starting to get weak. Cherry used a blast of energy to drive Krispin back into a corner and with two powerful swings was able to get his sword out of his hand. Cherry wasted no time in driving her blade directly into Krispin's heart.

"NO!" Arctic yelled. Krispin fell dead.

Arctic rushed toward Cherry, not knowing at all what she would do. Cherry simply flicked her wrist and Arctic went flying, crashing down next to Krispin. Arctic quickly looked him over and let out a bloodcurdling scream. There was no pulse, no breathing—Arctic knew that Krispin was dead.

"He's dead," Arctic screamed as tears began to fall down her face. "He's dead. Why did you kill him?"

"I'm going to kill all of you presently," Mala said. "But it will be so much better if you are all alive to watch me defeat my sister…again."

"You cannot kill me, Mala," Ashlynn said. "Not even your little Nature Watcher is strong enough to kill me."

As Ashlynn finished speaking she drew a knife from her clothing and threw it at Mala, hitting her in the chest. She threw another at Mystic Seven and a third at Cherry. Seven fell to the ground in a pile but Cherry caught the knife that was thrown at her. Cherry threw the knife back at Ashlynn, who was able to dodge it as Mala started to laugh. Mala stood, drawing the knife out of her chest. She looked at the knife, then the wound that wasn't bleeding.

"You really believe that a little knife would be strong enough to kill me?" Mala asked. "Tell me, what kind of poison did you place on the tip? Something slow acting so you could gloat over me as I died? No, looking at how fast Mystic Seven died it must have been something very quick. I can feel it in my veins right now. It's tingling…hot. Tell me, what did you use? You must know that there isn't a poison that would be able to kill me."

Ashlynn stood with her mouth open. She couldn't believe that her poison didn't work. She was even more amazed that Cherry was able to catch the knife in midair. Both the women were so intently focused on each other that they didn't see that Jade had taken something from Captain Creature and then quickly moved over to where Krispin and Arctic were slumped against the wall. Jade gave Krispin something to drink, forcing it down his throat. She checked over Arctic—she was crying, so upset with Krispin's death that Jade couldn't console her.

"I've had enough of all of this," Mala continued. "Cherry, kill her."

Cherry rushed toward Ashlynn and the pair crossed blades. They were moving quickly around the room, slashing and defending against each other. Neither could get an advantage until Cherry reached into a pocket, and in one fluid motion, pulled her hand out while throwing dust in Ashlynn's eyes. Ashlynn screamed and tried to rub her eyes, allowing Cherry to behead Princess Ashlynn. Ashlynn's body fell to the floor in a pile and Mala snapped her fingers, causing the head and the body to disappear.

"Sent it to the bottom layers of hell," Mala said. "Where it will never return. Now, I killed your father already…but the question is, which one of you am I going to kill first?"

"How about me?" Krispin said, from behind Mala.

Mala spun around on one foot, stunned at what she saw. Krispin and Arctic, standing tall behind her. Krispin was holding his sword and he was now in strange clothing—royal clothing. Blue and white tunic and tights—the clothing of the Former King. Krispin looked so confident, so powerful, that in that moment, Mala felt a twinge of fear pulse through her body. At first she didn't understand but then she caught a glimpse of Captain Creature, still behind her magic force shield.

"The mighty captain always has a bottle of water from the Immortal River on his person," Mala said, with a laugh. "I should have known that he would try something like that. Captain Creature, you and I should marry. We could rule this land with ultimate force. No one would dare stand before us."

"You under estimate everyone who stands before you, Mala," Captain Creature said. "You think that you can rule here but you are sorely mistaken. King Krispin will cut you down before your reign even starts."

"King Krispin?" Mala scoffed. "Now I've heard everything. This pup will never amount to anything. He should go back to the world he came from and enjoy it. I plan on destroying it once I have Cerrado secure."

"It's time to defend yourself," Krispin said, as he began to walk toward Mala with his sword drawn. "I will not permit you to live after the crimes that you have committed."

Mala smiled but brought her sword to her hands and began to cross blades with Krispin. Unlike when Krispin fought Cherry, this time he was amazingly good. He was quick, on the offense, and not letting Queen Mala have any offense. Mala signaled for Cherry to get involved, but Jade prevented her sister from doing anything. Cherry turned and began trying to fight with Jade but all three Nature Watchers together trapped Cherry and wouldn't let her help.

When Mala realized that Cherry was of no use to her, she began to use her magic. Mala tried everything she could, throwing magic at Krispin, but he was able to defend and deflect everything. There was nothing she could do. Mala was starting to get worried—starting to get scared as Krispin was moving faster and faster. Finally, when Mala was on the verge of exhaustion, Krispin's blade pierced her black heart. Mala fell to the ground.

"You think that a little sword to my heart will defeat me?" Mala asked. "You cannot strike me down. You do not have the power to do so."

"No," Princess Arctic said. "But I do."

Princess Arctic rushed to Mala and drove the unicorn horn deep into the wound. Arctic twisted the horn in the wound as Mala, sprawled on the ground, started screaming. No matter what Mala did, she was in extreme pain. Arctic pulled the horn out and Krispin stood in front of Mala with his sword drawn.

"When a unicorn gives its horn to a pure girl," Krispin said. "That girl can decide if the horn is used for life or death. Arctic just used it for death."

Mala's eyes got big as Krispin raised his sword and dropped it across her neck. Mala was killed and her body instantly turned to dust. As a wind blew the dust out the window, the force that was holding the others, disappeared. Sir Bromas rushed to the window and jumped before any of the children could get to him. Cherry fell to the ground, and when she stood she was back in her cherry colored dress.

"I don't get it," Princess Ambriss said, looking at Krispin. "You were dead. How did this happen?"

"She was right that I was given water from the Immortal River," Krispin said. "But before that, Jade showed me who I really was...the Former King."

"What?" Everyone seemed to gasp in unison.

"How is that possible?" Arctic asked. "You are a strange boy from another land."

"Jade showed me a truth," Krispin said. "My mother is Mary, but before she was Mary she was Tala—the eldest sister and the one truly in line for the throne. When Mala tried to kill her, Tala ran to Captain

Creature and Jade for help. They devised the plan. The Former King had been on the throne but we all knew a battle was coming. Mala had stabbed the Former King with a tainted unicorn horn, in effect killing him. Whether it was luck or destiny, my father walked through the arch and found this land. He was found by Captain Creature. Once Kale had told his story, he and Tala married. When she became pregnant they allowed the spirit of the Former King to take this body. I have all of his memories and knowledge, along with my own. My parents went back to my father's land where I was raised in safety. They knew it would take this much to be rid of Mala once and for all."

"What about Bala?" Ambriss asked. "Why did she become Princess Ashlynn?"

"After she saw the power Mala had, she wanted it for herself," Krispin said. "She had study necromancy before and had enough power to put herself in Princess Ashlynn's body. She gained much more power by killing her family and some of the people in the outer villages."

As Krispin was about to continue, Princess Ashlynn appeared in the room. Like the spell on Cherry and the magic force holding the others back, once Mala was dead, her powers didn't have any effect. Ashlynn wasn't fully dead, and she started to charge right at King Krispin, who had his back to her. As she was almost on top of Krispin, Lacey DuLake drew her sword and engaged Ashlynn, quickly taking her to the floor. Lacey wasted no time in driving her sword into Ashlynn's heart before Arctic drove the unicorn horn into Ashlynn's chest. Ashlynn's body turned to dust and blew out of the room, allowing the sisters to join each other in an eternity of hell.

"Thank you, Lacey," Krispin said.

"I guess you were ready for your big moment," Hibit said. "You are a brave knight."

"You are a king's knight, Lacey DuLake," Krispin said.

"To that point," Ambriss said. "How do we know what you're telling us is the truth? You have defeated our enemies but we do not know if you would become a new enemy. Father was the only one to see the sword of the Former King."

"A just question," Krispin said. "I believe that Prince Alos also knows what the sword looks like. Alos, will you look at my sword?"

"I did see it once," Alos said. "Father wanted to be sure that even if he wasn't here the Former King could still peacefully take the throne. Show me your sword and if it is the sword of the shepherd, then you are the king."

Krispin showed them all the sword with the relief carving of the shepherd with his sheep. All the children were very pleased. Alos was the first to bow.

"I pledge my life to you my lord and king," Alos said.

The others all followed suit.

"First order as king is to absolve Cherry of her crimes," Krispin said. "She had fallen under the spell of Queen Mala and was not acting on her own powers. The treason she committed was that of Mala, not her."

"Thank you, King Krispin," Cherry said, bowing.

"I hope that this can be the beginning of an alliance between Cerrado and the Nature Watchers," Krispin said.

"It will be," Cherry said, as Cinnamon and Cobalt nodded in agreement.

"The king needs a queen," Captain Creature said. "And I think if we don't hurry we won't make it to the wedding. Holly and Chester are about to walk down the aisle."

"Yes," Krispin said. "A king needs a queen. Captain Creature, Jade, Lacey, and Princess Arctic, you will accompany me back to my village. The rest of you, head to the Cerrado Castle and to the Honor Throne. Tonight will be a night of much celebration."

Krispin, Creature, Jade, Lacey, and Arctic rushed out of the room. If Arctic knew the plans that Krispin had, she might have worn a smile on her face. As it was, Arctic looked on the verge of tears as the other Nature Watchers took the group back to the castle.

Chapter 34

On the banks of the Lazy Brook, near the Moon Forest, a grand wedding was about to take place. Rows and rows of benches had been constructed, with a large arch that was decorated with multicolored vines and flowers. An aisle was laid out with flowers and shrubs. Candles and lanterns were burning even though it was a bright, sunny, cloudless day.

Holly couldn't have asked for a more perfect day for her wedding. It was warm, but not overly hot—a clear sky, and a pleasant breeze. All the flowers were in full summer bloom. The guests had been arriving for the past half hour. They were sitting on the benches waiting for the event of the summer to take place. Everyone in the village had heard about Krispin's proposal. They were interested to see if Krispin was going to make an entrance and woo Holly away from Chester.

Chester and his four groomsmen were prepared for the arrival of Krispin. They were all wearing swords with their suits, looking like knights, but they were no more than decorations. Chester was not going to lose Holly to some kid who'd traveled for three months. Chester looked over the crowd that had arrived, trying to spot Krispin, trying to figure out if he was going to arrive. As he was looking over the crowd he saw that Kale and Mary Risdell, Krispin's parents, were walking up to him.

"A fine day for a wedding," Kale said, shaking Chester's hand.

"It is, Sir," Chester said, slightly confused. "Have you heard any word from Krispin?"

"There hasn't been anything," Mary said, with a tinge of sadness in her voice. "I'm so worried about my boy. I wish that he would have sent us something. He knows the wedding is today. I can't believe that he would miss this."

"I sure he'll be here," Chester said. "Why don't you two sit right up in the front row, that way you can have a good view of everything that happens."

"A good idea," Kale said. "I wouldn't want to miss this."

Kale and Mary walked to the front of the benches and took their seats. As they sat, the wedding started. A four-piece string band started to play the wedding march and the groomsmen escorted the bridesmaids down the aisle. Four pairs, one by one, slowly walked as all the eyes were on them. After the wedding party was in place, a small priest in brilliant whites walked to the front, standing under the flowered arch. Chester made his way down the aisle and stood before the priest, looking back to the small hut that had been built for Holly on this day.

All the members of the crowd stood as Holly's father knocked on the door. Holly exited the hut in an amazing, flowing white dress. Her hair was piled up with flowers and a tiara fixed in. Holly's father escorted her down the aisle and gave her to Chester. As all the audience sat down and Chester and Holly took their place in front of the priest, something amazing happened.

A gust of wind came from nowhere as a bolt of lightning lit up the sky. A crack of thunder shook the ground something fierce. The guests looked around. A few started gasping, looking past the bride and groom to the river where a large ship was starting to form. The ship was massive, with three masts, multi-levels, many colored flags flying, and many pirates standing on their decks. Everyone was stunned, not knowing at all where this ship had come from or what it was doing here.

As the ship came into full view, a gangplank was lowered from an upper deck to the shores of the river. The first person off the ship was Lacey DuLake, dressed in her full knight's outfit, carrying a large sword with an ornate, gilded handle. Lacey's hair was flowing as she walked off the ship, looking beautiful and powerful, with a smile that went from ear to ear.

"All rise for Captain Creature and his mistress, Jade, the Lady of the Water," Lacey powerfully announced.

The crowd complied as Captain Creature and Jade made their way to the wedding. They were both cleaned up and wearing their best clothing. Everyone at the wedding was stunned silent to be witnessing this. No one, not even Chester, knew what they should be doing. They could only watch and be stupefied at the massive ship and the strange people coming off of it. Captain Creature and Jade walked to the front of the crowd.

"And now," Lacey announced. "All bow before Princess Arctic and King Krispin the Brave."

The crowd looked confused. Krispin's parents were the first to bow before everyone followed. The last person to bow down was Chester, who had a look of disbelief on his face as Krispin, in full king's clothing, shimmering and clean, walked down the gangplank. Princess Arctic, in her wrapped dress and snowflake embroidered cape, was walking beside Krispin. She paused by Lacey as Krispin walked to his parents first and motioned for them to rise up. Krispin hugged both his parents.

"We knew that you would succeed," Kale said.

"We love you so much, Krispin," Mary said. "I'm so proud of you."

"I understand why you didn't tell me any of this," Krispin said. "I had to discover who I was on my own."

"You have done well," Kale said. "Good job."

"You must have had one hell of an adventure," Chester said, as his eyes shifted between Krispin and the boat.

"Tell me what happened," Holly asked. "I can't wait to hear it."

"No," Krispin said. "I'm not telling my adventure."

"No?" Holly, Chester, and Arctic all said at the same time.

"Well, I don't care about your adventure," Holly said, looking over Krispin as she walked to him and placed her hand on his shoulder. "I just want you. Sorry Chester, but I'm going to marry Krispin."

"Wonderful, great, amazing, whatever," Arctic said, sarcastically. "Can I go now?"

"You're not going anywhere, Princess Arctic," Krispin said, as he took Holly's hand off his shoulder. "Holly, I learned something on my adventure. Love doesn't require an adventure. Love is fussy, messy, and sometimes can be confused with hatred. But it also is true, marvelous, and you feel it deep in your core. You can marry Chester. You and he are perfect for each other. I just came here to get my parents."

"As a wedding gift, you two can have our farm," Kale said. "I don't think we'll be back this way any time soon."

"A wise decision," Krispin said.

"Thank you," Holly said. "We have a farm now, Chester. We'll be very well off."

"Other than the fact that you were ready to marry Risdell here without even hearing about the adventure," Chester said. "I think this is far past due."

Chester pulled his sword out and pointed it at Krispin. Before Krispin could even get his sword out of his sheath, Lacey DuLake had engaged Chester, knocking his sword out of his hands and dropping him to the ground. Lacey had the point of her sword aimed right at Chester's heart.

"Shall I kill him?" Lacey asked.

"No," Krispin said. "Leave him be. He meant nothing by it."

"Hang on a moment though," Arctic asked. "If you're not going to marry Holly...who are you going to marry?"

"You," Krispin said. "If you'll have me. Princess Arctic, I love you and I want you to be my queen as we guide Cerrado to peace and prosperity."

"Yes, yes, yes!" Arctic shouted excitedly as she rushed to Krispin and kissed him.

The pair embraced and kissed as the crowd began cheering for them. Krispin and Arctic waved to the crowd before they walked back to the ship, followed by Kale and Mary, Captain Creature and Jade, and Lacey bringing up the rear. They got on the ship and with a crack of thunder and a bolt of lightning, the ship disappeared—never to be seen on that river again.

###

In a grand ceremony, one without equal in the history of Cerrado, Krispin Risdell was crowned King Krispin the Brave then married to Princess Arctic. The entire population of Cerrado had flooded the city and castle to witness the events. Krispin took his place on the Honor Throne to rule the whole of Cerrado with his loving wife by his side.

On the night of their wedding, before the marriage was consummated, Jade gave Queen Arctic a special gift—water from the Immortal River. Arctic, like Krispin, would now live forever—never aging. Krispin and Arctic welcomed the Nature Watchers, Captain Creature and his pirates, Lacey, and the other royal children into their court.

Krispin had his adventure, which led him to love—just not in the way he thought it would. He never again thought about Holly, only his wife Arctic. Krispin and Arctic went on to guide Cerrado to be very prosperous and all the peoples of the land loved the as their rulers.

But Krispin and Arctic couldn't rule forever. When the youngest of their eight children turned eighteen, Krispin and Arctic turned the rule of Cerrado over to the eldest. Krispin and Arctic spent some of their days with Captain Creature on his new ships and some with the Nature Watchers, helping keep the worlds in balance. Krispin and Arctic checked in on their descendants to help when needed—and the pair did have an adventure, from time to time.

About Author

Leif Erickson was born and raised on a grain farm outside Wheaton, MN, just a stone's throw from White Rock, SD, which served as the inspiration for the Ghost Town series. From a very early age, Leif knew that he was going to be a farmer, just like his father and grandfather. As he grew up, Leif learned everything he could about farming, always riding in equipment with his dad and helping out wherever he could.

After Leif graduated high school he attended North Dakota State University in Fargo, North Dakota, where he achieved a BS in Agricultural Economics along with a minor in History. During his time in college, Leif networked with many other farmers from across North Dakota, South Dakota, and Minnesota, while advancing his knowledge in all aspects of agricultural. With a diploma in hand, Leif returned to the family farm and started his career as a farmer.

The first season was very successful and stood as a testament to the hard work and education that Leif had received. All signs pointed to a lifetime career as a farmer until a family tragedy struck and the family farm was dispersed. For the first time in his life, Leif didn't know what he wanted to pursue for a career.

Leif returned to Fargo, ND where he began his career as a stock and futures trader. It was during this time that he began to become serious about writing. With one computer watching the markets, Leif would be on the other, writing. Leif quickly realized though that Fargo wasn't the city or location that he wanted to make a home in. Less than one year since he moved there, Leif moved to Plymouth MN, in the Twins Cities area.

Continuing with the trading and writing, Leif began to learn everything that he could about writing, about storytelling, and about the hero's journey. Leif spent his spare time reading novels or books about writing. It was during his time in the Cities that Leif wrote many, many different stories, getting the outlines and first drafts finished. In the three years that Leif was in the Cities, he wrote the first draft for over fifty different stories.

Leif received information about a career opportunity that was back in his hometown of Wheaton so he returned to go to work for the local grain elevator. The work was hard and the days were long without much time for writing. Leif missed being able to write every day. He had so many more stories that he wanted to write. Being aggressive and a hard worker, Leif quickly moved up the ladder in the company and within six months he was in a management position.

Although Leif had met and dated many women when he was in the Twin Cities, it was in Wheaton where he met the new Science Teacher at his old High School and within fifteen months of meeting the pair were married at Good Shepherd Lutheran Church in Wheaton. Many have described the pair as absolutely made for each other, and they spend much of their time hiking in State Parks or canoeing the local lakes and rivers.

Being back in Wheaton, Leif used his free time to polish up and finish some of his stories. He got two stories to the point where he was satisfied to bring them to the marketplace and share them with others. Although he still works for the elevator, Leif looks forward to the day when he can write fulltime, offering more novels and screenplays to entertain and delight others.

Throughout his life, Leif was always quick to be able to tell a story. He had an uncanny ability to quickly make up a story on the spot (sometimes to the dismay of parents and teachers) and to pull people into the story with wild characters, amazing locations, and fantastical storylines. Although Leif focuses on science fiction, he's written stories in many different genera's including mystery, horror, teen comedy, western, and even a little romance.

Throughout Leif's writings you can see traces of his farm life and his love of nature. Being an ecologist and former farmer, much of Leif's writings feature forests, lakes, and nature in general. Leif has always been interested in science and what's possible for the human race, pushing the envelope of technologies, and finding how far humans can go. Much of Leif's science fiction writing explores these themes and ideas.

When he's not writing, Leif and his wife Brittany can be found working on their goal of hiking in every State Park in Minnesota or on the lakes and rivers in a canoe. The pair have some big canoe adventures planned, and have already canoed, from end to end, big lakes such as Lake Traverse and Big Stone Lake. Every once in a while, Leif will pull out his old Disc Jockey system and play a dance as the 'Leif of the Party DJ Service.'

Leif has been influenced by many different writers and stories. His all-time favorite story is 'Sleepy Hollow' by Washington Irving, a story that Leif reads every Halloween. Other influences on his work are the 'Dune' series by Frank Herbert, 'The Lord of the Rings' by J.R.R. Tolkien, and anything related to the Arthurian Legend. Leif also enjoys many other authors such as Charles Dickens, Michael Crichton, John Steinbeck, Isaac Asimov, Neil Gaiman, and F. Scott Fitzgerald just to name a few.

Thank you for checking out a book by Leif Erickson. Please visit his website at www.leifericksonwriting.com and purchase the other books that Leif has written. They will take you on a journey that you will never forget...

http://leifericksonwriting.com/